GUARDIANS
OF the
SINGREALE

GUARDIANS
OF THE
SINGREALE

Calvin Miller

1817

Harper & Row, Publishers, San Francisco

Cambridge, Hagerstown, New York, Philadelphia
London, Mexico City, São Paulo, Sydney

FIRST EDITION

Designer: Jim Mennick

Library of Congress Cataloging in Publication Data

Miller, Calvin.
  GUARDIANS OF THE SINGREALE.

  I. Title.
PS3563.I376G8   813'.54   81-47852
ISBN 0-06-250573-4   AACR2

---

82 83 84 85 86 10 9 8 7 6 5 4 3 2

Contents

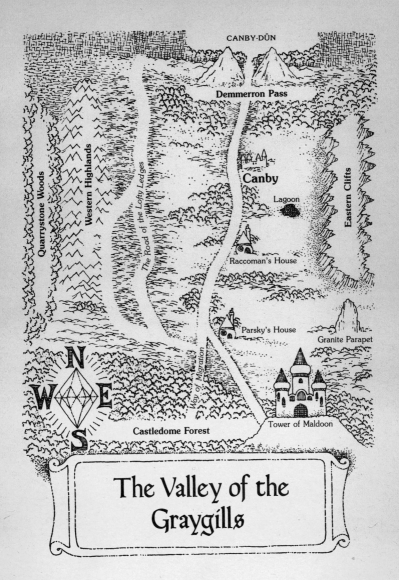

CANBY-DŪN

Demmerron Pass

Quarrystone Woods

Western Highlands

The Road of the Lofty Ledges

Canby

Lagoon

Raccoman's House

Eastern Clifts

Way of Migration

Parsky's House

Granite Parapet

N
W   E
S

Castledome Forest

Tower of Maldoon

The Valley of the Graygills

Earth holds a strange power that ties feet in the dust,
So that ponderous men are bound to her crust.
But the winds whisper tales of a force in the sky,
And those with the courage to scorn dust can fly.

CHAPTER I
The Tilt Winds

*T*HE TILT WINDS vaulted into the sky. It was time, and Raccoman stiffened his body as though he were having a seizure. With his arms straight out, he fell prone into space. The wall of red cliffs hurtled past him. His arms were tense, waiting for the jolt. He could see the canyon floor rushing angrily upward, but he was unafraid for he knew that, in a moment, his plummeting would be arrested by the winds.

When the winds came, they tore savagely at his arms. It seemed his arms would be ripped out of their sockets. He stopped instantly, his body suspended for a split second in mid-air before the whole falling process reversed itself. Now the red cliffs rushed back into the valley floor and he shot by them at a velocity that amazed even him as he rocketed into the sky.

Up, up, up—until he could no longer see his good friend Parsky, who waited at the cliff's edge to take his turn at this same curious process. Raccoman realized it would be useless to call out, for he was already too distant to be heard. The winds roared like a hurricane, but he moved so near their speed that he scarcely heard the roar. Raccoman adjusted the strong foil sheets tied to his arms and checked the push of the updraft that had flung him from free fall into the icy blue.

Parsky was much lighter than Raccoman, and he shuddered at the blast of cold winter air. He, too, held his arms stiff and forward and endured the same pretense of a mock seizure. His plunge resembled a dive. The winds caught him more quickly than they had caught Raccoman, and since he was both lighter and further from the face of the cliff, Parsky shot like a missile past Raccoman, who was frantically trying to stabilize his glide. Neither of them had calculated such a vertical trajectory and they found it difficult to control their flight.

The air twisted Parsky's flat foil wings so much that he had to strain his thin biceps in the straps to bring the wings level again. The problem with surfing the wind was that the foils had to be lashed so tightly to the surfer's arms that he could not reach across to undo them. Surfing could, therefore, be dangerous. However, both Parsky and Raccoman had lived through nearly a thousand seasons of gliding and long ago overcame their fear.

Inch by inch, Raccoman brought his wings forward and gently rose, while Parsky tipped his foils to the rear and gently settled. The subtle navigation brought them closer to each other until they were flying side by side.

"Hah-hoo! Hah-hoo!" laughed Raccoman Dakktare. He had never stopped to defend his unusual laughter. He was aware that everyone has his own style of laughter. Most preferred, "Ha-ha," some "Ho-ho," but Dakktare usually laughed, "Hah-hoo!" His laughter now was prompted by the exhilaration he felt lying prone against the sky, with the wind fluttering the hair of his gray moustache.

"Hah-hoo!" he repeated. His friend Parsky turned his head to speak to him.

"Dakktare, we're drifting too far south. I had hoped we might end up closer to your house than mine. I have very little in my pantry, I can tell you, and I'm always dreadfully hungry when I finish battling these winds."

Raccoman acted as though he hadn't heard. He pulled into a dive that astounded Parsky. He plummeted away by moving the wind foils closer to his body, and then he stiffened them outward again and shot upward. Finally, he pushed his silver wings forward to execute a triple roll, before settling back next to his comrade and exclaiming:

"It's a glorious wind
And a vigorous test;
But no winds would dare
To threaten Dakktare,
Who can soar with the best
Through the turbulent air."

The two rose higher and were delighted with the view. The cold had cleared the air and it seemed they could see forever.

"There's Maldoon in the snow," shouted Raccoman, moving only his head to indicate the crumbling towers of the old fortress.

Raccoman and Parsky were so familiar with the landscape that they didn't bother to comment on everything, but the bold relief of new snow gave the wind-surfers a clear view of miles of the terrain.

The round houses of Canby village lay directly beneath them

with the smoke of half-a-thousand fireplaces curling upward and disappearing. The brightly colored dwellings looked like painted pebbles in the snow. The smoke and the distance obscured most of the cone-shaped roofs that were typical of Graygill villages.

Far to the north, they could see the two sentinel mountains that marked Demmerron Pass, and to the west were the high ridges that prevented them from seeing the woods they knew lay beyond. But they could easily see the high, broken domes that jutted through the majestic silver trees of Castledome Forest.

"We are drifting, you are right," called Dakktare. "The winds will force our flight to your home tonight."

For a second time, Parsky grumbled something about how low his pantry was. However, he shouted down to his companion, who was now traveling just below him, "Yet what the winds ordain must come to be." Then he smiled lest he seem a poor host.

By mutual action, they turned toward Parsky's home.

The drift was more serious than they had thought, and it soon became apparent they would miss even Parsky's house by a couple of miles. Neither of them relished the long tramp home through the snowy fields. They scanned the sunny meadows that ran to the edge of Castledome Forest where Parsky lived. It was fully ten miles from the home of Raccoman, who lived in the grasslands just south of the village of Canby.

Winter was all but gone, which meant it was the season of the tilt winds. This was not particularly a welcome time of the year, for most objected to the disagreeable down-drafts that slammed against the open valley floor and then lifted with such sudden force that it was impossible to keep a hat on. Indeed, nobody wore a hat during the season of the tilt winds, for the winds made all headgear a nuisance. Most had rather risk frostbite than chase caps sent vaulting upward by a stiff gale in ricochet.

But seldom were the winds so detestable that they would not afford the mid-winter delight of zephyr-surfing. Wind foils, which were plentiful on the planet, served as the conveyance.

Wind foils had been so named by the Graygills for their metallic rigidity and lightness. They were really the leaves of ginjons, the magnificent trees of Castledome Forest that towered above all other plant life on the planet. Further, the great trees were a curious cross between botany and metallurgy. Their leaves glinted silver, whether they hung aloft or lay on the ground protruding through the white of winter. Ginjons were so tall that only the ancient Castledomes were taller.

The ginjon leaves were impossible to separate from their branches, for the same metallic fibers that made them glisten caused them to cling with steel-wire loyalty to their trees. But winter separated them naturally, and when the snows came, the old leaves fell first. They were so light that they never fell straight down, for the slightest breeze turned them into sail planes and often sent them far from the forest. A ginjon leaf in a violent storm would hurtle skyward and then drift for miles before settling softly on a distant part of the planet.

The leaves could be punctured with an awl and a mallet. A windsurfer could then insert hemp-thongs through the holes and tie them to his forearms. A large foil could be tied to the chest and around the waist. In this fashion, the ginjon leaves became for the courageous a kind of glider for surfing the eddies during the season of the tilt winds. It was the only time of the year when the winds deflected at such an angle to make surfing possible.

"Let's settle in," shouted Raccoman as he pushed his arm foils downward and stabilized his descent.

"Wait for me! My wings are smaller!" Parsky yelled, unable to duplicate the steep dive that his companion had managed.

As Raccoman descended, Parsky seemed far away. The blustery updraft carried sound with it, so that Raccoman had but to whisper to seem like he was shouting to his friend, while Parsky's shouts seemed like whispers to Raccoman.

The sky was blue crystal and devoid of all birds, since none of them were willing to risk themselves in the gales of the tilt winds. Whole flocks could be blown away in the menacing winter turbulence.

The lonely sky was a lofty and private playground for Raccoman and Parsky.

Within an hour, however, they were skimming in, cold and fatigued. In an expert fashion, they had kept to the north edge of the ginjon trees and were able, in a lull of wind, to skim north and thus regain some of the lost distance.

Landing was tricky. The idea was to hold the wind foils level and try to come in parallel to the ground. The horizontal foil on which a wind-surfer lay had to be kicked free just before impact so that there could be the full use of the legs. And it was important to pick a field as free from shrubs and rocks as possible to avoid injury. Raccoman was the first to land, just as he had been the first to leap from the eastern cliffs. When he was only twenty feet above the ground, he kicked off his ventral foil, which tumbled into the snow. He hit the snowy ground only seconds later and tumbled awkwardly into a drift, in spite of his determination to stay upright.

Parsky's ventral foil almost hit Raccoman as it fell, and Parsky himself tumbled into a deep drift a few yards further down the broad meadow. The pair may have lacked grace as they landed, but never while they flew.

Raccoman was brushing the snow from his bright, yellow mackinaw when Parsky came up.

The friends were nearly the same height, but Parsky was by far the trimmer of the pair. Parsky had a thick, black crop of hair that shagged out around his pointed ears. He was a Blackgill and, as such, the last of a race—a noble race, so he said, and since lying was unknown on Estermann, a man's word was, indeed, his bond. The Blackgill, like Graygills, had a naked chin and wide sideburns that crossed his face mid-cheek and jutted over the edge of the jaw in a thick canopy of hair. Above each sideburn was a heavy lock of hair that dangled just before his ear and fell all the way to his upper chest. These bold locks—too thin to braid and too thick to curl—were known as sidelocks.

Parsky was an intelligent Blackgill, and he was well accepted by his Graygill neighbors. However, the Graygills of the planet related color to nearly everything and felt that the darker the hue, the greater the tendency toward evil; for this reason, they generally despised black. While this did not affect the way they felt about the fair-skinned Parsky, it did make them stand-offish about the color of his gills.

In spite of the Graygills' acceptance of him, the thin Blackgill lived far from Canby Village, for he was by nature a loner. He wouldn't have minded "a lassie in his home," as he always said, but the truth of the matter was that he was doomed to bachelorhood by a double fault. First, like the Graygill men, most Graygill lasses were taken aback by Parsky's deep black hair. And second, they were in short supply. There had never been a population explosion on Estermann because only one out of four babies born was a girl. This was the natural course of things there—no one asked why—and it was a lucky man who had "a lassie." The Blackgill, though handsome and naturally endowed with good features, was not among the lucky, so like Raccoman and the others, he accepted his bachelorhood unquestioningly for it was the way of life for most men on the planet.

This trim Blackgill was old—but his eye was not dim nor his vigor sluggish. He had seen the snows of hundreds of winters. Even those who knew him well knew his great age was unmeasurable by the younger souls of the highlands villages. And everyone was younger; Raccoman was so much younger that he seemed a youth by comparison. Often Parsky had told him of things that swam the edges of unwritten history.

The edges of history were a frontier of puzzling facts. In a world where everyone lives to be at least 1,500 years old, no one asks why. They did not wonder that they enjoyed such long lives, for not knowing any other basis of comparison, their lives seemed to them all too short. There was no natural disease on the planet and all of the children born survived infancy. Adolescence began around the one-hundred-and-fiftieth year, and marriage usually occurred—when it occurred at all—around the three-hundredth year. Thus every marriage that existed observed their millennial anniversary.

Raccoman was not concerned with his own age. Since he was still under a thousand years, he was really at the prime of health and appearance, or should have been. His physical well-being did not suffer like his appearance.

Raccoman was obese for his height. Roundness and tallness never go together, for round people never appear tall nor tall people, round. Thus, Raccoman Dakktare had lived beneath a double curse for all his years of bachelorhood, being both too short and too round. He was gray, but gray hair had nothing to do with age on Estermann because, except for Parsky, all Estermannians had gray hair; even their gills were gray to the very last whisker. Raccoman's hair, too, would have been gray if it had not been largely absent. He was bald down to the fringe of gray follicles that shagged out over his ears. He was a splendid example of all the gray-whiskered men of the planet who were called "Graygills." His overlarge ears projected through his gray fringe of hair. All Estermannians had large pointed ears, but Raccoman's ears set the standard for the planet.

Both men were unmarried, but it was Raccoman who had fallen into the evil habits of bachelorhood. He was a metal-worker, a sedentary sort of occupation, and he grew quickly out of breath with the slightest exercise. He overslept because he always stayed up too late. He ate all the wrong foods, and right or wrong, he loved all food.

His hands dangled from stubby arms and were clotted on the ends with short, fat fingers. His cheeks were red spheres set close to his snubby nostrils. Words fail to describe him because Raccoman Dakktare was beyond description. He was congenial, but unlike Parsky, he could not be called handsome. His gremlin appearance would crack an ordinary plate, and yet he was blessed with such an overbearing arrogance that he believed himself both handsome and intelligent. Although arrogance is sometimes a clear fault, it is seldom dangerous, and his likeable egotism never wanted for friends.

More annoying than Raccoman's appearance was his affected way of speaking. He had a quick enough wit to speak many of the things he said in rhymes. His short phrases and exclamations sometimes escaped his doggerel speech, but he liked proving to his friends that he could make up a rhyme or a ballad on the spot. He never seemed to see that his customary way of speaking was more an impediment to good conversation than an incentive. If he was angry or afraid, he might, in the press of emotion, forget this curious habit of speech.

"It's a long walk, chum," said Parsky as he walked in the direction of his house. Raccoman replied:

"The snow shall show our footprints home
And bear us swift to Castledome."

Parsky winced. The doggerel was as unpleasant as the weather. The eager and biting cold never stopped his friend's rhymes, but it did slow his own poetic mood.

The pair said nothing as they crunched homeward.

"Look," Parksy said at last, pointing to the base of some snowy shrubs.

A family of tiny congrels appeared to be nibbling at some berries. Congrels were numerous on the planet, but the cold tended to make them huddle in their burrows, which they rarely left in the season of the tilt winds.

The congrels sat quietly on their haunches. They were gray-red in summer, but the color of their fur brightened to orange in the winter. Their ears were leathery and bent, and their eyes set oddly underneath their cheeks. Their mouths were small and drawn up in such a way that they always appeared to be smiling—though smiling was not a conscious part of their lives any more than frowning would have been.

For reasons ordained by nature, they always stuck vertical sticks, like miniature porticoes, in the ground around the openings of their burrows. They lived in small villages, where all of their tunnels opened to the sun; the scene appeared a Roman marketplace or palisade. The sky-surfers took notice of this group of congrels, an orange clot huddled in the snow.

"They must be frozen!" said the Blackgill. "In this cold weather, I always keep my congrel cages on the sheltered side of my house."

"What? Congrel cages? Why? It's not traditional. No one would agree that any living thing should ever be caged—even congrels."

Raccoman had referred to an old unspoken—and for that matter, unwritten—custom that declared there could neither be jails nor zoos on Estermann. "Besides," continued Raccoman, "for table scraps and little else you'd have to drive them from your door."

They had put down several snowy footprints before Parsky answered, "You're wrong, chum. Congrels will not come to the edge of the forest. It's as if they're afraid of something. So I've taken those I have played with in the fields and brought them home. I am lonely at night, and my little caged friends are excellent company. Don't begrudge me the cages."

Raccoman had found Parsky a delightful friend for many seasons. Besides, the Blackgill's logic was always good and so plaintive that he made Raccoman feel ashamed to have questioned it; and in this case, Raccoman was all the more ashamed, for being a bachelor himself, he knew what loneliness was.

Soon they caught sight of Parsky's house. Raccoman had been there a thousand times across the years, but the house always caught him by surprise. It was square. The Graygill villagers thought the shape of Parsky's house was as odd as the color of his gills. Their houses were all round to the very last dwelling, and Parsky's house was a geometric affront to the architecture of the village. In addition to Parsky's gills and his square and remote hermitage, there was the issue of his occupation—he had none. But when any of the villagers asked Parsky what he did, he shrugged his shoulders helplessly. Sometimes he told them he was a stew-cook, but this was not really considered an occupation. Since every Graygill bachelor cooked his own meals, none of them would have considered stew-cook a valid occupation.

Not that the Graygills had any reverence for the way any of their kind made a living. They were a simple race who esteemed all labor. In the village there were stone-workers who laid the stones in all the dwellings, wood-workers who constructed simple furniture, and metal-workers who fashioned ginjon leaves into various kinds of furniture and implements. The building of a Graygill house required all three.

Outside Graygill villages the only occupation was farming. There were no herdsmen; since no animals were domesticated, none were seen to be wild. Farmers planted and harvested the crops with hand tools and pulled their own small carts by hand. They then sold their wares in the central oval of the village. (City squares were rejected as distasteful geometry.)

Here and there amid the Graygill countryside were observatories for watching the stars, an occupation that, although it held as much respect as any other, was seen by many workers as having little *practical* value in the commerce and conversation of Graygill life.

Although Parsky's occupation—or lack of one—seemed unusual to the hard-working Graygills, it was cause for comment, not concern.

Estermann was a happy planet where suspicion was unknown, and Parsky was quite personable, quite good looking, and quite the life of any party. Parties were as much a part of the Graygills' lives as the round dwellings that composed their neighborhoods. I must not give you the impression that Parsky was all that different from others. Like other Estermannians, stew was his favorite food, and he had his favorite color as well. It was red—a violent, aggressive, and scarlet red. Thus his red, square house stood out like a bright parcel against the white snow and the silver foil leaves of the ginjon forest behind it.

They soon were at the red square door.

"Home," said Parsky, lifting the latch and walking in. It was never a custom to lock a home on Estermann. People would not think of breaking into and entering a home for any reason. There had never been a burglary, nor was there likely to be one.

"It's as cold in here as it is outside;
Was the glass ajar or the door flung wide?"

The question was needless, and even as Raccoman asked it, he began gathering wood and flint to start a fire. Parsky's fingers were blue from the cold, but this did not prevent him from gathering some vegetables together to pare so the stew would be ready for the fire when the fire was ready for the stew. A cold half-hour later, both the fire and the stew had made friends, and the chill had gone from the room. The Graygill backed up to the flame and turned his yellow breeches rearward to the fire, holding his thumbs in the corners of his back pockets to direct all the heat he might against his body. He took off his yellow boots when the floor was warm enough, and he wiggled his cold feet within his yellow leggings.

Parsky's red boots were soon comfortably beside Raccoman Dakktare's yellow ones, and the two friends moved only to put the black poker into the embers and nudge the fire up towards the bottom of the stew kettle. "My muscles ache," said the unemployed Blackgill to the Graygill welder. "Sky-surfing tries every muscle, but oh, the exhilaration of the tilt winds when they fling you skyward."

Raccoman nodded. His fatigue was obvious in his silence, and it was a drowsy silence at that.

He yawned and said, "I cannot decide when the fire is ablaze whether I am more hungry than I am weary or weary than hungry. The bed or table—which do I need? I'm eager to rest, but I've never been able to sleep well on an empty stomach." He yawned again and soon dozed. Somewhere in the midst of his hearthside dream, he heard the cook calling. Parsky sounded far away on the other side of the sky, as the Graygill welder soared through a kind of slumber. In his exhilarating fantasy, Raccoman turned and rolled mid-air, soared and rose. Again the voice called. It was nearer, but the wind was far too loud for him to hear it well. He sang in the ether of his delirium:

"Dakktare, you're the model sky-rider they say,
High-surfing the wild, gale-swept skies.
The wind where you soar is a zephyr of joy
That washes the air where it flies."

A brave falcon swept the void near him and then turned, tipped its wings, fell away, and rose alongside him once more. The falcon's great wings tipped slightly as if he signaled Raccoman from the airy chasm. His beak opened and he screamed through the Graygill's misty stupor, "Beware Maldoon!"

A bowl slammed down hard.

"Hey, chum, the table is spread!" laughed Parsky, waking the metal-worker from his cold and lovely flight and restoring unto him the sight of his own yellow boots and the warm fire.

The Graygill stood, wobbling on legs that obviously had not awakened as fast as the rest of him. He stumbled groggily to the table, while the Blackgill laughed at his clumsiness.

"Let's eat!" said Parsky, digging in with his spoon and slipping it just under his nose to take advantage of the first real smell before he took the first real bite. After savoring the aroma, he placed the spoon into his mouth.

"Hold there, stew-cook! Haven't we forgotten the creed of the plate?"

Parsky, having his mouth full, was embarrassed to have forgotten.

"You say it for us," said the Blackgill, who swallowed hard as the Graygill picked up his bowl. Raccoman raised the bowl towards the ceiling and repeated the words without which he never began a meal:

"To the maker of the feast
To the power of loaf and yeast
Till the broth and bread have ceased
Gratefulness is joy!"

Then they ate.

It was a simple broth of such vegetables as grew on the planet. Estermann's vegetables were quite different from the vegetables that grow and are eaten on younger worlds, but they were tasty and marked by the excellent aroma that surrendered itself in the cooking. There was no meat in any broth on Estermann, for meat was unknown there. Animals all were vegetarian, and not one animal on the planet preyed upon another as his source of food. Neither did the Graygills ever consider hunting and killing animals merely to enjoy the taste of flesh. Indeed, not only the taste but the very idea of eating animal flesh would have been repulsive, had it been possible for the thought to occur to them.

In a world where slaughter never occurs, meat is neither discovered nor desired. So their vegetable stew was delicious. It was so delicious that Parsky and Raccoman had soon helped themselves to generous second portions.

It was the second time they had eaten together in a ten-day week. Raccoman's business was not all that good in the windy season, so he took advantage of the lull to enjoy Parsky's company. It was a mutual joy, for good friendship is always mutual and always joyous.

"Parsky, tell me again, while we have ourselves a cup of cando-let tea, how you came to Castledome." Though Raccoman had often heard the Blackgill's story, he always felt there was more to it, and so he kept asking in the hope that he might one day hear a longer version of the tale.

Holding his teacup beneath his nose and savoring the candolet vapors, Parsky seemed lost in thought. Of the many kinds of trees that grew in and around the valley of the Graygills, the candolet was most practical. It had two layers of bark. The outer, woody, heavy layer could be burned in the fireplace and the inner, tender layer was used to make a tangy hot tea that was the social beverage during the long Estermann winters. The blue-green vapors that rose from the red tea opened the eyes and welcomed the snowy traveler. The outer candolet bark made the fire roar with magic visions. Something wonderful always happened when candolet bark produced the flames that brewed the candolet tea.

Raccoman waited, and at last Parsky told the same story he always did. The Blackgills had died in a famine, which he, through a long series of trials, had managed to survive. But only he had managed to survive and come to live here on the fringe of Castledome Forest with a square house, a black moustache, and a jobless existence. In a world of more industrious Graygills, none could understand Parsky's house, his gills, or his contentment with his idle life.

The Graygill would be leaving in the morning and soon both of them retired.

"It was a good stew—firm vegetables and a hot broth. A perfect ending to a perfect day in the air," said Parsky and then complimented Raccoman on his sky-surfing. "You're good in the sky!"

The Graygill answered the compliment by complimenting himself even further with a new ballad:

"I am natural there
When I'm soaring in ease
Over Maldoon and Canby
And silvery trees.
Parsky, old chum, again and again
I'll affirm myself first
As the proudest of men
Who can ride the wild sky
And challenge the wind."

Parsky had heard his lyrical outbursts as often as Raccoman had heard of the Blackgill famine.

Being tired, they decided to forego the Graygill custom of dancing before the hearth. And lying down in the small, square house, they fell asleep and slept through the long night into a brilliant but frigid dawn.

When morning came, Raccoman rose first. He stoked the embers of the not-quite-dead-fire and pulled on his yellow boots. He went out through the back door to get some wood, and in returning, he noticed the congrel cages. The beasts looked cold and frightened. One of the cages was empty and the door swung easily in the slight breeze.

"Good, they have escaped," he thought, carrying the firewood and going inside. No new snow had fallen during the night, but the cold seemed even more intense than it had the evening before. Raccoman found Parsky up and dressed in his red breeches and boots.

"Black bread and tea?" asked Parsky.

Raccoman repeated the question before he answered. "Black bread and tea? Yes, black bread and tea. Two slices," he said.

The Blackgill cut four slices as the Graygill heaped the cold wood on the grate. The fire nibbled at the dry wood.

While the black, iron teapot simmered on the fireplace crane, Raccoman meditated upon the two wonderful meals he had shared with the Blackgill in the week just passed. Parsky was a great cook and a delightful companion. Raccoman yelled across the room to Parsky, who was absorbed in the act of making tea.

"One cage is undone
And the congrels are gone."

Parsky shrugged his shoulders as he replied, "It doesn't matter.

There are more in the meadow."

Raccoman felt uncomfortable with this unfeeling reply, but decided to change the subject.

"Parsky! Once more before the tilt winds die, and winter is gone, I want you and me to take to the sky.

"This time we will soar on the edges of light,
As the wind and the stars and the magic of night
Shall leave constellations the footprints of flight."

They sat down while Parsky thought it over. They exalted the loaf with the same words that they had used to consecrate their congenial stew the night before. The Blackgill took a sip from his tea and answered, "All right, ten nights from tonight we will do it again. We'll meet north of the fortress Maldoon and take the high river road over the steppes. This time we'll jump from the granite parapet."

"We'll swim by night in the spangled sea from the parapet to the galaxy," said the welder, lost in the reverie of all he imagined.

"Providing there is wind," reminded the Blackgill.

"Providing," agreed Raccoman.

"It will be our last time this year, I'm afraid, for the season of the winds will soon be gone. Dress warmly."

Raccoman nodded. Then he gulped down his breakfast, put on his coat, cap, and gloves, and walked to the door to start for home.

On the way to the door, he stopped by Parsky's mirror to admire himself.

"What a proud Graygill," he boasted. "What a—"

But he stopped mid-brag, stunned by a little discrepancy in the image gazing back from the glass. In a moment of honesty, he blurted out: "Look, Parsky, look! My face! Some of the hair in my locks has turned black." It wasn't a major change of color, but it was clear enough to see. And though the change didn't worry Raccoman, he couldn't help but wonder what had caused the discoloration: the altitude, the cold, or frostbite? He waved good-bye to his unemployed friend, turned on the heel of his yellow boot, and, pulling shut the door, he started off for home. In the remote distance he saw the broken towers of Maldoon and remembered his dream and the falcon's warning. He thought he heard Parsky laughing at his superstition, but knew he had to be mistaken. The snow seemed suddenly cold and winter eternal.

How long we've feared the scales and fangs,
And the grinning head where the forked tongue ran.
But the deep black slits in the yellow eyes
Once gazed in love when time began.

CHAPTER II
The Guardian

$\mathbf{D}$OLDEEN HAD coiled up before the hearth. She usually liked a cold room, but she was getting older and this winter was particularly harsh. There were no tilt winds here in the highlands, and the surrounding trees of Quarrystone Woods almost completely shut out the straight winds. The trees did not prevent the cold, however, and Doldeen felt its severity. In the evening when the hearth fire was at its zenith blaze, she lay in the corner and stretched out to avoid too much of the heat. But as the fire died on a cold night, she slithered up closer and closer to the weakening flame, and on an early winter morning, she could always be found coiled up right next to the unsure embers.

She knew this was a special day, for her mistress Velissa would have to go out into the cold morning to run an errand for her father. So Doldeen took it upon herself to wake her mistress to be sure she got an early start. She uncoiled and slipped noiselessly across the floor. The blue rock tiles of the floor felt like ice wherever they touched the scales of her underside.

She shivered.

"What am I to do?" she thought. "A serpent in winter lives only for the hope of spring. May it come soon," she said half-aloud as she reached the bedpost, twisting herself around it as she rose from the cold floor to the warm comforters of Velissa's bed.

Coiled heavily upon her mistress' stomach, she said, "Awake, Velissssssssssa!"

Doldeen was old, and all her life she had tried to eliminate the "esses" from her speech, but they "persissst to ssstick in every essssey word," she always said.

"Now? It's so early and cold," protested her mistress.

"You musssst! Bessssidesss, if you think it isss cold here, try ssssleeping a night on the rock tile before the hearth."

Her family had built her two beds to keep her off the floor in winter, but neither of them had proved to be satisfactory. One of the beds was only a few inches wide and several feet long. It was not only strange-looking, but most uncomfortable to sleep in. Doldeen had protested the curious piece of furniture, insisting that no

"sssserpent could ssssleep ssso sssstraight and sssstretched out."
The second bed was square, offering her room to coil in slumber,
but she could not coil peacefully in a square bed. The miserable
geometry of the whole thing kept her awake nights, so she went
back to sleeping on the floor.

Velissa shuddered at the thought of rising and pulled her heavy
comforter over her head to shut out Doldeen.

Doldeen was hard to ignore. Her scales were mirrorlike, gold
and scarlet, and they caught the morning light and reflected it like
the facets of the diamond that she guarded. Her eyes were slits of
light that could flash like oval beacons to any who ignored her.
Upon her head, she possessed two small horns that had been fitted
with ornamental silver knobs. She was beautiful but obstinate.

"Pleasssse get up and build me a cozy fire before breakfasssst!"
she begged loudly enough for the sound to penetrate the coverlets.

"Oh, all right!" complained Velissa, suddenly sitting upright.
Doldeen flopped to one side, nearly falling off the bed.

She got out of bed, revealing her true height to be only half
Doldeen's length. In fact, Doldeen, now uncoiled, had to lie in a "z"
shape to fit Velissa's short bed. The bed, however, was quite long
enough for Velissa, who would never have thought of describing
herself as half-as-long as Doldeen.

"Brrrrrr," Velissa said when her bare feet touched the cold
floor. "You are right, Doldeen—the floor is cold. I'll warm it up for
the both of us before breakfast."

Doldeen was not a pet. She was a being—a member of the family. Her sensibilities and moods could not have allowed anyone to
think of her as a house animal or a loyal old lap dog. She ate what
the family ate and coiled across from them at the table on her own
stool, enjoying their conversation and talking so much that she always finished last. She could sip a cup of tea with finesse, lowering
her regal head with a kind of elite excellence, and eat everything in
her bowl or on her plate with not a hint of crude demeanor or
unpracticed etiquette.

Velissa pulled on her slippers and scooped up her long friend,
who was still lying in an uncomfortable "z."

"Oh, thank you, misssssstresssss. I could get a ssssssevere backache trying to find resssst in a Graygill bed—and when I get a
backache, it hurtssss inchesss and inchesss."

Velissa laughed at her old friend and hurried to the hearth. She threw in two powdery chunks of candolet bark and stoked the gray embers, which yielded a bright red promise. The flames leapt upward to the bottom of the cold kettle that soon sang in steam to be delivered from the fire.

"Where's father?" asked Velissa.

"In the obssssservatory. He'ssss getting together a bundle of documentsssss for you to take to Krepel'sssss."

Both Velissa's father and Krepel were star-watchers and thus slept all day to be able to watch the heavens by night. Winter was the season for astronomy, for despite the cold, the air of Estermann surrendered its haze and fog in winter. The clarity of the view brought even the smaller stars close enough to be picked like fruit. Velissa's father always said that the stars were so close in winter that they bumped the end of his great scope.

Velissa knew the house would be quiet after she left for the day, and her father would find his owlish slumber sweet. The astronomer didn't talk much to Doldeen. It wasn't that he didn't like serpents, but he found talking with Doldeen a little "essey" and, worse than that, scientifically shallow.

He had inherited Doldeen after the siege of the Castle Maldoon. She had slept for three thousand years at the base of a pedestal before the castle throne room. She was millennia younger then and, therefore, more alert in those days. She once had been assigned the eternal task of guarding the great diamond, Singreale, which was the treasure of Maldoon that the marauders had attempted to seize as their own. But their effort to take the stone had failed, and now the Singreale was all that survived of the ancient treasury. It had come, through time and circumstance, to belong to the star-watcher.

Sometimes when the star-watcher tripped over Doldeen in the dark, he would complain about the foul luck that was his to inherit a snake. At such moments, Doldeen always reminded him—for it was not like her to be silent—that:

> *"Them that getsssss the diamondsssss*
> *Must take the Sssssnakessss, too."*

They related best when they ignored each other, which is what they did most of the time. Irritated by her cumbersome speech, he often called her "Esssey," which she didn't seem to mind, even though it was a direct slur on her snakey way of speaking. Velissa and Doldeen, on the other hand, spent a lot of time together, especially in winter.

Doldeen still watched the great diamond Singreale as she had in fortress Maldoon. It was her one legacy of concern. She had been hatched in a rocky den near Demmerron Pass, and some said Singreale had been found in the cavern near the same place, but Doldeen could not remember much more than a thousand years and, therefore, could remember neither her own hatching nor the origin of Singreale. Her first memories were of the fortress where she had been the sole protector of the massive diamond, which gleamed in a timeless splendor.

Velissa of Quarrystone Woods was part of the feminine fourth of the planet's population. She was a saucy lass who loved parties, dancing, and riding. Her femininity made her a tease that had intrigued a score of suitors. But she held herself aloof from all serious entanglements and managed a coquettish flight from every proposal to marry. Her hair was Graygill gray, as were her sideburns and sidelocks. Her cheeks were over-red and dimpled, and freckles skipped across her petite nose. Her body was trim, and she flitted about every Graygill shop with such a lithe step that every Graygill lad above a hundred and fifty years couldn't help but look overlong in her direction.

On that very morning, as Raccoman Dakktare was leaving Parsky's for his own home in the fields south of Canby, Velissa rose determined to run a lengthy errand for her father. The nature of her errand would be time-consuming, requiring most of the day. The slower revolutions of the planet Estermann resulted in days that were more than twice the length of any day on earth. Thus, the Graygills became twice as tired as they might had they been blessed with fewer hours of light. Fortunately, their nights were equally long and, thus, perfectly assuaged their doubled fatigue.

Velissa and Raccoman were not completely unaware of one another. In the passing of the centuries of bachelorhood, Raccoman, like the other Graygills, knew of those lasses eligible for marriage. But the season when most males married had now passed Raccoman by.

Velissa knew of Raccoman too—he was generally regarded as the best dancer and ballad singer in the world of the Graygills—but he was older and they had only met a few times. Their homes were widely separated and Raccoman's occupation kept him tied to the commerce of Canby, in the valley lowlands. A high ridge of mountains erupted between the plains of Canby and the highland forest known as Quarrystone Woods. A road lay to the south of the ridge, and since it provided a less arduous climb to the forested plateau, most people avoided the ridge. Though Raccoman did frequent the eastern edge of Quarrystone, he seldom entered the forest itself. Quarrystone did not intrigue him. Its trees were not ginjons and, therefore, were less impressive than the towering monarchs of Castledome Forest. Still, the candolet trees and minion shrubs provided thick, red foliage all through the snowy winter. None of Estermann's plants were green, but this was not even a curious issue on a planet where green plants would have been startling and unnatural.

Velissa grew excited about the day as she dressed. She prepared a modest meal for herself and her father and, of course, offered a slice of bread to Doldeen. "Thankssss, Missssssey," said the snake, her silver-knobbed horns flickering with reflected light.

"Velisssssssa . . . I mean, Velissa," said her father, taking a sip of tea, "bundle up well and don't over-ride Collinvar. Too much cold air in his nostrils could chafe him. The water will all be frozen along the way, so be sure he has plenty at this end and at the other before you start back. Build a good fire so Doldeen will be warm all day and not have to wake me up before you come home tonight."

He took a small brown object from his pocket and handed it to her. It was a piece of paper wrapped around a hard and delicate core.

"I am lending this to Krepel. It is a star-scope lens. Be especially careful with it."

"Yes, Papa."

"And, darling, ask him if he knows a metal-worker across the ridges in Canby. The right cradle on my scope has a hairline fissure in the metal slide. I must have it welded before it breaks."

He gave her a bundle of papers and notes, then got up and threw some wood on the fire, and plunged the poker into the grate. Doldeen jumped at the sharp noise.

"Ssssettle down, Esssey," he laughed and turned on the heel of his blue boot and went off to bed.

Velissa pulled aside the blue curtains and looked out the windows to the barn. She stood lost in thought for a moment, then went for her riding clothes. Once she had pulled on her boots and heavy gloves and thrown her cape around her shoulders, she picked up the parcels and was about to leave the house when her father yelled from his bedroom, "Oh, yes! Velissa, ask Krepel if he's heard reports of smoke around the west tower of Maldoon. I think someone's living in the old place."

Maldoon was situated across the southern highland in such a way that if he pulled the support pin on his giant telescope, the barrel would lower and he could see Maldoon quite clearly against the high southern horizon on a winter's day. But he had not mentioned this phenomenon before.

Doldeen rippled uneasily. "Sssssmoke?" she asked.

"It's probably nothing of importance, but something seems to be going on in the old ruins," he said in a loud voice from his bedroom. Velissa heard both of his heavy boots hit the tile floor.

"Good-day," he said, which is what he always said the last thing before he retired. Considering the hours that he slept, it really had the force of "good-night."

Velissa said good-bye to Doldeen and opened the outside door into the clear morning.

She walked to the barn, which was as bright a blue as the outside of her father's house and observatory. She soon had saddled Collinvar and led him out into the bright and cold sunlight. Collinvar was a majestic five-horned centicorn, and "majestic" was indeed a fair word for him. His silver horns sparkled like a ginjon forest, and although he was magnificently large enough for two Graygills, Velissa usually rode him alone, sitting always in the forward seat of the double saddle.

Centicorns were so blue-white that they appeared opaque. There were just a hundred of them on Estermann, and hence the herd, widely dispersed over the planet, had been called centicorns. Collinvar was used to Doldeen's company as well on sunny afternoons in summer, for on such days Velissa never left the old snake at home. Doldeen usually rode coiled about the saddle horn, but she preferred to ride encircling Velissa's midriff. The steed's long and graceful strides were smooth as glass and never roughed the old serpent. Still, Doldeen was uncomfortable on the saddle horn and oft complained to her mistress that, twisted around the hard horn, she felt like a "hoop on a sssstick!"

But the weather this day was too cold for Doldeen, so Velissa rode alone with her heavy blue cape fluttering into the wind behind her. What a shame that there was no one around to see her, for the whiteness of her mount and the whiteness of the snow set the beautiful Graygill lass riding in a kind of azure splendor.

The cold of the morning added to the redness in her cheeks. She was striking in her beauty. She knew, as do beautiful women in any world, that she was pretty. There were in her reverie a thousand thoughts—they came and went as Collinvar's silver hooves thundered over the ice-paved trail.

Velissa was aware that she had reached that time of life when she should be married—but to whom? Almost every Graygill lad she had danced with so far could be easily forgotten.

Collinvar crossed a snowy bridge, and his hooves set a hollow rhythm that made Velissa think of the odd sound that men's boots made when they did the claxton on a wood floor. She wished there was a way to decide how to make a choice of suitors in the never-ending list of those who showed interest in her. The bridge was crossed and Collinvar's hooves quieted again as they struck only the felted fields of new and shallow snow drifts.

The woods gave way, here and there, to open meadows. When the forest closed in again, she urged Collinvar on beneath the red arches of the trees that created patterns of shadows on the snow.

Velissa's breath was a fog of vapor in the cold air, as was the centicorn's, and when they rode with speed, the vapor condensed in frost upon her bright, blue cape. Before long, the forest dwindled to shrubs and then opened onto a wide, snowy, windswept plain of unbroken white and sun-bleached fields.

Ahead of her, Velissa could see the round orange house of the star-watcher, Krepel. Surrounding it was a series of other orange buildings, which made the rather large dwelling seem a mother hen, snuggled in a snowy nest above her cold brood.

Collinvar closed the distance swiftly, and Velissa gratefully dismounted at the gate post.

Things were as silent as she had expected them to be. Krepel had obviously not used the front entrance, for the deep snow was unbroken. Velissa was half-frozen by the brisk ride and couldn't help but feel sorry for a family of congrels she saw bedded under a little shrub. Each of the little animals was attended by a breath of fog and frost, and their fur was so clotted with ice that they looked like small, crystal monsters. If the day had been warmer and if her fingers had not been frozen, she might have stopped to play with them, for her friendship with Doldeen demonstrated the love she felt for all animals.

She patted Collinvar on the haunches and crunched her way through the ice-crusted snow to Krepel's front door. She raised the huge latch and called inside.

"Krepel! It is I—Velissa!"

There was no immediate reply, but she heard soft footfalls thump down on the bare floors. They moved in a felted crescendo in her direction.

"You must come in, child," said the scientist. "Wake me up midday, would you? This had better be important."

She had expected that the old bachelor would be grumpy. He was usually quite jolly, but after all, he had been up all night at the scope. How unscientific a star-watcher could look when he was awakened in the middle of a day. For a moment she forgot the aching cold in her unbending fingers. Krepel's nightcap wound around his head like a turban and yet rode high on one side where his scruffy gray hair rebelliously poked out above his square jaw. One of his pointed ears jutted out from under his turbulent turban. And while all Graygills had large ears, even they would have said the astronomer had very large ears.

Krepel was as close to being a wizard as Estermann would ever come. He was old, for one thing, and could remember the days before the seige of Maldoon. Yet his brow was smooth and would have made him seem quite young, perhaps less than a thousand years. But the corners of his eyes betrayed it all, for there the little laugh lines broke into fissures and cracked his temples with deep creases of wrinkles through which had flowed the rivers of the passing centuries his clear old eyes had beheld.

The orange observatory that stood to the south of his house was a landmark, visible from the highlands to the west and the mountain villages to the north. It was seen to be a crossroads to the Moonrhymes north of Demmerron Pass and the forest villages of the Castledomes far away to the south. People never stopped at the orange observatory in great numbers, but across the centuries that Krepel had lived there, his lonely outpost often became an oasis for those who needed a night of lodging and a warm meal.

But better than either his food or bed was Krepel's wisdom, and those who despised their pasts or despaired their futures saw the orange observatory as a cheerful refuge—an amber stake driven into the high mountain snow. This white morning, however, the shivering sage was beset with chills and goosebumps, and Velissa smiled at his quaint appearance.

"Well, what brings you here?" he grumbled. "It's cold . . . burrr!" His teeth chattered from a blast of frigid air that blew in through the doorway where Velissa still stood.

"This!" said Velissa, extending the parcel in her frozen fingers as she entered the room. "It may be cold in here, but, Krepel, it is a thousand times colder on the high plains. Could we feed the fire?" She moved rapidly to the hearth as the outside door swung shut behind her.

The star-watcher made the flame blaze in splendor with such simple things as a poker and two large chunks of candolet wood. Velissa warmed herself and then prepared a large kettle of water to offer the centicorn before they began the trip back.

Velissa could not help studying the Moonrhyme Graygill. There was more to the man than she knew—indeed, there was more to him than anyone knew. He moved in certain ways that seemed to say he knew of a life that has passed from the planet in the eras of upheaval that had gone before.

Krepel had come from the high cliffs north of Demmerron to the service of the King of Maldoon centuries ago. Everyone knew that much about him. He had mentioned that he was born in the Grand Cavern of the upper cliffs. But he had never really told anyone his age, and, thus, all supposed it to be great.

There was a question of what life and being had preceded the Graygill settlements in the valley. Krepel had even intimated that there had been an upheaval in all of life before the collapse of Maldoon. This unrecorded cataclysm had destroyed all except the cliff dwellers, whose rocky dens had saved them. But some felt there was more to the story than the wizard had revealed. If Moonrhymes had survived some early cataclysm, it was useless to ask the Moonrhyme astronomer when it had occurred or what the secret of Moonrhyme survival had been.

"Father wanted me to ask if you know a metal-worker who could repair a fissure in the cradle of his scope," Velissa told Krepel.

"I have a nephew named Raccoman Dakktare who's a fine welder. Tell your father I'll send him over before winter has ended."

Velissa's eyes brightened at Raccoman's name. She had never thought of him as a metal-worker; in her mind the thousand-year-old Raccoman had one great attribute—he could sing and dance—a double bonus for a man clearly past the age of marriage.

While Krepel replied to her question, she busied herself in making a hot cup of tea. Through much of her activities, the bachelor astronomer sat silently. He yawned repeatedly and tried to rub the daylight out of his eyes.

"Really, Velissa, I have worked in the observatory all night. I may have to . . ."

He yawned again and shook his head.

"I understand," said Velissa.

Krepel looked relieved as he rose to go back to bed. He passed the brisk fire, warmed his hands, and reminded her to be sure the door was tightly closed when she left.

"Tell your father I've nothing to return, and thank him for the lens," he said as he moved toward his bedroom door. His nightshirt was so long it trailed on the stone floor in the back. Velissa thought him comical but managed to suppress the temptation to laugh at him. He was all but gone from the room when suddenly she remembered her father's question.

"Krepel!" she fairly yelled through the bedroom door after him, "Father also wanted me to ask you if you had noticed any signs of life around the towers of Maldoon."

It took a moment for her question to penetrate his nightcap, but when it did, he re-entered the great hall.

"Life at Maldoon?" He seemed troubled. "More than that," he said. "A week ago when the tilt winds were silent in the valley, I saw a spectre I cannot dismiss from my vision. It came on a day when the west tower of the old ruins was shrouded in smoke. Near evening I trained my scope on the mist and saw through the blue haze that there appeared to be a fire in the tower. I could see a flickering light, but the blaze was shrouded in so thick a gloom that I soon felt unsure of what I had seen."

Velissa was amazed at Krepel's confession.

He was suddenly alert as he continued, "Whether there really was fire in the tower, I can't be sure, but this I know: I saw a figure riding the neck saddle of a catterlob that was running twice as fast as I have ever seen your Collinvar run."

Although Velissa was from the highlands, she was familiar with the huge beasts of the plain. She had even seen catterlobs on occasion and knew how formidable they could appear. She suspected that Krepel was simply overdramatizing the mounted rider.

"I can't see the 'spectre' in this," she said. "The Graygills of the plains always ride catterlobs."

"True, but this was a huge one, and it appeared to be wearing spiked chest-plates."

"An armored catterlob?"

"Yes, and not only the beast was armored, but its rider as well."

"A Graygill in armor? It's not possible. What need would a Graygill have for armor?"

"It was dark, but I am sure it was an armored Graygill, and I know the beast was dressed for war."

"But with whom? There has been no fighting since the Battle of Kendrake a thousand years ago."

Krepel never liked being reminded of history that he already knew.

"I know the dates of the war," the old Moonrhyme replied, feeling even older when he remembered the final struggle of Kendrake. "Still, I am sure of what I saw. Tell your father I saw an armored catterlob with an armored rider."

He turned to his bedroom again and yawned as vigorously as he had told his short tale.

Velissa took some warm water outside to Collinvar, who showed his gratitude by drinking. When he had finished, she went back into Krepel's house to warm herself by the fire and make a second steaming cup of candolet tea.

She sat in the scientist's overstuffed chair to rest. Having gotten up early that morning, she was terribly fatigued by the ride. She grew drowsy before the fire, and though she tried to stay awake, she could not. What should have been only a brief nap extended for more than an hour.

When she awoke, she felt a kind of rested shame. The guilt of leaving Collinvar so long in the cold made her feel even worse. She quickly tied on her riding cape and pulled on her boots and gloves, made warm by the orange-red hearth.

Remembering Krepel's admonition to shut the door tightly, she tested it as she left the warm house. Dutifully, Collinvar had waited for her and soon they were on the high steppes again.

The wind was now against them, and Velissa felt angry at herself for extending her nap for so long. She could scarcely be home before dark, and this guilt which she inflicted on herself made the cold seem all the more brutal—a kind of atonement for her reluctance to leave the hearth. From her reluctance had come the ill-timed nap that would result in a dark ride through the woods.

The cold was severe.

The dark all too soon came on.

Velissa tried to sing while she rode, but the cold wind and the growing darkness was stealing from her all possibility of song as she entered the woods. The dusk of the plains became all of a sudden a forest gloom as Collinvar thundered on into the woods. The crusted snow of the forest trail played a hollow and clicking accompaniment that sounded as eerie as the flint hooves of the centicorn devouring the frozen road.

The smooth strides of the steed obscured a strange movement of the frozen earth, and while Collinvar himself was aware of it, Velissa was not. But soon even she noticed the growing tremor that was not caused by the glassy strides of her mount.

The tremors grew to a groundswell of thunder so loud that the wary Collinvar wheeled without Velissa's permission and, disobedient to his silver bridle and reins, turned from the road and quickly hid in a heavy thicket of trees.

The dark was close, and the woods shook with an awesome quaking. In the near distance there was a thin gleam that moved rapidly toward them. The sound became intense. The light emanated from a torch in the hand of a strongly armed warrior, and the thundering came from the foot treads of a catterlob larger than any Velissa had ever seen before. Old Krepel's words rang even louder in her mind than the denizen tread that now paralyzed her. The beast wore huge armored plates riveted together by knifelike barbs of steel. In the dim angle of the torchlight, Velissa could see that, on the side plates which fell out over the beast's powerful shoulders, there was a strange, spidery insignia emblazoned in the steel.

The amber light fell on the back of the beast's ugly head and illuminated the face of the warrior in the saddle. Yet it was impossible to tell what the rider looked like, and Velissa was suddenly so terrified that she dared not look at all. The fear of being discovered left her with such a paralysis that she forgot the biting cold of the night. The security that she usually felt in the friendly red trees of Quarrystone Woods was gone.

The demon beast passed and then stopped still. Raising his scaly head, he turned in the direction of the thicket that hid Velissa and Collinvar. Velissa refused to breathe for fear they might be discovered. The rider held his torch in their direction but seemed to see nothing. At length he shouted, "Holga!" and the catterlob thundered on into the forest.

When the light had died away and the thunder of the beast was gone, Velissa urged Collinvar back onto the trail once more and they started on for home. The way went slowly, for Collinvar could not move so fast in the starlight. It was difficult for the centicorn to pick a path that avoided the deep indentations which the catterlob's ponderous feet had made in the snowy trail. Yet only once did the sure-footed steed ever stumble, and then not seriously. Velissa was suddenly and terribly aware of the night cold, but its effects on her could not erase the spectre of the armored beast that had passed them in the dark like an omen. The vision occupied her mind until at last in the clearing ahead she saw the lights of home.

Collinvar was as comforted as she.

The dreadful catterlob tracks had not ceased, and now in the starlight she could see that they ran all the way to the very yard of her home. Gratefully, nothing was damaged, or so it appeared. She took the centicorn to the barn and covered him with a warm blanket after she had given him a drink of water. Her father had prepared the water and the stable for Collinvar's return. She was about to turn and leave the stable when she became aware of a figure in the doorway. Only for a moment did she fear it.

"Velissa."

"Papa!"

They embraced.

"Papa, I saw an armored catterlob on the trail."

"I know. . . . His rider came to steal Singreale."

"Did he succeed?" Velissa's concern was more than obvious.

"I think so. Doldeen is gone as well."

"Oh, Father, are you sure?"

"Reasonably so. I can find neither one, and Doldeen cannot survive these temperatures for long."

"Oh, Father, why did she leave the house?" lamented Velissa. They closed the door of Collinvar's stall and then the barn door and turned toward the house.

"It was her protective instinct towards Singreale that caused her to leave." The astronomer had answered her question belatedly and was taken with a kind of fatigue that bore like a lead weight upon his frame.

Shuffling toward the house, he took Velissa's gloved hand in his own and drew her very close as he continued, "I was about to go to the observatory after I had eaten my meal when I heard Essey—I mean, Doldeen, cry 'Singreale!' She bolted for the diamond as the door flew open. A monstrous figure in black armour came through the door as Doldeen, with the gem in her fangs, raced out into the night. The intruder turned back outside and there was scuffling in the darkness before the warrior mounted the catterlob and rode away. Once the hideous beast was gone, I looked in the snow for both Singreale and Doldeen."

They arrived at the door of the house and went inside. The cold of the late afternoon ride forced Velissa to move quietly to the hearth. She warmed her hands and removed her cold cloak to enjoy the full benefit of the heat.

Soon both she and her father shared a cup of candolet tea. In grieving the loss of Doldeen, they said nothing to each other.

Gradually they became aware of a faint tapping at the side door of the house.

"It's the wind," said the scientist.

Velissa said nothing but let her silence concur. With the wind coming up as it now was, her hopes for Doldeen's survival grew faint. The tapping continued.

"No," she cried, "it's not wind!"

She ran to the door and flung it open.

The silver-horned head half-reared itself from a snowy set of coils.

"Doldeen! You must be frozen!"

"Yessss, Missssy," the serpent cried, and when she opened her mouth to speak, her jaws formed the setting for a most welcome sight. Beneath her graceful fangs glowed the crystal splendor of Singreale.

There are worlds unseen by naked eyes,
And pompously our science tries
To call us to some telescope,
To see what best is viewed by hope.

CHAPTER III
Night Flight

As they had agreed, Raccoman and Parsky met on the snowy trail north of the crumbling fortress. Raccoman had risen against a darkness so deep that it afforded no horizon; but he knew the ancient roads quite well and thus walked with a yellow-booted briskness into the morning.

The morning was still, and the heavy clothing that he wore was as cumbersome as it was warm. But it was easier to wear the extra clothes than to carry them, and when the tilt winds came in mid-afternoon, he would need all that he wore.

Raccoman could not imagine why Parsky had taken an indirect route from his home. He wished the Blackgill were with him for the companionship they always enjoyed. The stew-cook so detested rising early that he had chosen to camp for a night in the empty and eerie halls of Maldoon; he preferred to make a two-day trip of a more casual pace than to expend the vigor required to walk to the eastern cliffs in a single day. It was, indeed, an arduous walk that would make the flight back seem fleeting.

In his pocket Raccoman felt the note he had received from his uncle who lived on the edge of the Western Highlands. The request excited him. He would be glad to go to Quarrystone and weld the cradle of the scope. It was not an urgent request, and the job could be done after the worst of winter was over and spring had all but begun.

His mind was as active as his feet while he trudged eastward. A hundred-thousand boot prints brought him steadily toward the cliffs, and by noon he could see the granite parapet. He hoped to be there by late afternoon and certainly by dark. He stopped near a small grove of trees and ate a raw, cold, vegetable sandwich. From his elevated vantage point, he could survey the trail up which he expected the Blackgill to come.

The winds had not yet begun. In the distance he could see Maldoon, the tops of whose towers were shrouded in mist or smoke. He strained to see the red form of the Blackgill against the sunny snow.

Raccoman had never been good at waiting. He was always fidgety and soon had traced a complex set of footprints into the snowy hilltop. He paced and waited, and chided his absent friend:

"Parsky, you dawdling and piddling chum!
While you should have arrived, you still have not come.
You offend every moment and break every date,
And keep your appointments a half-a-day late!"

Behind him, someone cleared his throat and he wheeled to see the Blackgill grinning at his criticism. Raccoman shifted on his feet, trying to keep his startled verse alive.

"Parsky, I didn't expect you to be
Spying on me from the snow-covered trees."

His rhyme was a near miss, for "trees" and "be" didn't quite form the jingle with the poetic perfection he would have liked, but the Blackgill's sudden appearance had rattled his mind.

"That is obvious," said Parsky. "Well, let's see . . . six foils and hand straps."

Parsky always brought the foils with him since he lived near the ginjon forest and had a plentiful supply. The large foils were all lying neatly stacked and interlocked.

"Shall we go before the winds begin?" the Graygill asked. The Blackgill nodded his agreement.

Parsky picked up the foils and they moved off through the small grove in the direction of the granite parapet.

"The air is gloomy
Above the bulwarks of Maldoon."

It was another near-rhyme.

"Mist, not gloom," said the stew-cook, clearly irritated.

"Just mist?"

"Rain-fog and snow haze," said Parsky. "With all that mist, you should see the ice crystals that form on the upper towers. The icy outer stones trap light and speed it through the gleaming hallways. I camped last night in the ancient throne room of Singreale, where stalactites of ice hung from the upper vaults and dripped light from long-dead evening stars."

Raccoman was intrigued by the image.

"You make it sound so frigid-fair
I am not sure that I would dare
Resist the urge to visit there."

"Oh, I wouldn't," Parsky strongly protested. "It sounds magic, but the palace is a haunt of icy spirits that bleed and screech at midnight. I quaked! In the frozen light, I saw the ghost of the vanquished king, Singreale, as transparent as the lost diamond that bears his name. He was pale as frost and stalked the icy labyrinth where he once had ruled. He looked exactly as he had the night the siege broke through the double walls and the castle fell to the marauders."

Parsky smiled as he told the story. Then he quickly wiped the smile from his face, embarrassed that he had found his somber tale so amusing.

On a higher rise, Raccoman paused and looked back at Maldoon. The sight was even more foreboding. The welder could not take his eyes from the dense cloud that all but completely concealed the distant fortress. Parsky turned and looked with him, and in their silent stare the eerie cloud seemed to darken. At last Raccoman said:

"This fog that sculpts ice and guilds the frozen towers,
Looks not like mist at all but more like foundry smoke."

"Mist!" cried Parsky, angry that Raccoman had cared to disagree with him when he had just spent the night in the sparkling citadel. He smiled as if to make amends for the hostile tone of his voice, turned on the heel of his red boot, and started to walk.

"Great distant ginjon forests, bound in silver wire!
The western towers of Maldoon have exploded into fire!"

Parsky wheeled to look. "What?" he asked, staring hard at the distant cloud.

"For a moment, Parsky, I would swear
The smoke gave way and fire burst there.
The western towers became a flare."

"Nonsense," Parsky replied." I was there just last night. The towers are solid ice. Come on! The winds will be beginning all too soon and then the going will be slow."

Parsky was right. Raccoman decided that he must have been mistaken, for as hard as he stared into the distance, he could see nothing more now than smoke or mist. He was foolish to have imagined anything else. Still, if only the tilt winds would come early, the gloom would be blown away and he might behold a true glint of fiery light upon the towers of ice. Besides, he would rather question his own senses than doubt his friend.

He turned from Maldoon and followed his red-coated companion up the narrow lane that crossed the broad, white plains. They fell into more casual conversation as Parsky confessed that he would not have arrived late had he not found a lone catterlob and rode him north. Raccoman lamented that the two of them had not come across so recent a piece of fortune. The beasts by now were all taking refuge in various breaks and groves, for they knew and feared the icy discomfort of the tilt winds that Parsky and Dakktare were planning to surf.

Their path for the next two hours wound ever closer to the granite tower ahead of them. It was late when Parsky shouted suddenly, "Here it comes!"

Both of them braced themselves and listened. There was a strange howling in the sky above them. Raccoman hastily pulled his heavy hood forward. Parsky took his free hand and did the same, and then grabbed the foils firmly in both hands and cried again, "Hang on, Raccoman!"

"To what?!"

It was a fair question. There was nothing nearby that either of them could cling to.

The howling skies were screaming in pain, and their screeching agony deepened into thunder and then exploded in fury all around Raccoman and Parsky. The first gales hit the eager sky-surfers with such force that they both were knocked flat on the ground. With tenacity Parsky held to the giant leaves while Raccoman cheered both his grip on the foils and the fury of the slanting zephyrs.

It was cold!

The pair made their way in pain the last three miles to the base of the granite parapet. They began to climb. The steep passages made them feel like insects frozen to the high and unguarded precipice they ascended. They felt as icy as the stone itself, for the wind had made the cold unbearable. As the gales intensified, the sun slipped behind the western cliffs and night swept the empty sky with icy air. The two friends looked forward to the time when they would eagerly commit themselves to the wind, for the only way to battle the gales was to ride them.

It was completely dark by the time they reached the top of the monolith. They did not stand on ceremony, having already decided to leap as soon as possible, if only to warm up. The stars above the eastern cliffs were blue-white and sparkled like frozen blips of burning snow in the black night sky.

Quickly they strapped on their foils. As soon as the knots were tied Raccoman replaced his heavy, yellow gloves and called over his shoulder:

> "Good-bye my friend!
> I'll join you there
> In the upper wind."

The rush of night air tore at his face as he ran to the edge of the parapet and dove like a swimmer into the invisible gales. The air halted his defiant dive and hurled him a thousand feet upward into the stars. He felt immediately warmer. The stars gleamed and the constellation of the Grand Dragon sparkled all around him.

Parsky had not yet "jumped free," as he always said. At least Raccoman could not see him, and thus the Graygill enjoyed his solo in the empty sky. He loved singing, and the exhilaration of space lured him at last to mingle the tones of his robust ballad with the flickering eyes of night.

> "I have come to the arms of the evening sky
> To swim the empty track of space,
> Where the dragon stars of brilliance lie
> White woven into flaming lace.
> Hail to the light of the fiery night
> Where the crystal constellations soar
> And the blue-white beams of the starry streams
> Are washing galaxies ashore!"

In the ecstasy of his flight, he turned and rolled, drew back his foils and plunged a thousand feet into the black. His dive ended in resolve that pulled the foils straight out and the obliging winds again hurled him straight up into the womb of space. Once more he rocketed into night and rolled and catapulted into the studded, black of the earless void that was a galactic sea of eyes.

He rolled again and seemed to stop as if he hung on silver wires. A star stuck to his shoulder and another to his foot. He had never been so high. A swarm of tiny, white-hot comets passed through his very soul. They stung like flecks of sand in a wind storm, but the liveliness of their burning did not deter his song.

> *"Come, you cold, fire-spangled sea*
> *And sting my eyes as amberoids!*
> *Glow blue, you snow-hazed nebulae*
> *Like fields of lava asteroids.*
> *There's a planet coiled in fiery rings,*
> *And a nova glutting on the night.*
> *When the sun retires, the stars are kings*
> *As I, Dakktare, am king of flight."*

His singing possessed an eerie thinness as he soared aloft, but his tendency toward arrogance was as thick as ever. Among the stars, he congratulated himself in a laughing jingle whose near melody slid along his foil wings and fell upward, snagging on nail points of light.

> *"Sky Prince, you're the best of all those who fly,*
> *The superb silver rider who tames the wild sky.*
> *All winds must surrender their swift moving air*
> *To the genius flight of the Graygill, Dakktare."*

His congratulation was barely out of his mouth when a gust of tilt wind flung him even higher. He was no longer cold. Indeed, the heavens seemed mysteriously warm, as he looked in vain for the Blackgill. The night below him made it impossible to see his missing friend, but he was not worried, for he felt certain that Parsky was enjoying his own lonely quadrant of space.

Raccoman rolled to his back and stroked gently with his yellow feet until he slowed to a stop. He wiggled his hands from under the straps and held the wind foils, as one of the light blips stuck to his moustache. He blew it away and it soared like a glistening seed puff, tumbling into other blips of light and then floating slowly to a stop.

Raccoman closed his eyes for a moment.

When he opened them again, a wondrous vision caught his sight. There was a moving starfield that approached him. It was difficult to tell how many stars were in it, but there appeared to be hundreds. The advance of the stars increased their intensity and their size. The spectacle was breathtaking; Raccoman finned the upper silence and watched.

In but a moment, the starfield had become a gathering of lights, then men on huge, winged creatures. The men were not Graygills, but tall and angular titans dressed in light armor. The light came from within their massive beings and shown out, and they crossed the outer sky only a short distance from Raccoman but seemed to take no notice of him at all.

The vanguard were all standard carriers, and their banners, floating from tall silver staves, bore a single phrase: "The Desire of Ren!" One of the banners bore the word *Rensgaard,* and the titans moved along, singing something about the Reign of Ren on Estermann.

Raccoman listened until the anthem faded into silence and the flying, mounted titans became only a starfield once again. He watched until the small blips of light disappeared into the black beneath the constellation of the Grand Dragon and were gone.

Raccoman reflected on the vision, which he felt was more than a vision. The huge men were real and sang of the Desire of Ren and his reign on Estermann. Could this planet hold some continent beyond the one where Graygills lived? Were there other lands and other people? People different from those who lived in the valley of the Graygills?

His musings about lost lands suddenly congealed in fear. His fears became a threat, for he was high in the heavens and he felt the tilt winds falter, then fail. His field of vision swam in the vortex of swirling colors as he tumbled through the black sky toward hard collision. He rolled over and over, mixing the hot white lines of star streaks with the red and green of his delirium. He tried to move his arms in the foils, but they were useless. He was caught in the deadly pull of his own planet, with not a hint of tilt winds now to break his fall. The world he loved seemed now an alien killer.

The rush of air was so furious he could not even call out as he neared the moment of impact.

Everything went black. But the darkness was not silent. He saw the Star Riders split the air near the high cliff openings of the Moonrhyme caves. The dead sky above Demmerron held a huge falcon as black as the night through which it soared. The winged sentry was carrying a huge diamond in one talon and a serpent with glowing eyes in the other. The black came on deeper and deeper—the wind was oppressive. Raccoman felt an intense and sudden pain and then nothing.

A kind of blackness that holds no symbols occupied the Graygill for what seemed like a short time but was really a long time. And when he finally began to feel cold, he at least considered that a life sign. A coma on any world is like death, and feeling cold is much better than feeling nothing. After the cold came a sharp feeling of pain in his back; that too was a welcome pain.

Into his foggy focus came a long, black thing, with two small spheres of light. Gradually the black thing became Parsky's gills; the two spheres became the bachelor's eyes.

"What happened?" asked Parsky.

"Where am I?"

"Flat on your back; otherwise your face would be buried in the snow."

Parsky's logic was at once reprimand and humor. They both laughed, but Dakktare's laugh ended in a groan. He had hit the ground with such force that everything hurt.

"I ran into a moving starfield that turned into titan soldiers twice our size who rode on flying beasts."

"Your head's been injured in the fall," said Parsky. "You had best be content with wind-surfing, and no more this year; the winds are through, and so, I hope, are such wild visions."

Sure enough, it was calm, and because there was no wind, the pair felt very little cold. That was always the problem with the winds; they could die as abruptly as they began and drop Graygills out of the sky onto hard meadows.

"I saw a lighted legion of titan knights whose king is Ren of Rensgaard. I believe Rensgaard may be another continent on Estermann, Parsky."

Parsky shrugged and smiled at his words. "There are no other continents on Estermann. Remember what our forbears said, 'Ours is the perfect world built perfectly; Estermann: one continent, one sea.'"

"I always believed that. Now I am not sure," said the Graygill.

It was pointless to argue, so while Raccoman could not deny his experience, he did drop the subject. A glorious idea had been born in his mind—though he knew there would be little use in discussing it with Parsky.

"Where are we?"

"Look."

Even in the dark Raccoman could see Parsky's red square house against the ginjon trees.

"Home!" he cried.

"My home, at least," laughed the Blackgill. Raccoman expressed his relief in verse:

"I'm glad I had the common sense
To manage this coincidence."

It was a stroke of luck in a cold, dark night, rest assured, for soon the pair were inside, basking drowsily in the heat of the hearth. They enjoyed a warm half-cauldron of stew. To Raccoman, his friend's stew had seemed a trifle lumpy of late. But he ate it in the good faith in which it had been offered, and it left them both warmer in the fatigue that had made them all the more eager for bed. They slept ever so soundly.

They woke on a quiet and wind-free morning.

The fire had died, and Raccoman got out of bed and went directly into the frosty morning. He left the cold interior of the house for the ever-cold exterior through the same side door he had used on his last stay. This time he was amazed to see that all of Parsky's congrel cages were empty except two on the very bottom row.

"Escaped! Escaped!
The doors are wide, the congrels are set free,"

he thought as he bent over the woodpile to pick up a few snowy chunks of candolet bark. Then, with his face close to the ground, he noticed a frosted pile of small sticks. He poked the pile with a piece of bark. The mound fell apart.

"Bones!" he cried.

Sure enough, it was a stack of bones from some small birds or animals. Raccoman had come upon an occasional animal skeleton in the meadows in summer, but never had he seen so many little skeletons all at once.

He looked at the empty cages. The two remaining congrels looked frightened. He poked the pile of bones again and both of the animals shivered and turned their faces toward the dark interiors of their cages. Sensing their fear, Raccoman was bewildered. He reached into one of the occupied cages to pet and comfort the creature, but it snarled viciously at him. He had never heard one of the lovable animals growl, much less snarl. He withdrew his hand quickly and shut the cage door.

He kicked the small mound of bones before he returned to the house and built a roaring fire.

The Blackgill and Graygill talked long after they had finished breakfast.

"The congrels are all gone," said Raccoman. The statement was not quite a question, but it invited reply.

"Like winter, itself, they are gone. I've set them free. Free for mating in the fields of Canby. Free to raise their young. Free to enjoy the warm summer sunlight.

"Free as the trees
And the summer."

Raccoman stood up, walked to the hearth, and brought the big black kettle back to the breakfast table. He poured himself and the Blackgill a second cup of tea.

"Parsky, near the woodpile
By the earthen gray stones
There's a curious mound
Of tiny white bones."

"I know, chum. Though I haven't the foggiest notion of their origin. They have puzzled me as much as I am sure they puzzled you." Raccoman pressed the subject:

"Further, your captured congrels are ill behaved,
They are savage or frightened or very distraught.
One flew in an instant to snarling
When I attempted to reach in his cage."

Parsky fidgeted, then slammed his fist on the table in anger.
"Did you open the cages?"
"I, I," stammered Dakktare.
"Did you?" shouted the Blackgill.

"Yes, but—"

"Did any escape?"

"No. But there are only two cages left with any in them."

"I told you I set the others free!"

Parsky's face stood out in glowing red above his black gills.

The metal-worker had seldom seen the stew-cook in such a sudden fit of rage. He decided to change the subject.

"While I was surfing stars last night,
My eyes beheld a sea of light—
Flaming fiery soldiers twice our size!
In light, they hurtled out of sky
And flew where only titans fly,
Returning to some continent
Of this, our present world."

Parsky cocked an eyebrow and drummed his lean fingers on the table.

"Delirious poet! There are no flying titans twice our size. It only seems that way when your mind is cold and the tilt winds dump you a thousand icy feet into the hard snow. You did not see these imaginary men and then fall. You hit the hard world and imagined all you think you saw in space."

"Untrue, Blackgill! There are starfields made of men,
Whose banners tell of their allegiance
To fly the edge of sky."

"Your head is full of clouds, not stars. There are no other continents. You'd best do all you can to enjoy this one, for it is the only home you'll ever know."

Raccoman finished his candolet tea. The morning had become somehow disagreeable. He wanted to go home. It was pointless to argue with the Blackgill. Besides, arguing was not much of a sport to Graygills. Even when they won, they were so tender of heart they could not stand to see their antagonists lose.

Raccoman put on his coat and gloves and walked out into the morning sun. It was warmer than it had been in a month. He called out a farewell to the grumpy Blackgill as he started for home. Soon he could see the round yellow house he loved so much. His house was as bright as his boots and his entire world view. In the field beyond his house, he could see his oval barn and, beyond that, the eastern cliffs above which only last night he had seen the tall and beautiful inhabitants of a continent unknown to him, a vision that had so ignited his imagination he was not sure he could ever be content again with the home where he lived.

He walked into his house and removed his yellow mackinaw and muffler—it was too hot for them anyway. He ran his hand into his coat pocket before hanging the coat on a wall hook. There he found the crumpled note from his uncle regarding the welding that needed to be done west of the highlands. He stuffed the note between two cups on a lower shelf and turned toward his cold fireplace. It was midday and not very cold, so he decided to wait a while before he built a fire.

He passed a bronze mirror, and his egotism forced him to have a look and create a verse to celebrate himself.

> "Dakktare, you know you're a devilish bloke,
> You're handsome and winsome, a real Graygill rogue.
> Admire me, you plain;
> Esteem, you who lack—"

He stopped short, moved closer to the mirror, and inspected his face. "Esteem, you who lack," he repeated, then continued,

> "It must be the cold of the upper night air
> That freezes the locks and darkens the hair.
> Determined to make the Blackgill Dakktare."

He shuddered at the thought.

From the mirror a face loomed out above his own. It grinned, then sneered, then grinned again. Then the horrible face tilted backward and laughed a free but horrible laugh, and the laughter fell out of the reflection and filled the room with so much sound that Raccoman covered his ears and squinted, as though he hoped the clenching of his eyelids would shut out the sound. When he uncovered his ears again, the sound was gone and the evil face had left the glass.

(45)

Let the çentaur play while his gold hooves prance.
Let his man part sing and his beast part dance.
He's a schizoid beast whose man eats bread
While his hungry hulk craves straw instead.

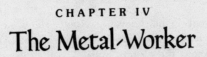

CHAPTER IV
The Metal-Worker

RACCOMAN DAKKTARE was not disobedient to his heavenly vision. He woke early, peered through the window, and exulted in the bright blue day erupting pink-edged above the eastern cliffs. The day was so beautiful and still as to make him doubt that there even were such things as tilt winds. The distant silver forest glistened like a thin ribbon of light under the pink horizon that fled upward into the blue glass dome of the Estermann sky.

Winter would soon be gone and spring would speed his new vision to completion. The only thing that stood in the way of beginning his new dream was a slice of black bread and a cup of tea, which he laid near the hearth while he pulled on his yellow boots and tunic. He then went to admire himself in the mirror, and his admiration only served to deepen the affection and esteem he had always felt for his glorious self. By the time he was finished at his mirror, his bread was quite hot, which was exactly how he liked it. Like most bachelors, he gobbled rather than ate his food. He was still chewing the last bite as he pulled on his cap and walked outside.

On a day like this he would allow nothing to frustrate him.

Almost nothing! Raccoman realized that if the trend he had been observing in his mirror continued, he would not be a Graygill much longer. There were even more black hairs in his gills now than there had been just a week before. Thus, he walked along, kicking the snow and mumbling to himself:

> *"If the trend continues, my whiskers will grow,*
> *As black as the bark of a ginjon tree;*
> *And Parsky will swear he is brother to me."*

He scowled at the thought of looking too much like Parsky.

He trudged on. The last snow had begun to look old, and while there might still be other snowfalls this season, they would not come today. Raccoman's energy was fired by a new dream. Nothing mattered now but the vision that had fallen upon him out of the stars. A man's dreams become the man and etch themselves on the soul until they become a reality.

Less than two miles from his yellow house was an old and neglected barn whose once-yellow paint was sadly chipped. In a spirit of zeal, Raccoman Dakktare entered the abandoned barn as though he were stepping directly into the future. As long as he could remember, the barn had stood in the meadow.

It was nearly noon when Dakktare entered the old barn. The barns on Estermann, like the houses of the planet, were never square with gabled roofs. They were not even rectangular. They were round or oval shaped with peaked and conical roofs. Sometimes they were nearly spherical with brass spheres set in finned tiers that rotated with even the slightest breeze.

By afternoon, the bright sunlight of the morning was less intense, and a slight chill in the air suggested a gentle snow might now be gathering in the west. In the dim light of the rickety old barn, Raccoman strained to see the large pieces of wind foil strewn about. Gaps in the tin roof permitted the sun to fall in blips of light all over the floor. These splotches of sun gave Raccoman the impression that he was walking on the ceiling of an inverted sky. But it was only the world of Raccoman Dakktare which, up till now, had been right side up.

In most ways, the barn was inadequate for the project he had in mind. The lighting was terrible and the splotches of daylight would make every mathematical calculation a nightmare. The leaky roof would let snow and rain fall upon his remarkable effort, and the ground would be fouled around the area where he must work. Only one part of the old barn was weatherproof—a lean-to shed where his tools would be stored. But suitable space or not, he went to work. Nothing could daunt his enthusiasm. He lifted one of his shaggy eyebrows and studied the great, steel sheets of wind foil and smiled. The gleam of light from his overly large teeth was evidence that his genius was at last to bloom on Estermann.

He constantly talked to himself when there was no one else at hand. He worked best when someone complimented his efforts, and since he was going to be working alone, he would have to supply all the approval he needed,

"This is my day,
What a day to be free!"

He laughed and slapped his knee; then rollicked hysterically and waltzed through the barn in his obese glee.

> *"All Estermann will marvel and stare*
> *At the genius art of*
> *   the Graygill Dakktare.*
> *I'm handsome and clever*
> *   as ever you find.*
> *I'm brilliant, efficient,*
> *   and honest and kind,*
> *I'm strong and robust*
> *   in body and mind."*

He said nothing of humility and that was at least honest. He then spoke to the scattered foils.

> *"Where do we begin, my little steel friends?*
> *Ah, come to me, and you will be*
> *The wonder of this world."*

He set himself to gathering the wind foils and welding them at right angles.

His torch was lit by steel-fire—old-fashioned by every standard of Estermann. Most metal-workers agreed that wind foils should be welded by star-steam, which never made a faulty seam. But that sort of welding equipment was far beyond the budget that the Graygill had set for himself. Besides, the steel-fire worked nearly as well, and so he continued gathering foils and welding them until the long hours of afternoon sun were finished and the light splotches on the floor were almost black. He had worked in silence and the clink of his welder sounded loud when he stopped at last and hung his torch on the charred hook against the black wall.

He stepped back and surveyed the odd object he was bringing into being. It glistened with hairlike silver welds, and even in the half-light, it was clear that Raccoman was a superb craftsman. He stroked his whiskers and addressed his embryo invention:

> *"If you had not been welded*
> *Then what would you be?*
> *A pile of old wind foils*
> *Stacked under some tree.*
> *You'd soon be all rusted*

In Estermann's air.
You're lucky you met
With the torch of Dakktare.

Dakktare, you're the standard
All men should be.
You're the heartbeat, the center,
The substance, the key;
An idol deserving of idolatry."

Saying nothing of modesty, he turned on the heel of his yellow boot and left the barn.

The day was beautiful, or rather had been. Raccoman had spent most of it inside. A poor poet may be a good welder—indeed, an excellent welder—and our Dakktare felt heroic, for a good day's work is its own reward, and a man who marvels at himself may oftentimes be justified.

It was not far across the fields, but the walk was a reasonable challenge to Raccoman's stubby legs. The sun was almost gone, but it never occurred to anyone on Estermann to be afraid of the dark, for the dark was as friendly as the light.

There were as many kinds of animals and birds on Estermann as on earth—probably more, but everything on Estermann was more so than on earth. Colors were more colorful and fur more furry. There were great creatures that lived in the forests of the planet, but their size did not make them fierce. The animals of the planet never stalked each other, for all were vegetarian. Large animals roamed the fields as well, but they, too, were all friends of the Graygills.

The largest of all Estermann creatures were the catterlobs. They were dragonlike but as kind as they were awesome.

The catterlob had a huge ridge of bone that passed behind its slender head to form a natural saddle-shelf for the adventurous. Its nose was long and ran the entire distance from its wide-set, oval eyes to its flaring nostrils. Two long tusks hung from its underjaw, which looked fearsome but served no malicious purpose.

Catterlobs could rise on their haunches to a towering height equal to the combined height of three Graygill homes. But they never came near the towns, preferring to spend their summers and winters in the well-watered plains around Canby.

On his way home, Raccoman passed a trio of the beasts trying to graze in the snowy meadow, and one of them was a calf of the size that Graygills used for an evening of sport riding. The beasts were usually amiable to the instant whims of Estermannians, but Raccoman had no time for sport now that he had begun his great invention. While he did not intend to become fanatic about it, he knew the morning would come early and he would have to return once more to the old barn.

It was all but night when Raccoman finally arrived home. His house was as quaint as he himself. As it squatted under a burdensome nest of yellow vines, it looked like a pile of stones with a blonde and unkempt hairdo. The shutters were open, and through the glass, Raccoman could see his blazing hearth. At a distance, he had seen the flickering of the fire and became excited, for he knew only one person who would enter his house and build a fire without permission. He was surprised that Parsky had come so soon after their recent trip to the eastern cliffs. In the anticipation of the greeting, he set his stubby legs in motion and bolted through his own front door.

"Parsky! Bless my uncle's nephew!" Of course, he was but blessing himself.

> *"Parsky, you rogue*
> *You old catterlob*
> *You underweight Blackgill*
> *You underfed snob!"*

This greeting took some amount of brash nerve, since Raccoman was as round as Parsky was thin. But Dakktare never ran short of brashness.

Parsky was carrying a large kettle of soup which he had just taken from the fire. Before he could set the kettle down to greet Raccoman, it nearly capsized in the vigor of their embrace.

"Ah, Raccoman," Parsky said, "I bring you good news." His eyes were lit from within. "The moving starfield you said you saw may be real. Your uncle Krepel was playing with his star-scope recently and saw masses of moving light."

"Where?"

"Close," said Parsky whose coal-black moustache was twitching underneath his flat nose. "In the Southwest quadrant of the evening sky."

"How do you know? Have you seen my uncle?"

"There was a letter in my box before you left yesterday. I didn't find it till you were gone."

"What did my uncle's letter say?"

"He says he cannot understand the riddle of the moving stars. He was puzzled when he first began to track them, for they appeared only random blips of light. Then, before his very eyes, he saw the distant moving stars fall into an organized formation—like a moving constellation—and then, locked into that fixed configuration, move off over the horizon and leave the viewing field of the orange observatory."

Parsky's mind wandered to the time he first met Dakktare's Moonrhyme uncle. It was hundreds of years ago at the Survival festival of the Moonrhymes. Parsky was troubled by something deep and painful in his past, something he had never confessed to Raccoman but told the wise and kind Krepel. The star-watcher had earlier tried to get the angular but handsome Blackgill to seek the affections of Velissa of Quarrystone Woods, but Parsky was disinterested. Now Parsky's past was too remote to trouble him, but his visits to the orange observatory were as frequent as ever. The star-watcher talked mostly of the heavens or of his Moonrhyme past, while the congenial Parsky cooked and listened.

"I tell you, Parsky, seen close enough these stars are not stars—they are flying titans," Raccoman interjected into Parsky's reverie.

Parsky cocked an eyebrow. He was willing, on the evidence of Krepel's scope, to accept the reality of moving starfields, but he was not yet ready to accept his friend's visions seen on the night he had hit the earth and jarred his imagination with wild reports.

"Do you suppose I could have a look through Old Krepel's glass?" Raccoman asked, changing the subject. "He's fussy about his scope, but surely he would never refuse his own nephew a turn at it."

Though Parsky was trimmer of physique than Raccoman, this alone could not distinguish him. Everyone on the planet was thinner than the arrogant metal-worker Raccoman. But Parsky was lean, and something stiff and foreboding inhabited this thinness. Everywhere that Raccoman was gray, Parsky was black, and the black sometimes seemed sinister to the Graygills. The Blackgill's eyebrows were pointed and drawn upward on his white forehead. His hair was a shaggy carpet of disobedience and incredibly thick.

Yet the jolly metal-worker and the thin and nervous stew-cook had become friends through Parsky's relationship with Dakktare's star-watching uncle. The three of them were a triumvirate of hilarity and great parties. Still, Raccoman could see that his uncle and Parsky shared something special in their relationship that did not include him. However, a Graygill's best friend was always the person he was currently with, and Raccoman and Parsky had been together much.

Parsky picked up the pail of soup again. His hands were long and tapered, and his fingers were so thin they seemed to twine around the bail of the fragrant cauldron. He carried the great kettle to the table where he promptly poured half the contents into one huge bowl and half into another bowl. Then he walked back to the big oven, took out a loaf of blackmeal bread, and set the loaf in the center of Raccoman's round dining table. His thin and willowy legs made a final and rapid trip to retrieve the knife and butter.

"I shall slay the loaf, Dakktare," he announced.

Raccoman looked away, embarrassed to hear such a strange and forbidden expression.

"So it is slain!" Parsky laughed as he plunged the huge knife into the bread. The laugh resounded to the corners of the room, making the metal-worker want to cover his ears. Raccoman ignored his discomfort and complimented his friend.

> "Parsky,
> You can make a table shine
> And wake a dead man in the steam
> of this delicious smell."

But Parsky seemed not to hear him as they pulled out their chairs and sat down.

Then Raccoman raised his eyes and spoke the Graygill customary words before beginning the meal.

> "To the maker of the feast
> To the power of loaf and yeast
> Till the broth and bread have ceased
> Gratefulness is joy!"

Parsky looked annoyed. He waited out the verse in impatience.

They began to eat, smiling broadly through the steam that rose from their bowls. It was after the second spoonful that Raccoman bit into a strange, firm lump in the broth. The lump had a taste familiar to Raccoman after the last few stews Parsky had prepared for him. The flavor of this ingredient was distinctly different from the vegetables Raccoman used for his own stews, and the texture of the lump, as he chewed, was sinewy. Yet it was tasty.

"All right," he said. "Parsky, what is new in the stew?"

"Congrel," the Blackgill answered, not looking up.

"Congrel!" cried Dakktare, gagging as he swallowed. "Surely you do not speak truth."

"On the contrary, I do. I took them from the cages back of my house."

"And you killed them?"

"They would have drowned in the stew if I had not," laughed Parsky.

"But we are not permitted to murder nor eat meat," protested Dakktare with an earnestness that made him forget his affected way of speaking in rhyme.

"What's a congrel?" argued Parsky. "It's nothing more than a . . . a—"

"A living beast with no defense system. Where is your sense of fairness? Suppose the beasts were to set upon *us*."

"Congrels?" asked Parsky, still laughing.

"Well, then an army of congrels!"

The idea of these gentle, lop-eared creatures mobilizing a fearsome army on Estermann brought a faint smile through Raccoman's indignation.

"An army of congrels!" taunted Parsky. Both of them sat silently for a moment. Then Raccoman threw down his spoon and pushed his large bowl of soup to the center of the table.

"I will not eat murdered congrels!" he said firmly.

"Think of it as meat! If you think of congrels and animal executions, nothing will taste good. Think only of meat!"

"Meat?"

"Yes, meat and vegetables—tell me, Raccoman, did you taste the lump on the first bite?"

"No, the second!" said Raccoman.

"And did you enjoy the first bite?"

"Well, yes," he admitted reluctantly.

"And on the second bite, after you had tasted the meat, did you enjoy it?"

"Well, yes—till I found out what it was."

"So, it was good, wasn't it?"

"But congrels, Parsky? Helpless little congrels?"

"But they are delicious, and they make a soup so much more than it might otherwise be. Quit being silly and finish your soup! Besides, the last three times you have eaten at my house, I have served you the same congrel stew."

"I will not eat!" Raccoman said, angry that the Blackgill had tricked him on three previous occasions into accepting what was forbidden.

"Eat it, please, Raccoman. I have cooked for you the entire day. The broth is good. Let's eat it and we shall enjoy ourselves as we always do. There's no need to be afraid of the meat. It shall add as much to our friendship as it does to the stew."

"But meat is a murdered beast!"

"Please, Raccoman, let's eat it together. No one will find out about it. Only we shall know."

With all Parsky's pleading, it was hard for the Graygill to say no. Somehow the stew had been good, and Raccoman was hungry. He pulled the bowl back toward the rim of the great round table and picked up his spoon again. He was suddenly aware of Parsky's black moustache and fascinated by the color of it. Parsky had been eating vigorously before the argument broke out, and his moustache was clotted with soup.

"Parsky, why is your moustache black?"

"Now, you're an odd lot—first you protest my stew and then my appearance. My moustache is black because every hair that makes it is black."

Raccoman felt ashamed. His lack of esteem for off-color moustaches was clear even though he tried to hide it. He felt he had wronged Parsky. He wanted furiously to eat the soup and reassure Parsky that he really had not meant to offend him by pointing out the color of his gills.

Parsky looked hurt.

So Raccoman dived into his bowl and ate the stew—vegetables, meat, and all.

No sooner had he finished than the wind began to blow. He hurried outside. He usually loved snow storms, but he wished to protect his windows and so he closed the shutters against the gale and went back inside his house. When he had warmed his backside at the hearth, he sat by the fire feeling most queer.

Parsky smoked his pipe and smiled contentedly.

It was near the end of winter so there would be no tilt winds, but it was not past the season when storms swept the Graygill country. Raccoman was glad that he had made it home from the old barn before the snow had come.

The flames leapt while the last snow of winter sang and danced at the frosted glass. It was a gentle blizzard, and the warm fire soon had Raccoman dozing in his easy chair with his hands clasped on top of his spherical middle. He snored intermittently with such vigor that it seemed as though the winter winds were inside his house.

His yellow boots stood beside his footstool where he frequently left them. All Graygills were fond of their boots, made of warm, brightly dyed candolet fibers and lined with the fleece of talmonar seed puffs. It was customary to keep one's boots nearby even when one slept. Except when dancing the Claxton, no Graygill ever left his boots more than two paces from his bed, for everyone despised going barefoot, even on a warm, wooden floor.

When Raccoman was sound asleep, Parsky took his friend's yellow boots, stole out of the room, and hid them in the second drawer of his bureau. Parsky was impish at heart. Then he took a little vial of oil from the top of his own red boot and pulled the stopper. The dozing metal-worker never knew he owned or carried such a vial. The aroma from the opened vial was wonderful, and the smell declared itself above the delightful odor of the burning wood. Parsky tiptoed over to Raccoman and put a single drop of clear liquid from the vial on the end of Raccoman's gray and black moustache. At last Parsky removed his red boots and lit his pipe once more.

Raccoman Dakktare usually considered dreaming a waste of time. Storyless sleeping was his favorite way to spend a night. But either his gnawing guilt over having eaten the congrel stew or the pleasant odor from Parsky's vial filled his brain with soothing images that all too quickly turned to terror.

He was barefoot in his dream and walking in his own meadow. He saw a family of congrels munching flowers in the shade of a small tree, and he could not resist going to them. He loved playing with them and holding them close to his own round cheeks and stroking their soft fur.

As Raccoman moved closer, they became aware of him and did something he had seen them do only once before. They bared their teeth at him and growled exactly as those imprisoned in Parsky's cages had. Raccoman recoiled from these gentle creatures who were so much his friends when he was awake. He felt unsettled and did not know whether he should approach them.

Boldly he extended his hands to one of the little animals. It leapt at him and sunk its tiny teeth into his forefinger. Dakktare leaped back in fury yet in slow motion, since all such dreams are in slow motion. The frightened, cornered congrels fled in slow-motion terror, and Raccoman fell back aghast when he saw a pile of fur. They had been devouring one of their own. There was a queer mound of white bones like the mound near Parsky's woodpile.

Raccoman stared at the bloody flesh and remembered that, not long ago, he had eaten that very kind of meat. He felt a terrible chill. Why had congrels turned from munching flowers to cannibalizing their own kind? Why did these gentle creatures flee from him in fear?

The mists of his vague dreams swirled about him, and he turned to see through a swale of blue fog the terrifying form of a catterlob charging down upon him. His legs seemed leaden as he turned in terror. It is hard to run for your life in slow motion, and yet his legs would not hurry through the dreamy mist that resisted him. His muscles were dead and his bare feet were cut by sharp stones on the meadow floor. The hot breath of the great lizard beast burned his back as he fled. He stumbled over a huge rock and tumbled into a ravine, rolling over again and again until the rocks on the sides of the canyon seemed to bruise his deadness and leave him bleeding like the animals. The roar of the wind tore at his face as he plummeted away . . . and away . . . and away. Titan soldiers rushed out of the moving starfields as Raccoman fell through.

His delirium was like what he had experienced the night the tilt winds stopped and he fell into a trance when he hit the earth. Once more he saw the flying falcon, heard him cry, "Beware Maldoon!" The falcon's warning was almost drowned out by loud laughter that broke through his dream like the laughter from the image in his glass. Dense flames exploded against the homes of the cliff dwellers, spreading itself against the windows, licking at the cowering inhabitants, and through the stupor of his dream, he wondered, "How can the cliff dwellers stand this? What is the secret of Moonrhyme survival?" Nothing tied the pieces of his vision into wholeness but his fear.

Then the fire died out and Raccoman continued to fall until he felt himself impaled on the stone spire of the lofty tower of Maldoon. Red washed his vision before everything went black.

Raccoman promptly hit the floor and gratefully awoke.

"Parsky!" he cried. "Where are you?"

"Here, chum!" the Blackgill answered.

"Parsky, I had this horrid dream."

"I know," Parsky said smiling, still holding the unseen vial in his hand.

Intrigue is an apple whose shiny rind
We know is dipped in iodine.
But it woos us with a haunting cry
To cherish, fondle, eat, and die.

CHAPTER V

The Cauldron

R ACCOMAN AND PARSKY rose
early the next morning. Raccoman Dakktare decided that he would
postpone going to the old barn, for he was more determined than
ever not to share his work with Parsky. The two friends decided
that they should straight away visit Uncle Krepel to learn more of
his discovery.

The handsome Blackgill considered his appearance to be good
enough as it was—though "as it was" that morning was worse than
usual. As Raccoman was grooming himself standing before his mirror, he inwardly lamented that so much black had appeared in his
moustache. He was uneasy about the changing color of his gills,
fearful somehow of being the Blackgill he was rapidly becoming.

Parsky enjoyed seeing Raccoman hunt for his boots, which the
Graygill was disturbed to find in the bureau drawer. Dakktare debated with himself about how they might have traveled so far from
their customary bedside place. But the night had been unusual
enough, and he had the feeling that misplacing his boots was a little
grievance compared to his horrible nightmares.

The friends ate black bread with butter and dark tea, and then
bundled up for their trek to see old Krepel, who would revel over
their unexpected visit. Dakktare's fat, yellow mackinaw and knit-
ted cap fit comfortably over his fat personality and capped his
boots with custom. Parsky was as red as ever in both mackinaw
and boots. The pair, like all Estermannians, despised pastels and
turned from any color that would not proclaim itself.

Ah, color! Estermann was a poster color world whose reds and
blues and yellows were gaudy as a kaleidoscope. And the second-
ary colors of the planet were so independent that they refused to
harmonize in any sense with the rainbow universe they inhabited.

The travelers closed the door and walked out into the new snow.
Snow, like sky, tended to bring out the song in the Graygill. Still it
was the none-too-musical Blackgill who began singing first. Parsky's
thin chest did not prevent his baritone exuberance. As he walked,
his melody roared out:

"Here nature comes a ripping night,
For Estermann is sipping white
To bleach the forest in delight,
So . . . o . . . o . . . o . . . o."

He stretched out the "O" as an invitation to Raccoman to join in the winter rondelet.

Raccoman felt incriminated by the color of the snow. White was all around him, but no longer in him. He thought about Parsky's congrel stew and the changing color of his gills. He thought about the terror of his nightmare and felt that both he and his world had changed for the worse. He didn't feel at all like singing.

"O . . . o . . . o . . . o," continued Parsky, oblivious to Raccoman's moody reluctance to sing. "O . . . o . . . o," Parsky sang, turning blue from lack of air and his fruitless entreaty.

Finally Raccoman turned from his inner conflicts. He decided that he would no longer forestall his own urge to sing along and thus his silence burst into harmony.

"O . . . o . . . o . . . o . . . o . . .
The rollicking winter is here.
Sing grandily, bandily, handily gay,
And the cherries are buried, so carry the cheer
This glorious, hoary, uproarious day.

It is grand just to stand in Estermann's woods,
And to sing 'Fra-loo-ling, snow is king for the day!'
The whiteness, the brightness, the lightness is good.
Let none delay fun who may sing rondelet."

Their voices were as full and as round as Dakktare's mackinaw. So they sang two sets of stubby footprints into the forest.

It was no slur to refer to Raccoman as fat, nor was it condemning to speak of such matching characteristics as fat mackinaws, fat voices, and fat arms. Fat was ever a sign of well-being on the planet and the ideal of Estermann contentment. Even Raccoman's footprints in the snow bordered on fat.

They crossed a large ditch. With snow piled high on each side, it looked as though some giant plow had cut a furrow through the white. But the ditch was only the snowy track of a catterlob, and the enormous lizardbeast had long since gone.

Crossing the ditch became an occasion for playfulness, and Parsky promptly pushed Raccoman over the brink. Raccoman tumbled headlong into the shallow ravine, laughing and shouting.

"Parsky, you're rotten, you ill-gotten tramp!
You vagrant, you kluttzer
You rascal, you scamp!"

He laughed so hard that he could scarcely speak. But he did, of course. It was not like Raccoman to confess that he was out of anything, and certainly he would never have admitted to being out of words. He continued his insult through spasms of laughter that resounded through the forest.

"You wimp and unkempt
Little red-booted shrimp.
I'm going to give you a terrible whack
For shoving Dakktare in a catterlob track.
In the future you'll run from all conflict with me.
I'm peerless in battle: TAKE THIS MR. P!"

So shouting, he hurled a fistful of new snow that caught Parsky full in the face and clotted his black whiskers together in ice. Losing balance, the Blackgill tumbled headlong into the track himself, striking Raccoman full in the chest and bowling him over like a tenpin. The two laughed harder than they had in many a snow.

They had awakened a family of sleeping congrels who soon threw themselves willingly down into the track to join in the merriment. Parsky picked up two of the downy, orange creatures and hurled them at Raccoman who caught them and cuddled them next to his chin. The congrels loved flying through the air and the sport of the new snow, and thus they pleaded in soft whimpers for Raccoman to return them exactly as he had caught them. Back they flew to Parsky, who snared them mid-air in glee. The snow and wind of the later winter morning was as pure as their laughter. Remembering his evil nightmare, Raccoman hugged the congrels close from time to time to assure himself that nightmares never become reality.

They had a wonderful time until the Graygill grew weary. Then the two friends left their little forest friends, climbed out of the track, and passed on through the forest. The congrels climbed to the edge of the snowy ditch to watch them and listen to them singing their way into the trees.

At length they walked in silence till Parsky brushed the snow from a fallen tree trunk and both of them sat down to rest.

"I don't see how you could," said Raccoman.

"How I could what?" replied Parsky.

"How you could catch them and put them in the stew."

"But they are good that way. Tell me, Dakktare, you liked them, didn't you?"

"I only said it to please you."

"Well, I shall surprise old Krepel with a new stew."

"Will he tolerate meat?"

"Of course, with more ease than yourself."

By noon of the long winter day, they had traversed most of the forest, and by night they arrived at Krepel's house. It was a quaint habitat—round with a conical roof and as orange as Raccoman's house was yellow. The roof was interrupted by two chimneys that indicated a large hall with fireplaces at either end of the house. It was a much larger house than Raccoman's, but then everyone's was. The astronomer, like Raccoman, was fond of large parties.

Wifeless and fun-loving, this trio—Raccoman, Parsky, and Krepel—regularly enjoyed their bachelorhood together. None of them any longer lamented the single life, as common to them as it was to the planet. A Graygill lass was always a welcome sight, for a daughter was a treasure in a Graygill home—and it was a lucky man who had a wife to share his round house and deliver bachelorhood to companionship.

It had not snowed as much west of the forest, so there was less on Krepel's housetop than on Raccoman's roof. Back of the two-chimneyed house was a small orange building that was nearly a cylinder. The smooth lines of its conical roof were broken by a large star-scope that jutted out just to the right of a small chimney. The tube was oddly heaped with snow on the upper end, so that it resembled a great custard cone. The scope had a welded ladder extending up the side, and as night was soon to approach, Parsky and Dakktare were not at all surprised to see old Krepel climbing the scope to brush the snow from the upper lens.

He looked like an orange roach on a stovepipe as he climbed upward. His mackinaw was plaid squares of amber and black. He was as handsome a Graygill as ever existed. He was trim of physique—a state of health he had acquired from years of climbing the tube. His moustache was well groomed and held nothing carelessly left over from his hasty breakfast. His eyes were a scientific gray and his brow was a handsome tan. There were the customary laugh lines at the corners of his eyes, which is enough to say that even Estermann's scientists liked merriment. Krepel's heavy eyebrows shaded his eyes, but could not hide much of their lively sparkle.

Krepel was still furiously brushing the snow from the upper lens of his scope when Raccoman spoke:

"Uncle! Look, it's me—
The great Raccoman D!"

The snow continued to fly, and "young" Raccoman remembered that his dear uncle was largely deaf—and never more so than when he stood on the barrel of his great scope, his lifetime affection. So Raccoman repeated his greeting:

"Uncle . . . halloo there, I say—
Look over this way!"

"Ah, halloo, nephew!" cried the Moonrhyme star-watcher. At that moment a large clot of snow slid off the roof and onto the very heads and shoulders of Parsky and Raccoman. Enough of the cold white slipped down their necks to cause them both to shudder. Krepel surveyed the whole scene, laughing so hard it seemed he might vibrate himself off his lofty perch.

"Go on in and I'll come down," he cried in half-speech between the ha-hoo's that were his and Raccoman's much-used syllables of laughter.

Before long they were all inside the large house, standing between the two great fireplaces, embracing and laughing over pewter tankards of hot berry wine, which was especially tasty after having had snow dumped plentifully down their collars.

"It's to be a clear night after yester-night's snow. I've something new to show you through the glass," said Krepel between sips.

"But first," cried Parsky, "I will make a pail of soup. Soup such as you have never had before!"

"Ah, I have eaten your soup a thousand evenings—but you are the best cook I have ever seen for a—."

"A Blackgill?" Parsky finished Krepel's statement. "Why can Graygills not tolerate any other color of whiskers but gray?"

"No harm intended," insisted Krepel.

"He makes too much of his moustache," remarked Dakktare.

"Gray! Gray! Gray!" ranted Parsky, suddeny becoming so angry that he stomped the floor planks. "I have had a gill-full of trying to be liked on Estermann. A Blackgill can never be at home in a world where little men measure friendship by the color of hair and gloat upon the paleness of their whiskers."

Raccoman remembered the black he had lately noticed in his own moustache and tried to put the issue aside.

"Now, now! Is this worth a row? Come, Parsky, and let there be no further cracks on the subject of black."

"Yes," agreed Krepel. "I apologize. Please fix us the stew—just like you always do." Krepel looked embarrassed that his words had accidentally rhymed. He was quite content to let his nephew the welder "do the jingles," as he always said, for he felt that jingling was unscientific and not to be done by a star-watcher. There was nothing more reasonable about a poetic metal-worker than there would have been about a poetic star-watcher, but Krepel was content to speak plainly. This, he somehow felt, was in the best interest of science. He realized what a tangle the world would become if scientists tried to be poets and vice versa.

"Raccoman, this fellow star-watcher in Quarrystone Woods—I wrote you concerning a fissure in the cradle of his scope."

Somehow Krepel's words fell out in disconnected sentences.

Raccoman sipped his berry wine and nodded.

"Well," continued the keeper of the orange observatory, "he keeps the blue observatory and is father to the beautiful Velissa, who has just passed her one hundred and seventy-fifth year. There is no end to her list of suitors, but as yet not a single Graygill west of the ridges has taken her interest."

Raccoman nodded again. "I remember her well. Would that I were younger!"

"Well," said the old astronomer, "I encouraged Parsky to pursue her, but he has shown himself a poor suitor. If you ask me, there's a chance that you . . ."

"Never mind, uncle," said Raccoman. "I'm nearly a thousand now. If I married the lass, I'd likely leave her widowed in half a millenium. I'm past the marrying age."

"Besides, he's too fat to keep up with a young one," called the Blackgill, who had gone to the kitchen and was chopping vegetables into the stew.

"Nephew, before the battle of Kendrake I loved a Moonrhyme lass. I thought I couldn't live without her. Funny, I was fat then, too. Who says the fat don't want a wife?"

"You were fat before the battle of Kendrake?" Raccoman asked.

"Ah, so I was—but more than fat, I was in love."

"And you thought you couldn't live without the Moonrhyme lass?" Raccoman asked.

"Well, I did, didn't I? For fifteen hundred years! Still, a Graygill shouldn't live alone unless he has to, and you may not have to, Raccoman. This star-watcher's daughter—you'll see her when you go to weld the cradle of this scope."

"You think I could weld and wed in one trip?" the welder gibed.

"Just be sure you don't burn your nose on the torch. Look up from your work and you might find yourself a new way of life."

Raccoman turned his uncle's words over in his mind.

"Nephew, Estermann lost much in the struggle of Kendrake and Maldoon, and I have known the pain of watching the stars to the exclusion of all else. But yours could be the fortune of a life companionship which I have missed."

Raccoman once more offered a disinterested nod. He would have much preferred to speak of the moving starfields he had seen than the unknown daughter of an astronomer in Quarrystone Woods.

Meanwhile, Parsky continued to prepare their evening meal. When the vegetables were cut and vapors rising from the kettle in the great fireplace, the Blackgill felt in his pockets and, to Raccoman's horror, pulled a tiny live congrel from his left pocket, then another from his right.

"Where did you get them?" cried Raccoman.

"I saved them from our game in the catterlob track. I'm going to chop them for the stew."

"What!" cried Krepel. "Chopped congrels?"

"They're tasty," the Blackgill responded. "Ask Dakktare."

"Have you eaten murdered congrels?"

Raccoman looked sheepish. "Well, yes. I mean . . . I thought of them as meat and—."

"A congrel is a congrel, and calling them meat will not make them palatable," said Krepel.

"I cannot bear to think of it," said Raccoman. "We were playing with these in a snow ditch this very morning."

He looked at the orange fur and soft brown eyes of the lop-eared and lovable creatures. He felt ashamed that he had already eaten their relatives in former broths, but when he considered Parsky's intentions his blood ran cold.

The little animals began to whimper as Parsky left the room with them both dangling from his left hand, while in his right hand he held the vegetable cleaver. He soon re-entered the room, walked to the fireplace, and tossed a double handful of whitish-pink lumps in the small cauldron of stew. Old Krepel shook his head sadly, and his nephew turned away, remembering a snowfield, gone now by an afternoon.

Parsky busied himself by setting the table as night closed in around the snowy house. Inside Krepel's home, the hearth was warm, but the steaming stew did not produce their usual merriment of eating together.

Krepel refused to eat, and Raccoman also left his meal untouched. But not Parsky—he ate heartily alone. Krepel vowed to have a slice of bread and butter later. For the time, he was content. The uncle and his nephew watched Parsky taking his meal. As it is not the nature of Graygills to bear grudges, their contempt for the congrel killer could better be called disillusionment. But even that soon subsided and they at last fell to discussing science.

At the second hour of darkness, Krepel slapped his knee and said, "Let's all go out to the observatory. I've something to show you." Only Raccoman followed him outside, while Parsky made himself comfortable before the fire. Inside the observatory, Krepel fumbled in the darkness for a flint stick. He scraped it on the stone to get a small flame, then lit a candle. In the uncertain flickering of the candlelight, the two walked to the lower end of the great scope. The handsome old Moonrhyme fitted his eye loosely to the eyepiece, cranked the small brass wheel on the barrel of the mechanism, and smiled at what he saw. And after turning a series of smaller brass thumbscrews, his smile grew wider and wider until Raccoman was driven mad to have a look for himself.

Raccoman's turn was shortly forthcoming, but first he had to be given the coordinates and star depth.

"A month ago, just after your last visit," Krepel told him, "I discovered a moving starfield. This roving field of stars crosses the sky at just this hour each night." The old astronomer continued, "These stars seem to move on no predetermined orbit. They behave like stars that had the wit to think and decide their own direction."

He stopped talking and placed his eye to the scope once more. Again he smiled broadly, and Raccoman was barely able to restrain the urge to push his uncle away from the scope and brutishly take possession of the eyepiece.

Finally he did.

He knew every part of old Krepel's mechanism. He adjusted the proper thumbscrew hastily and the distant starfield appeared before his eyes. He gasped, then looked again. His eye that was not pressed against the ocular had such a gleam in it that it was easy to tell his other eye beheld the confirmation of his earlier vision.

"Look again, uncle, they're not stars, but giant Star Riders.

They're beautifully handsome, as handsome as I.
The kings of the planets and princes of sky.

They're men—titans, I tell you."

The astronomer once again took his place at the scope. "By Singreale, nephew, I do believe you are right."

He drew back and rubbed his old eyes and looked again. "Now I see—riders!"

"Uncle," said Raccoman, "I have seen them as close as I now see the barrel of this scope. They are large men, twice the size of ourselves. Their flying beasts are magnificent. They fly beneath a banner that names their country as Rensgaard. Uncle, there must be another continent we Graygills know nothing about."

"Is it possible these night-flyers have passed undetected above our scopes for years?" The old man seemed not to be speaking to Raccoman but to the empty air as he stared vacantly ahead. Then he slapped his knee and, without waiting for a reply, answered his own question: "Yes, of course, they have—but never overhead. They have flown—there—on the horizon of the southwest quadrant. And they've always been there, but we have never set our scope quite low enough to see them until now."

The tiny blips of light soon moved down below the horizon. Raccoman and his Uncle Krepel went back into the house.

Once inside the cozy house, Raccoman brushed the snow from his feet. The scientist looked back to the edge of the candlelight where Parsky had fallen asleep—warmed by the unthinkable stew. He turned back to Raccoman after a moment's thought and said to his excited nephew, "Another continent? One cannot be absolutely certain, but the chances are good. Still, remember the old cliche: 'Ours is the perfect world, built perfectly; Estermann: one continent, one sea.' You see, my dear nephew, two continents would spoil the jingle."

This was a clear slur upon the poet's love of slogans and simple rhymes. But then Krepel grew kinder and conceded that perhaps there might be another continent in the ocean that engulfed the one where the Graygills lived. The seas had never been explored in all of the centuries that the astronomer had seen and studied his own land and its inhabitants.

Raccoman was tempted to tell his uncle about his work, but he decided to conceal the secret of the old barn in the catterlob meadow. Krepel was wise and, in his centuries at the orange observatory, he had heard the yarns and dreams of a thousand inventors and soldiers of fortune. Raccoman was reluctant to speak further of his idea lest his uncle should greet it with contempt or, even worse, ridicule, for Krepel's love of laughter and good times had done little to dampen his wizened spirit. He could see through foolish schemes and suffered from a distinct lack of tact.

Besides, Raccoman's experiment was based wholly on the untested idea that the old cliche that spoke of one continent only was wrong.

"Uncle, if there *were* two continents, we should have to name the one we live on, shouldn't we?"

"Yes, I suppose," replied Krepel.

"There can only be one unnamed continent per planet. Names distinguish, don't they?"

The astronomer nodded.

"How do you go about naming a continent? Could we draw the Moonrhymes and Canbies together and try to come up with a name?"

"Well, we're not all that sure there are two continents. Besides," added the wise man, "even if there are two, you can't just name somebody else's continent without asking their consent. I mean, how would you feel, Raccoman, if somebody named our own lands without even asking us?"

They continued to deliberate the issue until Parsky, overwarmed by the fire and bored by their conversation, fell back to sleep.

"Well, nephew," said Krepel, slapping his knee, "we've had enough about the rights and wrongs of continent-naming."

Raccoman had made his point before, but he felt that he should make it one last time. "Oh, but uncle, there is another continent! The titans live there and they defend the citadel of Rensgaard."

Krepel stood firm. The nephew had overpressed his own particular.

"I must remind you that, having missed the stew, I'm hungry at least for the bread," the old man said. They woke the disinterested Parsky and poured three bright red cups of candolet tea. Raccoman exalted the loaf and offered the customary thanks to the ceiling.

Somehow it was not as filling nor as satisfying as either of them would have liked, and they eyed their untouched bowls and the half pail of soup still steaming on the hearth. The star-watcher stoked the fire and Parsky fell to dozing once again. Raccoman felt a strong desire to eat of Parsky's broth but remained firm in his resolution.

What was the lure it held? Almost desperate to try the stew, he wished Krepel were not in the room so he could eat without being discovered. And secretly, old Krepel wished Dakktare would fall asleep so he could try half a bowl. But neither of them disclosed his unspoken desire.

Krepel surveyed the drowsy Parsky and remembered their first meeting at the Survival Festival of the Moonrhymes. As he looked at Parsky, his mind traversed the recent centuries of their companionship. Parsky's refusal to get a meaningful job was still a puzzle to him, as was his lack of interest in the opposite sex. In spite of his years, he was handsome enough to interest such lasses as were available, although most of the unmarried women would have looked askance at his lack of real vocation.

The vagabond Blackgill was Krepel's best friend, closer even than Raccoman, a relative with a trace of his own full-blooded Moonrhyme heritage flowing through his veins. He could not understand the intrigue he felt for the unemployed stew-cook. He only knew he could not bear to think of that distant day when death or circumstance might separate them. He relied so on their relationship that he felt no price was too great to pay for its keeping.

Krepel thought again of the congrel stew. He wanted to eat it, if only to be like Parsky, but he faced the age-old taboos on the killing of animals. He smiled above his drowsy friend.

"No," he resolved firmly in his mind, "eating meat is one thing I will not do to honor our friendship!"

They were firm but inner words; he meant them. He really was determined. Never, never, never would he end his lifetime of compliance by tasting the forbidden. Still, he looked at his sleeping friend and loved him all over again.

Presently, Parsky awoke and removed his boots and set them by the fire. He took old Krepel's lyrolian off the wall and handed it to Raccoman and announced, "It is time for the Claxton!"

"Yes," said Krepel, taking off his own orange boots. The bootless scientist and the cook were enough incentive to Dakktare, who promptly added his own yellow boots to the others, and soon the trio was barefoot and ready to dance. "This Claxton is in honor of the moving starfields," said the astronomer. Raccoman began to strum the lyrolian and sing:

"*Gliding the glen of the little men*
High in the middle of the candled sea,
The wind will spindle the golden candle
And handle the fire of the lightning tree."

There were other like verses, and the trim Krepel promenaded hand to hand and stepped brightly over the floor. Parsky continued to sing, but the overweight Raccoman, for all his love of dancing, soon tired and begged the more athletic star-watcher and cook to cease. Unhearing, Parsky and Krepel continued the dancing in a strange rapport of soul that often excluded Raccoman, but didn't bother him.

Although it was Krepel's custom to sleep by day, they all soon retired for the night and the fire flickered warm but low. Dakktare's mind was too full of the wonder of the tall men and idea of a missing continent to go immediately to sleep. He lay awake so long that his unsatisfied hunger began to gnaw at him once more. They had eaten the last slice of bread, and he could not help but wonder if the cook's forbidden soup was still warm. His hunger at last got the better of him. He reasoned that if he tiptoed to the hearth, he could fill his bowl quietly and return to bed and none would be the wiser. His guilt was less incriminating than it once had been. Once you have tasted the forbidden, a second serving seems less serious. Still, he would certainly never want the old scientist to know he had eaten the broth of murdered congrels right in his home.

Secretly convinced, he stole from his great wooden bed and crossed the rough-plank floor and moved silently toward the huge table.

He was stunned by what he saw there.

For the old astronomer was seated near the hearth with a bowl of soup in his lap and lifting the spoon to his mouth.

"No!" Raccoman cried. "Don't!"

But it was too late. The telltale evidence dripped from Krepel's thick moustache.

There are mysteries told of a misty sea,
Where lizards swam and the bearded trees
Beheld old wars of blue-green gore
And cried, "Beware what went before!"

CHAPTER VI
Parsky's Tale

THE MIND OF Raccoman Dakktare swam with a thousand images of his uncle's making. His thoughts passed from the mysterious Star Riders to Krepel's reminder that his late father had wielded a crafty torch. The sight of the trim astronomer eating stew by the hearth in the middle of the night haunted him. What was there about animal flesh that needed to be tried?

Parsky and Dakktare crunched through the snow that had begun to look old. They traversed the same lane they had so lately traveled to arrive at Uncle Krepel's observatory. A handcart had left deep ruts in the dirty snow and the enchantment of their earlier walk was missing.

When they reached the old catterlob track, it was soiled by the thaw and not at all the sort of place for frolicking that they had found it only a day before. So they crossed it in silence and moved through the trees. A little distance from the muddy track, Raccoman saw a family of congrels as they scampered across the trail and disappeared into a clump of bushes.

For diversion he hurried to the bush and reached in with his hand extended and his short, fat fingers open in entreaty. The congrels approached him cautiously as though they were afraid. He stroked them gently and tugged affectionately at their floppy ears.

Suddenly they caught sight of Parsky approaching and whimpered—one even cried out—and the entire family ran under a fallen log as fast as their furry legs would permit.

"Drat it," said the Blackgill, "I had hoped to take a pair home with me."

"It's as if they know you," said Dakktare.

"Nonsense! Congrels are ignorant animals. Their finest use is the juice they make."

"Really, Parsky—must you be so cruel? They're alive and a source of joy for the living."

"Better dead!" cried Parsky. "Dead, dead, dead, and digested—that's how I like congrels best."

They walked on for a moment without arguing the point. Then Dakktare changed the subject.

"You seem to have a special friendship with my uncle," Raccoman observed. "It's odd when you think of it: He's the only Moonrhyme south of Demmerron and you're the only Blackgill left on Estermann."

"For a while," said Parsky with a curl in his lip.

The metal-worker kicked the dirty snow distractedly and went on: "How does it make you feel, knowing you're the last—the very last Blackgill this planet shall see?" Raccoman felt uneasy asking the question, particularly because his own gills were rapidly changing color.

"I wouldn't be too sure," grumbled Parsky, still angry that the frightened congrels had eluded his grasp. "I could tell you of a time when there were more Blackgills than you could count. Back then, I'll tell you, this prejudice and ill-treatment did not exist. Before we both were born, my kind was as plentiful as yours."

"What were they like? What was their attitude, their temperament?"

If anything angered Parsky besides a slur on the color of his moustache, it was the reminder that he was prone to be out-of-sorts. Oh, he was capable of merriment and an excellent cook. He liked singing and dancing on occasion. But it was easy to come upon him suddenly and catch him in an unpleasant mind-set. The cordial and merry Dakktare tolerated his friend's changeable nature, for Graygills all held a cheerful tolerance. They loved with exuberance, and prejudice was beyond their cheerful acceptance of everyone. In truth, they never resented Parsky's black upper lip. It was the suspicion of prejudice that was held by the Blackgill, for the actual prejudice didn't exist. Graygills did not seek to prove how noble they were by giving up their prejudices. It was just that a prejudice like meat-eating never occurred to them until such an occasion as that unpleasant afternoon when Raccoman had questioned the strange lumps in his stew.

Now Parsky grew angry over Dakktare's question about the temperament of the vanished Blackgills. There was no judgment intended in Dakktare's query, but Parsky chose to take it as a reprimand for his own glum personality. He scowled for a while, then continued the tale he had begun.

"My grandfather's people once thrived in the forests south of Canby. They lived in the large fortresses now called Castledomes. They farmed the valleys where the forests moved back and gave them room to grow their vegetables. They were a happy, loving, industrious, and congenial people—not that I am not," he said, breaking his tale to affirm his own congeniality.

Dakktare grunted in assent, and Parsky continued: "Yes, they were the Blackgills of Castledome Forest. Here and there one could see the great, stone domes rising through the trees. Each of the fortresses was linked by roads that connected them to all the others. Then came the dry years."

He paused unexpectedly in his narrative as though he were about to quit.

"What happened?" asked Raccoman.

"I'm coming to that," said Parsky, annoyed by the interruption. "The dry years left the Blackgills with little to eat. It was useless to try and grow vegetables, and the orchards produced only withered fruit.

"The famine affected the people of Canby and those in the fortess of Maldoon, where it was believed some food had been stored. I do not honor what my people did as they laid siege to Maldoon. It was their hope to divide the food and grain that King Singreale had stored against the famine. But when the southwest wall was finally breached, we discovered to our dismay that Singreale's larders were as empty as those of the Castledomes.

"A band of ruffians tried to seize the king's diamond, which for centuries had been guarded by an old serpent hatched in the rocky dens of Demmerron Pass. The diamond, sometimes called the Fire of Singreale, was held in great reverence throughout the starving planet. Graygills and Blackgills alike believed it contained a mysterious power over life. In the siege of his castle, King Singreale was killed, as were all of his knights. The Fire of Singreale was stolen and the serpent disappeared, never to be seen again." All this had happened before Raccoman was born and he had heard it before, but now Parsky came to a part of the story he had never told the welder.

"My people were hated by the Graygills of Canby for the havoc of their siege. They decided that even in their weakened state they must leave Castledome Forest.

"Many of the Blackgills died, and the rest began a long migration to the Flandry Lowlands. They had received reports that water still flowed in the lowlands and food was more abundant. They found that vegetables did, indeed, grow there, but the great catterlobs that roamed the area devoured their first plantings. Thus my people awaited a harvest that never came. They could not endure the seasons until the second gathering. Nor did they have the stamina to retrace the long path of their migration.

"In the desolation of Flandry, the Blackgills passed a decree that was to save their stricken people till the rains fell again. They proclaimed the catterlob a vegetable. They admitted it was a very large vegetable, and even a roving and unplanted vegetable, but they declared it a vegetable, nonetheless." Raccoman broke in:

"But it was a lie.
Could starving men about to die
Believe their own deception?"

"Please don't interrupt! Not at first. Who can say if they ever believed? When you have not eaten for a year, it is easy to believe anything. The catterlobs were certainly not very plump vegetables—they, too, had become thin in their search for fodder that was virtually nonexistent. The meadows were desolate and the bogs and berry fields were pools of dust. So we hunted the great but gentle beasts and felt fortunate that the catterlobs had not proclaimed us to be vegetables. In their weakened condition, the creatures could not have run far, but it never occurred to them to run at all.

"Hungry though our people were, the idea of hunting the great vegetables did not appeal to them. Many said they would rather starve than eat them. Some did."

"Eat?" asked Raccoman. "Or starve?"

"Starve," answered Parsky, annoyed that his friend could not tell the meaning of his words. "Yes, starve! But some made spears and hid in the bushes until one of the craggy old catterlobs happened along. Then they all leapt out of the bushes and cried, 'Die, vegetable!' The unsuspecting animals died as very surprised vegetables, I can assure you.

"My grandfather was one of the old warriors. Having grown too old to fight, he stayed in the camp with the children. Once when our parents were hunting, they left us alone and we began to be afraid as the hour grew late. There were rumors among the children that their elders had been attacked by a savage herd of catterlobs and been destroyed. Although it was not the nature of the great beasts to kill, they realized they were facing extinction and, in their desperation, had begun a bloody war of retaliation. The rumor was confirmed and the children were very much afraid until my grandfather called us to the council fire that burned in the center of our starving camp. He gathered us dolefully about him.

"His voice broke as he became choked with the somber warning that was his to bear.

"'These are the last days!' he said with agony of soul common to old and grieving prophets. 'All life must end, for soon we will be at war.'

"'What is war, grandfather?' I asked.

"'War—war is the killing of living things by other living things,' he replied.

"'Killing?' the children cried and shuddered. 'But who would want to kill us?'

"'Even as we once proclaimed the catterlobs to be our food, now they have decided that their diminishing race must be defended. The last of the great animals are gathering even now to devour the last of the Blackgills. We must fight them, but the battle will not take long for they are large, and though they are weak with hunger, we are no match for them.

"'It is only because they were willing to be our prey that we have ever been able to subdue them. But if they come upon us with snarls and ripping teeth, we shall not long endure. My little ones, there is no escape. Flandry is dying—perhaps all Estermann. The vanquished will be the fodder of the victor—then death will leave everything in silence.'"

"So it was eat or be eaten?" Dakktare interrupted.

"That's right," continued Parsky as though he had not heard, for he despised to be interrupted in his tale. "I sat by the fire and listened, and I was afraid for I was old enough to know that war, as the old man referred to it, would destroy the final remnant of our people.

"'Do you think we will live?' I asked my grandfather.

"'Come here, young Parsky,' he said.

"I approached the center of the fire. The yellow flickering fell on the old one's face. His hair and moustache were as fine and deep a black as you can imagine."

"I don't know—I can imagine it was pretty black," said Dakktare. He had never liked the word *black*. It was an unclean word to the Graygills, and he felt suddenly ashamed to have used it.

Parsky never heard this second interruption nor noticed Raccoman's shame. It took much more to make him feel ashamed than it did the welder.

"As I stood face to face with the elder Blackgill, he reached out his hands. They held a leather thong, threaded through a large ivory tooth.

"'Kneel,' commanded the old man.

"I knelt.

"With his arms extended, he slipped this sharp amulet over my head. The tooth felt cold as it fell against my chest and rested above my heart. I could feel a tremor of cold moving across the torso of my young body and racing out into my limbs.

"'Will I die, grandfather?' I asked.

"'Die?' the old one answered my question with a question. 'Yes, son of my son—all that live must die. The treasure of Maldoon is lost! The king is dead! Some say he had a brother and that his brother yet lives and will come one day to restore Maldoon and thaw the ice from the frozen halls and throne room. But Singreale is dead and the diamond is gone, though the power of life that once shined in brilliant radiance from the huge diamond is still on Estermann.'

"The old man paused and lifted me to my feet. 'Here is the light of Singreale—it now lives in this amulet,' he said, rapping the tooth with his firm fist.

"I was still afraid and I looked up at my grandfather once again and asked the same question I had asked before with a stronger desire for insight.

"'Will I die *soon*, grandfather?'

"'All must die,' he repeated. 'But now there is a tooth at your heart. You have a chance to live. Have you eaten meat?'

"'I have not,' I replied.

"'What have you eaten?'

"'Only roots and what ferns and acorns I could find.'

"'Why did you not eat as we have?' the old man asked.

"'Because I could see the great beasts were not vegetables. I cannot bear the lie. I had rather die than call black "white" merely to enjoy its blackness. No, grandfather, animals are animals—we shall not stop their being beasts by tricking our minds into other labels.'

"'You are honest, Parsky.'

"'I am weak—I am hungry.'

"'You wear the light. The light you wear is the only hope you will have tomorrow when the great beasts come.'

"At this suggestion, the other Blackgill children, remembering their dead parents, stood and cried. 'No, war is hope. We will set our war against the beasts and win.'

"'We will be destroyed,' said the old Blackgill, ignoring their clamor. 'But now you, Parsky—you must return to Castledome. There are rumors that the famine in the North is over. You must leave tonight.'

"'He will be lost on the dark trail,' protested another youth.

"'He will make his way—this amulet will help.' Grandfather paused for a moment and then lifted up his voice and cried, 'Behold the Fire of Singreale!'

"I thought he was mad since everyone knew the Fire of Singreale was the lost diamond of the murdered lord of Maldoon.

"He held his right hand out and stood there. Slowly one of the embers floated up from the fire. It traveled in a wide arc and then settled white-hot in the palm of his open hand. He grimaced at the pain of its touch, and it seemed for a moment he would drop the ember. Soon I could see that the pain passed, and he took the white coal and approached me. He extended the ember until it touched the tooth hanging at my chest. The tooth began to glow and became brilliant. Blue fire moved around the radial ivory, but nothing burned, nor did I even feel the flames that rested right above my heart.

"'Go now and the Fire of Singreale will guide you!'

"I hesitated.

"'Go now, son of my son,' said the old man again.

"I knew I must obey, but still I hesitated. I felt the fire and cold at once.

"'Go!'

"I moved away from the council fire of the young ones as the light of the flame above my heart still played upon the amulet. I moved on into the leafless forest. The trees were twisted cadavers, rotted and leafless in the starlight. There was no grass beneath my feet. I crossed the River Kendrake, which begged its mountain source for one rivulet of hope. Just north of the river I ran suddenly and most unwittingly through the dale of the catterlobs. They were all sleeping, but even in sleep their breathing at close range made a dreadful noise, like the howl of wind in the mountains.

"I moved quietly, being possessed of the mistaken fear that the Fire of Singreale would wake them, for it blazed incandescent guidance from my chest. Its blue glare kept me from stumbling over the great, gaunt beasts. I passed within a few feet of their scaly heads, massive in the darkness. I beheld their great jaws and feared for the remnant of my people.

"As soon as I was safely through the camp of our enemies, I made my way on down the dry, dark trail, and yet my grandfather's gift of light was adequate. Soon you will ask me, chum, how indeed I knew I was on the right path."

Dakktare had wanted to ask him that very question. It always amazed him that Parsky knew exactly what he was thinking and what he would ask next. Raccoman loved conversation but always wondered how Parsky could possibly enjoy talking when he always knew what someone else was going to say.

"Indeed," Raccoman replied, then asked the unnecessary question, "how did you know which way was the proper way to Castledome Forest?"

"Whenever I would turn from the proper way, the illumination on my chest would dim. Thus I only walked where there was light. The night in Flandry is deep, and when the darkness stalks you and collects like a great web across your useless eyes, there is only one real companion—light!

"All night I made my way forward until at last the light of day began to break. By this time I had reached a high plateau, and leaning back against a tree, I closed my eyes and slept. I cannot say for how long. But when the morning was mostly spent, I was awakened by a mournful sighing in the wind, for there blew from beyond the River Kendrake a crying sound that filtered through my skin and settled in ice about my heart.

"I was cold with fear, knowing that the last of the Blackgills were dying in the war against the hungry beasts. I alone had survived. What did it mean to be the last of the Blackgills?

"Thanks to the light of Singreale, I was very much alive, though I had little doubt that my grandfather had perished with the foolish children.

"I wept.

"I pressed on into the dead forest.

"Day after day, night after night, I moved northward toward Castledome Forest, retracing the route of my people's migration. I was hungry and thirsty. Here and there I stopped to split a cala-dery shrub to drink what little water its porous heart contained.

"Within six days, I began to see some vegetation again.

"By the eighth day, some trees even had leaves. Thus I became certain that the rumor we had heard was true and that the long drought was over in my ancestral home.

"On the ninth day, I picked berries, plump and ripe. I stuffed my knapsack with fruit and continued. On the eleventh day, it rained. For each of three days thereafter, the rain continued. It felt wonderful. Finally at the end of one month, I spied the gleaming towers of Castledome Forest with their white stones jutting upward through the silvery ginjon trees and flinging their old and broken minarets into the morning sun. Only when the towers were clearly in view did the light of Singreale begin to dim.

"It never went completely out.

"I made a pouch of coarse cloth to bind the tooth inside, for even though it no longer blinded me with the same incandescence that had guided me through the flight from Flandry, it still was much too bright to permit me to sleep at night.

"Besides, I was alone in Castledome Forest, and I knew I must move on to the land of the Graygills, for now my people were gone and I despised to live alone. So by tucking the glowing tooth in the pouch, its light was extinguished and left me less conspicuous to the dwellers of Canby where black had now become obscene. I did not want the Graygills to be afraid of Singreale."

"What makes you think—" Dakktare interrupted only to have his interruption interrupted.

"What makes you think that Graygills would object to the light? Well, I shall tell you. Most Estermannians have a fear of too much light. Anticipating this, I hid the incandescent tooth in the small bag and made my way through the lofty ginjon trees to the plains of Canby Downs.

"Since that time I have lived here among you, Raccoman. It has not been easy being the only Blackgill, but I have managed. From time to time I take the tooth out of the pouch and gaze gratefully at the light of Singreale."

Dakktare felt a strange pang of conscience. He hated to question the Blackgill's integrity, but he could scarcely believe that he really owned the light of Singreale. He had never heard that the great Singreale would inhabit a tooth. The story needed something more to make it real.

"In Canby they would never believe that the missing Fire of Singreale now burns from an old tooth. They would still insist that his light is the lost treasure carried away by a giant falcon during the siege."

Parsky shifted on his feet and looked as if he had been accused of a falsehood. But he recovered his composure and answered the welder's question.

"No. King Singreale's great fire has left the diamond and become the prize of my ancient race. His light was salvation in the day of my people's destruction.

"I remained true to the light. I abstained from meat, which had been the folly of my race, until this very winter. Then for the first time I desired to know the forbidden taste that had damned my people. The catterlobs were unafraid of me, but they were too huge to eat. To slay a catterlob would be useless, so I focused on congrels.

"I was playing with a family of them when the ancient urge for meat came furiously upon me. I feared to kill, yet desperately I wanted to do so. 'Come, little vegetables!' I cried as I grasped one and tore its fur away while its frightened eyes looked up at me in confusion and terror. I crammed a piece of its exposed flesh into my mouth even as the little creature shrieked its last entreaty in horror. I smiled at the warm, red taste. I felt strong and secure, as though I could lift the planet all alone and I thrilled to the ecstasy of my surging appetite. It rippled along my nervous system, and I cried aloud in the indescribable zenith of the warm fulfillment.

"When the little beast was limp and dead, I felt shame. The only

(87)

contentment I felt afterward came in realizing that I was somehow united with the past. I held knowledge—I knew I was one with the ancient race that had died in the Flandry Lowlands."

Raccoman had sat silent for a long time. Then suddenly he blurted out, "Just raw? Raw like a vegetable?"

"Raw," replied Parsky, and he licked his lips as if he were delighted in remembering the experience. "Yes, I have tasted the ancient and forbidden food."

"Then tell me—" Raccoman started to say something but stopped.

"So," said Parsky, "not willing to live alone in my new desire for meat, I began to put it in your stew, too, and you must admit—you liked it."

"Yes," Dakktare grudgingly conceded, "but raw—never mind. How or when then did you start stewing them?"

"The primary question," said Parsky, "is not how or when did I begin stewing them, but why?"

"Then, why?" asked Raccoman.

"So you would find it possible to eat them, too. You would find only disgust in raw meat. Someday you, too, will eat them warm and red and find them desirable this way."

"Never!" cried Raccoman. "And further, Parsky, I cannot believe you wear Singreale at your heart, for his light is the life and health of Estermann."

Parsky's horrible confession left Dakktare desirous to change the subject. For sometime now they had been stopped and resting on a round, broad log. The snow was mostly gone, and the shadows were long as the sun grew pale above the western mountains. The two without speaking rose and walked on, but before they had gone very far, Raccoman Dakktare began to sing softly a tune that he was composing on the spot. It was a plaintive tune about the world he had once lived in, the only world he had ever known before his friend had deceived him.

If Parsky could tell a story—and he could—then Dakktare could sing a song. In the loose earth soaked by the dying snow he sang with muddy stains on his yellow boots:

"Once in the flowery woodlands I found
A small nest of life in the glen.
They frolicked through the forests of Canby Down

Where the sun and meadows were friends.
   Come play in the light
   Till the cool of the night
   Shall stop all joys we know,
   Sing tra-loo, tra-lay—
   Beg sunlight to stay.
   Ro-lolly, to-holly, ho lo!
When I picked up a fellow to hold to my face,
He bared his strong teeth to my heart
And he growled and snarled at my offered embrace
And tore my warm world all apart.
   Now the forest must growl
   And the woodland must scowl.
   Behold! Love is scarce as you know.
   Peace is a wreath.
   But the baring of teeth
   Can kill, dilly-nilly, ho lo!"

Raccoman looked at Parsky, who had trudged on ahead. The Gray-gill's gait became sluggish and his melody slowed to match his anguished stride.

"There are bones in the nests where the furry ones slept
Here and there are the tufts of soft hair.
The sun will not shine where the little ones leapt
For the odor of death swims the air.
Where are those who ran
Across Estermann
And played in the wintery snow?
Come back, little friends.
Oh, come once again,
Ro-lolly, to-holly, ho lo!"

"A sad tune," grumbled Parsky, as they approached Dakktare's house.

"Do you still have it?" asked Raccoman, coming down from the mood of his haunting air.

"Have what?" said Parsky in the same complaining tone that had characterized their long trip.

"The tooth. Is it still at your neck?"

"Of course, it is. It always is."

"Could I see it? I would love to see the Fire of Singreale."

"Do you not believe me, Raccoman?"

"Believe? What's not to doubt? I give you all the trust of Ester-mann, but I would like to see the glorious light."

"Oh, all right," said Parsky, "but remember, your eyes are not accustomed to such light, and I won't be responsible if it hurts your eyes."

He drew the little pouch out of his soft shirt. It was heavy.

"I haven't looked at it in several weeks. I have never showed it to another soul," he said, letting Raccoman know just how good a friend he was. Raccoman shielded his eyes to protect them from the light of Singreale.

Parsky's thin fingers untied the drawstring of the little pouch and pulled it away. The old tooth had turned black. There was no fire. Raccoman wondered if there ever had been. If there had been, he reasoned, it must have died when Parsky joined the soul of his evil past—perhaps the very day he tore the bloody flesh from the terrified congrel and devoured it warm and red.

"There is no light," objected Raccoman.

"Not now, chum. Singreale never spends himself uselessly in sunlight. Were it now night, it would be another matter."

But Raccoman suspected that the black tooth and the Blackgill were brothers in a kind of blackness that never honored any light. Perhaps it never had.

Sin is the offspring of weakness when men and serpents join league.
It is born in the lust of the moment and hatched in the womb
   of intrigue.
It denies all sense of denial to sacrifice all sacrifice.
It consistently ends all consistence like fire whose heartbeat is ice.

CHAPTER VII
Velissa of Quarrystone Woods

*T*HE WINTER DIED and the grumblebeaks returned to the lagoon east of Canby. The birds' gaudy plumage was glazed with silver feathers shot in double bars across their fuchsia bodies. Their beaks looked broken and, hence, the name they had worn for centuries. Their eggs were forbidden as food, but it was common knowledge that every egg contained two yolks and, thus, hatched two chicks. The chicks hatched green as the deep lagoon, but gradually their feathers deepened and turned fuchsia as they learned to fly and readied themselves for migration to their winter feeding grounds on the south of the continent—a continent that Raccoman now believed was only one of at least two.

In two successive visits to Uncle Krepel's, the scientist and his nephew observed the flights of the Star Riders and were able to predict their direction and vector, although they had no idea why the flights continued in the very same path night after night.

Parsky grew increasingly more scarce as a visitor and, throughout the long summer months, did not make a single appearance. Raccoman's moustache and, indeed, his hair too was now as black as that of the stew-cook, though many times he had wished it was not so. Raccoman knew that his special project would depend once again on the coming season of the tilt winds, and he had set the turbulent winter season as the goal for the completion of his work.

He could be frightfully absent-minded, and whenever he thought of making his journey to Quarrystone Woods to seek out the blue observatory, he told himself that he was too busy to take time off for a journey that would take three days by foot. Before winter was over, he had told himself he would finish the job in summer. Now by the same odd logic, he felt that he could best complete the job when winter afforded him the leisure.

He missed Parsky, but even more than missing him, he wondered what could have kept the Blackgill so preoccupied as to leave him no time for their friendship. Though he couldn't quite put his stubby finger on the issue, it seemed to him that Parsky had changed into something so sinister it frightened him even to imagine it.

Summer produced enough rain to make the meadows around Canby ideal forage for the catterlobs, which knew they had to grow fat enough in summer to weather the barren, snow-packed meadows of winter. And fat they grew, while the bachelor welder watched their feeding habits throughout the sunny months. Near the end of summer, one of the old cows gave birth to a set of triplets, who were born like miniature reproductions of the older catterlobs. Raccoman was compelled to watch their mischievous antics while they grew.

But by the end of summer, Raccoman was so absorbed by the powerful image of the Star Riders, he found little time for anything but his work. And the project that he had in mind would take his old uncle and himself in pursuit of the flying titans.

But the life of a metal-worker is one of toil—especially when he must do without the best of equipment. So *slow* went his seams that he knew he must rise early every day to begin his work. His strange project grew across the weeks and the fire on the tip of his antique torch seldom cooled. He was often haunted by Parsky's strange tale, but it never stopped his work. He sang constantly, having a song for every activity he performed: he had riveting tunes, songs for the steel-fire, and airs for the cold tips. Indeed, he had two welding songs: one was for fast seams and the other for slow ones. But wind foils were so light and easy to weld that his work made friends with his music, and his bonds were as tight and solid as his equipment was old. He sang as the carbon sparks ignited in the air about his stubby hands.

> *"In the fiery, frenzied finishing of all the*
> *flattened foils,*
> *Comes the fantasy of feeling for the final filigree,*
> *In the flame of flashing fortitude the gallant welder*
> *toils,*
> *To behold the glowing arc of his creativity.*
> *He is faithful, yet fanatic, as he fiddles at his game,*
> *And he knows that few have ever felt the fever*
> *of his art,*
> *Frisking frantically for fagots in the flickering*
> *furnace flame*
> *For the fusing of the band that can join the metal parts."*

Day after day, he sang this furious tongue-twisting tune while the strange invention took shape.

Parsky didn't come back till the beginning of autumn. By that time they were Blackgill brothers for their color was one.

Raccoman had become a hermit. Part of his seclusion was due to the fact that the Graygills of Canby had never seen him as a Blackgill, and he was embarrassed to face them. Still, he desperately needed welding supplies if he was to continue to work. He had plenty of wind foils but not enough silver rod to bond the star-steam arcs he used to fuse the wind foils.

He did not fear that Estermannians would mock him as a Blackgill, but he didn't like being different. He had never felt bad about Parsky's black hair; still, in a world of Graygills, black can leave one conspicuous. And he disliked the color on himself. "I know!" said Dakktare to himself, "I'll go to old Krepel and plead for him to go up to one of the Moonrhyme villages and buy me the welding supplies I need."

It occurred to him in a moment of enlightenment that, while his uncle shopped for the supplies he needed, he could go on to Quarrystone Woods and weld the fissure in the cradle of the broken star-scope at the blue observatory. So he set out on foot, and by sundown he arrived at his uncle's observatory with the scope sticking through the roof. Krepel was always home and always waiting for dark. Like the ganzinger fowl that nested in the huge gable of his home, he slept days and watched the skies at night.

As Raccoman approached, he saw pelts drying on the crude, wood fence that surrounded his uncle's home. The tiny skins made him cringe over the new status of life on Estermann where animals were no longer safe. Congrels were in the most danger of all for they had no natural defenses except for short teeth, which afforded them no protection.

"Hello, nephew!" cried the old astronomer. Raccoman turned from staring at the small congrel skins.

Whatever hope Raccoman had had for Krepel to do his shopping, it was now shattered. Krepel's moustache was blacker than his own! Instantly, he decided to conceal the true purpose of his coming. Hesitantly, he asked the astronomer. "How are the Star Riders?"

"Fine! There's to be a party tonight!" said Krepel, obviously changing the subject.

"Where?" asked Raccoman.

"Here at my house—welders are welcome!" Krepel said with cordial volume. "Will you stay? There's a fiddler coming."

"Krepel, your moustache is black!" Dakktare blurted out at last.

"Yours, too!"

"Will they never be gray again?"

"I think not. But come, nephew, let's not be glum. You've the good fortune to happen here on a party night. We will make this autumn evening live."

"But what will we do?" asked Dakktare, looking past the corner of the old house to the southwest horizon. It was an unfocused look that rests vacant eyes while the mind runs wildly away with itself.

There was a long silence before the metal-worker repeated his simple question:

"I say—what will we do now that we're Blackgills?
There are now only three,
You, Parsky, and me."

"But not for long—that's the purpose of my party—I've invited a hundred guests for a hundred bowls of steaming stew." He winked. There was a momentary flash of mischief across the old man's face that so resembled Parsky's expression that it unnerved Raccoman. Krepel went on, "Oh, I am glad the brisk weather has come early—for every Graygill is a hearty eater when the nip of autumn is in the air. Soup is always good on a brisk night."

Raccoman felt the bright sting of autumn and thought winter might come early. Secretly he hoped so, for winter would bring the tilt winds and a chance to try his hopeful theory and test the success of the work to which he had devoted himself in the old barn.

They walked the short distance to the house. Through the half-opened door, the smell of stew gushed out into the cool night. They did not enter the house through the oval-shaped front door by which Velissa had entered when she made her wintry trip to Krepel's station. They took the side door that faced the well-worn path to the orange observatory. Old Krepel entered first and Raccoman followed him into the kitchen. Passing through the great room of Krepel's house, Raccoman noticed that it had been gayly decorated and two long tables were set for a hundred guests. He could not imagine where Krepel had kept the tableware for such a magnificent feast.

No sooner had he entered the kitchen than Raccoman spied Parsky sipping red broth from a steaming ladle. The cauldron before him was friends with the fire that caressed its thick iron sides like a blazing octopus, whose amber arms fondly embraced the black kettle. The flames burned low in the rest of the fireplace, and these were the perfect kind of coals above which one might simmer the first fall cauldron of stew.

> "Parsky, you stew-cook—
> Unparalleled chef!
> You're the last great cook
> Our planet has left!"

The cook winked and rejoined:

> "None of your verse,
> Or I'll give you the curse
> Of your life."

Parsky grinned, then added, "This is going to be a great night."

Some of the new stew still clung to the black bristles of Parsky's moustache for he tasted every meal to be sure the seasoning was just right.

"What's in the pot?" asked Raccoman.

"Enough to blacken a hundred gills," his old uncle interjected.

> "Don't you think it best
> To tell the guests
> What's in the pot?"

"Now, Raccoman. . ." In a moment Parsky went on, "Would you like a bowl before the others arrive?"

"Not me, I am determined I shall never again taste your meat." Raccoman felt a little self-righteous, for he furiously wanted to taste it, but he continued on:

> "I live for the day
> When I hope that I can
> See my gills again gray."

"It is too late, Dakktare. You are a Blackgill now. You can't ever go back."

"I will go back!"

Raccoman's protest was firm and his firmness did not invite congeniality, nor did his cool resolve. His uncle looked away from the argument that was about to erupt.

Parsky slammed the ladle down and looked Dakktare in the eyes. "Fool, there is no going back to gray—the color is black! If you tell any one of our guests that there is meat in the broth . . ." Parsky picked up a huge knife he had lately used to carve the congrels' flesh from their bones. He looked at Dakktare, then grabbed him by his shirt and drew his face close to his own. He brought the huge knife to Raccoman's throat in a mock gesture of decapitation. "If you tell any of our guests that there is meat, I'll see that you thicken the broth at our next party."

Raccoman's eyes were wide. The almost one thousand years of his entire life flashed before him. His life had not been all that eventful, but it had been dear to him even if others considered it dull.

Parsky released him. Raccoman stroked one of his sideburns and thought of the old, round barn and the moving starfields. He knew that Parsky meant to carry out his prophecy with the stew for he was not the sort to make idle threats. He also knew the deception was the joint desire of Krepel as well. A few weeks ago there was only one Blackgill—now there were three. A stew-cook, a metalworker, and a star-watcher. He knew there would soon be a hundred more. Then five hundred. The forest would then be combed by Blackgills seeking meat in congrel nests, and when the little animals were gone, they would slay the catterlobs as the starving Blackgills once had done in the days of the migration.

Raccoman felt a chill—it was more than the drafty room. He left the kitchen.

He went around the tables in the great room and out the back door. He walked out to the observatory, climbed the old stairs, and looked through the eyepiece of the scope. There was something over the entire upper lens—or was there? No, the great lens was gone! Raccoman heard footfalls behind him and turned in time to see Krepel bounding up the stairs. Krepel picked up a huge axe that was lying on the floor above a pile of shattered glass.

"Where's the great lens, Krepel?" Raccoman asked, studying the broken glass.

"It fractured in a hail storm."

"There have been no storms."

"Perhaps on your side of the forest, but on our side we had a great storm. Hail stones larger than the eggs of grumblebeaks fell. They destroyed the scope," said the astronomer.

"Nonsense! Such stones would have destroyed the roof of your home as well."

"Do you say I lie?"

Dakktare looked at the axe. "No," he said, then paused and continued, "When will you order a replacement?"

"I have no plans."

Raccoman knew that Krepel was no longer Krepel. Looking at the stars had been his only love.

"No plans to mend the scope?" asked the nephew.

"None," replied the one-time astronomer.

"Then what of the Star Riders—how can we track them?"

"What Stars Riders?" asked Krepel.

"You do remember . . ."

"There are no moving starfields—we were mistaken."

"It's not true. I saw them, just as you did," Raccoman insisted. "They cross the southwest quadrant of the sky each night. I've been working ever since . . ."

Raccoman shuddered to think that he had almost revealed his secret project. Suddenly he thought better of telling his uncle.

"Working on what?" asked Krepel.

"Working on . . . on . . ." Dakktare struggled to find a believable subject. "On a long poem dedicated to the moving starfields."

He was proud that he had come up so quickly with a believable lie. It was the first he had ever told. Lying was as new to Estermann as eating meat. His lie was all the more believable because he was so widely known as a poet.

"Let's hear it," said Krepel suspiciously.

"All right," said Raccoman, pausing to collect his wits. He paused overlong.

"Well—let's hear it!"

"I'm trying to recall it," Raccoman lied as he attempted to compose something.

"The sky is a friend
That beckons to me.
It snuggles horizons
And fondles the . . ."

Again he paused, obviously searching desperately for a word.

"Well, go on," demanded Krepel.

". . . sea!" said Dakktare, suddenly breathing easier. "Do you want to hear more?"

"I think you just wrote that," accused the astronomer.

"You want to hear more?" Raccoman asked again.

"Never mind. It is time for the guests to arrive."

The astronomer turned and left the observatory. He placed his axe against the house and entered by the side door. Raccoman lingered a moment, reflecting upon his near-confession. He vowed to be more careful from now on and to keep his life work entirely to himself.

Lest he be suspected of trying to escape Parsky's stew, he went back into the gaily decorated house. Several of the guests had already arrived. They all wore coats against the autumn chill and busied themselves removing mufflers and coats. Each of them found a hook for their garments at the windowed end of the great hall.

It is never possible to chart the reasons for all the events that occur in life, but Raccoman, like his uncle and friend, had supposed that he would remain a bachelor to the end of life. Women Graygills, scarce as they were, had never seemed to be interested in him. Their appearance had always intrigued him, but their conversation was shallow and rarely took a turn towards the serious or the valuable. Could a Graygill bachelor—now becoming a Blackgill bachelor—ever change his mind? Raccoman Dakktare stroked his left sidelock and wondered.

At old Krepel's party, Dakktare met Velissa once again. He decided that Velissa was a musical name and fit her. Raccoman had danced with her at bygone parties and knew her to be the daughter of the astronomer whose star-scope needed to be mended. Her father had been for generations the close friend of his uncle. Her father was one of those unbelievably fortunate men who had known the blessings of both a wife and a daughter.

Velissa was a charming Graygill. Her sideburns did not detract from her femininity, since sideburns were common to both sexes. Her eyes were a deep-set blue, and her sidelocks, which curled on either side of her face, bounced with an intrigue that left Dakktare's eyes sparkling. He felt as he had felt at bygone parties. He found it hard to take his eyes from Velissa, and wished himself three centuries younger and as trim as the Blackgill.

The dress Velissa wore to Krepel's party had a tiered skirt of bright blue flounces. It was the perfect sort of dress that Graygill women wore to dances, and her affection for the deepest blue possible was no different than Raccoman's love of the brightest yellows he could find. After dinner they were shortly to dance the Lindon, a happy and fiery dance of Graygills that went perfectly with blue dresses and yellow boots.

Before long, Raccoman and Velissa were conversing like old friends. She told him of her father's scientific work in labeling stars in the second magnitude in the constellation of the Grand Dragon. She felt an immediate attraction to Raccoman, and inwardly she was glad to know that Dakktare was the metal-worker Krepel had recommended to her father to repair his scope.

As if he had read her thoughts, Raccoman said, "I hope to come and repair your father's scope before winter comes again."

"Plan to stay awhile when you come," Velissa urged. "My father's star-scope may give us an additional evening of your verses and ballads."

Raccoman sensed that she was sincere, although his age made him feel unworthy of her invitation.

"Tell me, Raccoman, have you learned any new steps to the Forest Rune?"

Hearing that he had, Velissa looked forward to the evening's entertainment even more eagerly. And since Velissa was one of the guests, Raccoman too was eager for the time when the tables would be cleared and the dancing would begin.

As the guests sat down to eat, Parsky appeared carrying a gigantic, steaming cauldron. Raccoman stood to say the universal words of Estermann gratitude:

> *"To the maker of the feast*
> *To the power of loaf and yeast*
> *Till the broth and bread have ceased*
> *Gratefulness is—"*

"Here! here! None of that!" interjected Parsky.

"But we always bless the loaf and broth," objected Dakktare.

The guests knew Raccoman to be right but decided not to take part in the disagreement since it was Parsky's feast and Krepel's house. Besides, Dakktare had said nearly the whole blessing before Parsky had interrupted him.

"Here's to the new stew!" Parsky exulted as he lifted the ladle. Guest by guest, the great scoop lowered into the broth till all the bowls were filled. Steaming loaves of black bread were brought and the Graygills agreed in appetite that never had they tasted such a delicious meal. Around the table passed a certain puzzled look, as though each Graygill had sampled something never before tasted, but none protested. The usual merriment persisted.

Raccoman and Velissa continued their conversation during dinner. Raccoman found her enchanting. Her eyes were innocent and their sparkle held his own. During pauses in the conversation, Velissa stared reluctantly at her bowl of stew and even lifted her spoon several times as though she would eat, but finally laid her spoon down and pushed the bowl to the center of the table. Raccoman did not even lift his spoon, for his determination was firm. Above the happy faces of the other guests, he noticed Parsky's face locked in a scowl as he watched everyone eat. Then Parsky turned his leering burning stare on Raccoman.

Raccoman was so engrossed in Parsky's disdain, he did not immediately notice that Velissa had not eaten either. When he became aware of her again, he asked, "Don't you like the meal?"

"I'm not fond of Parsky's cooking," she said. "I've never trusted him—my father told me tales of ancient Blackgills that would make a decent Graygill cringe. Besides, I'm puzzled."

"At what?" asked Dakktare, surprised that she knew the tales of the ancient Blackgills. But she did not answer.

"At what? What puzzles you?" he repeated.

"Oh, nothing," she said.

Raccoman did not know her well enough to be insistent. Besides, this was a party, and when the merriment began, there would be little place for the serious turn their conversation had taken.

"What, not eating?" said an all-too-familiar voice behind them.

"We're not hungry—or, at least, I'm not," said Raccoman.

The two bowls of stew had cleared of steam and were growing colder as they sat.

"He's not hungry and I do not eat because of an old proverb," said Velissa, apparently unafraid of Parsky. Dakktare was amused at her calm and courageous defiance of the leering Blackgill.

Velissa spoke: "I have lived on the border of Quarrystone Woods with my father all of my life. The people in the center of the woods tell of ancient griefs when the famine struck the Blackgills of Castledome Forest."

Parsky glared.

"What do they say of those who once lived in Castledome?" he asked.

"Never trust a Blackgill's stew," she said curtly.

The words so angered Parsky that he seized her lukewarm bowl and hurled it against the wall. It made a frightful mess. But worse than the mess it made was the stir it caused among the guests. Parsky, realizing that all eyes had turned upon his temporary tantrum, smiled and broke into laughter. His laughter eased the tension and soon the other guests laughed and continued eating. Still, Parsky's temper dampened the table conversation for a while. Krepel in particular was embarrassed by both the mess and the stir and was glad that the dinner was nearly over.

After a few moments he briskly clapped his hands and smiled. His moustache loomed black above his white teeth. Then he called out, "Clear the tables and chairs—it's time for the dance! The Claxton will be first and then the Lindon."

The room sprang into action. The table was cleared to one side, and the chairs were moved to the perimeter of the room. Three musicians found a spot near the end of the hall and their music promptly began. Their instruments resembled a fiddle, a mandolin, and a concertina. The concertina had a bright, reedy sound and the mandolin had more of a harp quality about it. The music was brisk and lively. Only the men of Estermann did the Claxton, for it was a vigorous dance. The Graygills, fueled by red broth and black bread, linked arms and danced in lively double columns, kicking their stubby legs until it seemed their boots could never stay on their furious feet.

Raccoman danced liveliest of all. At one point he entered a square of four men and clasped hands with Parsky, who still scowled at him as there was time in the fast stepping that the Claxton required. To the rest of the guests, Parsky seemed as congenial as ever.

The dance lasted rather long so that the overfed men were quite out of breath by the time the music stopped. The women applauded their vigorous performance.

In the merriment and hilarity none except Raccoman noticed that Parsky had slipped out the main front door, putting on his coat as he left the hall. Raccoman was not troubled by his leaving, but he wondered why he did so.

"It's time for the Lindon," cried someone.

"No, no. Let us rest, please," called the other men. "Let the metal-worker sing while we rest."

Dakktare was out of breath, but since he had not eaten the stew, he was not as winded as the rest.

"Sing the 'Forest Rune,'" cried Krepel, then turning to the musicians, he asked, "Do you know it, too?" They didn't even nod. Their answer was the bright melody that they promptly began to play.

"Stop," cried Raccoman, "play it lower or I shall never manage the high notes."

This request promptly stopped the music.

The shortest of the three musicians plucked a few strings and lightened the thumbscrew. Raccoman was grateful for the delay, for not only did the Forest Rune require breath, but it also required some stamina for the hasty stepping that accompanied it. No good Estermann songster worked his mouth only. The whole body served the tune and every animated song made the legs and arms do their part to aid the mouth and lungs.

The musicians began again, and stomping his bright yellow boots on the great stone floor, Raccoman sang:

"Walking and talking in Granover town
I'll come to the meadows of Canby Down
And there in the lea, where the beasts wander free
I'll dance with the rogues wherever they're bound."

At this point, Dakktare stepped briskly with the music and turned a complete somersault, never breaking the cadence. He set the black caps of his yellow boots to clicking on the stone and kept it up fully three minutes while the guests cheered his tuneful antics. The applause for a moment was louder than the clicking of his heels and the sound of his words.

"Come, dance with me, prance with me,
Clickety-clack,
Come stompedy-rompedy.
Never turn back;

We shall use for our floor
The catterlob track."

The welder's step now swaggered to resemble the beasts of Canby. The very reason the catterlobs left such deep grooves in the meadow floor was their crushing and burdensome weight, and the antic was so awkward that Dakktare did not continue the pondersome and tuneful swagger for long but was soon stepping brightly on the clicking floor.

"A rover once moved to the edge of the sea,
And built him a boat from a candolet tree.
He sailed past the Kendrake, he sailed past the moon,
And filled his own sails
With his own happy tune."

He swung his bright scarf and sang the refrain:

"Oh—
The singing is ringing the grumblebeak's tree
The forest's a chorus
Of glad harmony.
The shrubs are all singing
Uproariously."

Dakktare hooked his fingers before his nose to imitate a grumblebeak, his eyes crossed in the comic masque of his distortion. The merry Graygills laughed and slapped their sides. The cadence continued and so did the welder.

"Who can deny this delirious day?
A Graygill is gray as Graygills are gay.
When the moustache is gray, then a moustache is grand;
As long as it's gray, there is joy in the land."

He was about to begin the chorus when he noticed the guests snickering. Then they began to laugh. He had forgotten that the last verse did not harmonize at all with his new black gills. The guests did not mind the discrepancy, but they found it humorous that Raccoman's words and colors did not match. The laughter grew to such a pitch that Raccoman could barely hear the musicians.

"Come, where the rill is a thrill to the ear.
The clatter and chatter

Won't matter to me
A Graygill is gray as a Graygill should . . ."

Dakktare could not say the word *be* that finished the Forest Rune. It was too humorous and sad for a Blackgill to sing of Graygill life. Thus, the tune and dance and his honesty all came to an end at one time.

He covered his moustache, deeply ashamed of its color. The Graygills suddenly stopped laughing for they hadn't meant to hurt the welder nor to make fun of his appearance. Their laughter had come only in the interest of their own good time.

But for the first time in his life, Raccoman felt ashamed, stopped his song, and took his place along the wall. Velissa, seeing his discomfort, came quickly to stand alongside of him.

Velissa's presence at first cheered him, then left him insecure. He realized she was beautiful. He forgot both his obesity and his age, and he knew that his contentment with bachelorhood was ebbing.

The musicians called out a single word: "Dandonnarrie!" Velissa's eyes lit up at the word, and Raccoman in an instant forgot his embarrassment. He could see that she wanted to join in the dance. They were already face to face, so that asking her seemed terribly formal—instead, he simply took her hand and led her to the open floor.

The music began.

The fiery tempo allowed Velissa to display the blue, tiered skirt she had chosen for Krepel's party. The steps to the dance were brisk and at times invited the clapping of the hands interlaced in rhythm with the cadence of the loud and furious stamping of the feet. This exotic stepping was usually accompanied by a shuffling of the body and an elevation of the chin.

Raccoman had been tired when the song began, but found Velissa an enchantress whose seductive affair with the dance beguiled him into a steady gaze at her lithe form, which turned the flounces of her blue dress into a spinning intrigue of ruffles and coquettish invitation.

Then the music slowed to a close and seething tempo. Raccoman felt the blood pounding in his pointed ears. He slipped his arm around her waist, and their bodies touched, agreeing with the closeness of the music. Velissa felt the hypnotic tug of the welder's eyes, and he could not release her from the spell he so unwittingly had cast. Worse, for the first moment in his life, he was captive to a new set of feelings that stirred him and chained him to some necessity of closeness he felt he never could release.

They were suspended in time, locked by a long gaze that set Raccoman's empty centuries to begging. Nothing mattered but the moment. Somewhere the music ended and they both became aware that they were standing alone, still seeing nothing but their own reflections in each other's eyes.

Only when the guests began to snicker did Velissa become aware that they had lingered overlong. How long they were not sure. Neither of them wanted to break the silence, but both of them knew they must re-enter the world they had so recently left behind.

"It's time for the Lindon," she said. "Shall we dance?"

"No . . . at least not for a moment." He felt suddenly years younger, but admitted to being tired.

"Let's go out into the cool night as soon as the music begins," she offered.

Without answering her, he knew she was a friend. When the music began, the Graygills danced the Lindon, while the welder and the star-watcher's daughter slipped out into the night through the same side door by which Uncle Krepel had so lately entered. When the door had closed upon the merriment inside, the cool air seemed the perfect antidote to Dakktare's flushed cheeks.

"Velissa, do I seem a hypocrite?"

"How's that?" she asked in innocence.

"A Blackgill who sings of the glory of gray."

She still did not seem to understand. They walked in silence a little way from the old house and sat down near the observatory.

At last he broke the silence and asked her, "Why did you not eat Parsky's stew?"

"I cannot help it," said Velissa. "It's the first time I've ever had a Blackgill fix my dinner. I was afraid."

"Oh, that I had been as wise," said Raccoman. "I once tasted— oh, that I had not!"

"How long has it been since your gills turned from gray?" she asked.

"Since the night I first trusted a Blackgill's stew."

Velissa did not press for an explanation. He offered none.

"You came a long way to be at old Krepel's party," she said at last.

"I did not come for the party. I did not even know there was to be one. I came because . . ." He hesitated.

"Because?"

"Because I need some supplies and I was . . . I was afraid to face the merchants of Canby with black gills. Still, I must have rod and fire or I shall not finish my remarkable work."

"You're welding your work?"

"Yes," he said, again hesitating. "But tell me of your father's scope. Is it as large as Krepel's?" He changed the subject partly because he did not want to reveal his secret project and partly because he wanted to know more of the moving starfield.

"Oh, larger, much larger," she said.

"Tell me," he asked, "did my uncle ever mention the moving starfields—to your father?"

"Moving starfields?" she asked.

"Yes," said Dakktare. "There are stars that appear each night in the southwest quadrant of the sky—they migrate at steep vectors and soon disappear over the horizon."

"I know my father's sky maps. I am almost always with him in the observatory. I am sure he knows of no moving starfields. Do you remember the quadrant and triangular fixation?"

"Not exactly. It was deep in the early night sky. They appear near the constellation of the Grand Dragon." For the moment Raccoman decided not to reveal to her the secret of the Star Riders.

"Could you find it in the scope?"

"I think so, but I'm not sure."

"Then let's go to old Krepel's observatory and have a go at it," she said.

"Krepel has smashed his scope," he said.

"But why?" she asked.

"Who knows why. His behavior has been erratic since his gills began to turn black," said Dakktare.

"I, too, was dumbfounded when I saw that his gills were black," she said.

They sat in the silent darkness for a few minutes. Something was wrong. There was a chill in the air, and more than a chill.

Neither of them spoke until Velissa suddenly cried out, "I'm afraid. Could we go inside?"

"Listen," said Raccoman.

In the distance there was a muffled sound of heavy footfalls like those made by a great beast. The sound caused them to quake. It seemed to be coming nearer.

"Could we go inside?" she repeated.

"Inside is not best," he said. "Come. Let's move further from the house."

Velissa trusted him and walked with him to the edge of the wood. They sat down in the starlight. By now the noise had become thunder. The woods were splintering around them.

The noise had not reached those inside the house as the music and the dancing were still intense. The merriment of Krepel's party could be seen through the windows.

Little more than two hundred yards in front of Raccoman and Velissa the trees exploded into splinters. In the starlight the pair could see a monstrous catterlob. It was armored and bore an evil insignia painted on its shoulder plates. It lumbered across the dark yard and swung its giant forepaw at one of the chimneys of Krepel's house.

The noise of the crumbling stones stopped the music instantly.

The beast stepped into the roof and his huge tail swung into the window of the great hall.

The glass shattered.

The astonished Graygills cried in terror.

Raccoman and Velissa saw a shadowy form in armor near the corner of the house. A sword was strapped under his cape. He cried "Holga!" and the catterlob lowered its scaly head. The armored cavalier climbed onto the neck saddle. The beast then wheeled in the direction of Quarrystone Wood.

"No!" Velissa gasped half-aloud. "Doldeen! Father!" she cried in an agonized whisper, as the beast lumbered off into the darkness.

There are vistas where wind blows the stars.
There are ledges where daring may dare.
There are crags only claimed in abandon
By those unafraid of thin air.

CHAPTER VIII

The Upper Ledges

FEAR HAS TAUGHT even the sluggish to run, and Raccoman and Velissa ran as fast as any had ever run on Estermann.

Their flight was complicated by the tangled undergrowth of the forest. They tried in vain to find the road that ran through the thicket that surrounded the taller trees. In the distance they could hear the plaintive cries of catastrophe that only moments before had been a lively Graygill party. Shouts of terror and the sounds of splintering timber gradually gave way to a silence that was as ominous as the chaos had been. Soon there were no sounds at all on the night wind except their own hushed breathing as their flight continued.

"I wish I could see," whispered Dakktare. "For all I know we could be running in circles—completely lost. We must stop and rest."

They did.

They sifted the darkness for even a whisper of evidence that all that had gone before had really happened. Even the crashing tread of the catterlob was choked to silence by the dense, black foliage of the inky forest.

For half an hour no words passed between them.

"Raccoman," Velissa finally broke the silence, "I am afraid. The catterlob may be drawing near to my father's observatory. We must hurry forward."

He remained firm. "But what is forward, Velissa? Where is Quarrystone? We are lost. We must wait for the day," he insisted. "We will only waste our energy trying to find our way without light."

"Perhaps we can," said Velissa. "Have you heard of Singreale?"

"He was the great king in the days of the Castledome famine. He reigned from the strong and beautiful Castle of Maldoon."

"Certainly." She seemed pleased. "He ruled in the lush valley of the eastern steppes when the Blackgills first came to the ginjon forest. Three thousand years he had ruled the steppes. His power was manifested in his two great falcons that flew the morning mists and soared above the sunny fields. One was as black as space and the other as white as steel fire. Before the throne of Maldoon there was a crystal spindle that rose from the stone floor and supported a single small platform. On the top of the graceful column there rested Singreale, a great gem larger than my hand." The darkness was so deep he could not see how large that was.

She paused. At the mention of Singreale, a new wind rustled the night forest. It was soft and seemed to be crying. Still, there were no distinct sounds of danger, so she continued.

"The gem was the glory of Singreale, and the fire that swirled about the jewel was proclaimed by the king to be the pure fire of being. It was the radiance of the ideal, the source of life as it should be.

"When the Blackgills began to gather themselves for the siege against his castle, Singreale took the light to their leader and told them the good news. 'Trust the fire,' he said, 'and the light will change your lives. Walk in the light and you will know life and peace. You will have food without slaughter and love without fear. The forest and the plains will be a table of bounty where all may eat, and the land of the Castledome will be free forever.' "

Velissa and Raccoman listened in the darkness for the sound of any unfamiliar animals on the prowl. They heard the cry of a ganzinger fowl.

Dakktare's brain was now as dark as the forest. He knew that Parsky had tricked him into savoring evil. He even knew that both Parsky and his uncle had tricked a hundred innocent Graygills with the same deception this very evening.

Velissa continued, "The Blackgills rejected the king's fire."

"And they never accepted the light at all?" asked Raccoman, wishing he could see Velissa's face as she went on.

"They hated light. They left the Castledomes and marched eastward. They broke down the walls of Maldoon and killed the king."

"Singreale?" asked Dakktare.

"Yes," answered Velissa, invisible to him in the darkness. "They destroyed the white falcon. The great white bird was soaked in his own blood, but the black one escaped and flew away with the king's diamond in his talons."

"So the Blackgills never really owned Singreale at all?"

"Never," said Velissa. "They knew of the great light, but it held little interest for them. After the siege they began to crave killing, and in the days that came after the murder of the white falcon, they pledged themselves to the death of all animals. Soon they began to wear teeth and bones on leather strips about their necks. . . ."

"So that's where Parsky got the tooth," he interjected.

"What tooth?" she asked.

"The one he wears about his neck beneath his tunic."

"Have you seen this?"

"I have. He showed it to me on the way back from my uncle's only a few weeks ago."

"Then it is as I feared. Parsky was a survivor of the Blackgill war with the beasts. While the last battle was in progress, he must have crossed the Kendrake and made his way back to Castledome Forest. It was a long journey," she said thoughtfully. "I wonder that he made it at all, and especially alone."

"He would not have if it had not been for the light of Singreale that rode on the old tooth he has tied about his neck."

"Is that what he told you?"

"It is."

"Parsky is the great deceiver. The fire never rode upon a tooth. The Fire of Singreale has ever inhabited the giant treasure of Maldoon—the light in the talons of the sky. If only the Blackgills would have accepted it—they might have lived. But Parsky alone survived that ignoble race whose deceit and death survived with him. Now the terror of slaughter that made a waste of the Flandry Lowlands has come at last to the North."

These were heavy words—as heavy as the thick darkness into which they were spoken. The stars hid under clouds and made the recounting of Estermann's bloody past all the more a cold and chilling saga.

"Do you not see, Raccoman, that this pointless struggle of nature is set upon us again? Estermann will die. The destruction of your uncle's house is the beginning of the end. We are no match for the beasts."

"Is there no hope?"

"One . . . but it is slim."

"Then what?"

"The Fire of Singreale. I don't know how Singreale could save us, but there is always hope in the light."

"But where is the Fire?" he asked hopelessly.

"Here at my neck, in a little pouch of coarse cloth."

Raccoman was dumbfounded at her words. Could it really be true? The darkness was so great that he could not see her neck, or the pouch, but he did believe her.

"How did you come to have it?"

"The black falcon delivered it to my great-grandfather who had once been knighted in the ancient castle of Singreale. He grieved over the murder of the king and vowed to defend his vanished light until his own death, if necessary. The Blackgill marauders never seemed to know what became of the king's falcon and his treasure. Some felt it was hidden in the cliffs north of Demmerron, but none ever guessed the diamond had come to rest in a simple dwelling in Quarrystone Woods. We vowed never to disclose what we knew of Singreale nor to speak of it at all.

"On his flight from the sack of Maldoon, the black falcon had carried the diamond to the Western Highlands, along with its serpent-guardian Doldeen, who in the course of generation was to become my best friend.

"My father, sensing the danger of our times, gave the diamond to me this very morning, and I hold it in the pouch at my neck. Doldeen, for the first time in her life, agreed to let me become the guardian of her great prize. After her conflict with the armored marauder, she knew that the whereabouts of her treasure had been discovered. Perhaps she sensed her age and inability to defend the stone.

"Raccoman," she said, "I am going to take Singreale from the pouch. We must trust it through the forest."

"No!" cried Raccoman. "It is too dark to see it anyway, and should you drop it and lose it in this forest, our only hope of saving Canby from the deception of Parsky would then be lost."

"Your thinking is as dark as the forest. Singreale cannot be lost in the dark. For dark is dispelled by its light." She paused. "Do you hear anything?"

"Nothing," he said after a moment of silence. The darkness seemed to stop the ears as well as the eyes.

Velissa opened the cloth pouch. "I have it in my hand," she said.

"No, no. For the hope of light, put it back."

"Nonsense, it is for that very hope I take it out. Here, hold it, Raccoman."

She extended her hand in the direction of his voice, trying in vain to find his hand. She could not. "Speak to me," she said, "I must hear your voice to find you."

"No! For the love of Singreale, put it back!" he cried again.

She moved toward his voice. She tripped and fell clumsily against him. The large jewel rolled from her hand and dropped.

"I have lost it," she laughed. "But trust me, Raccoman, the ancient Fire is near."

They stood again in silence.

In the blackness they saw a single star. In the wonder of this pinpoint of light, they momentarily forgot the lost treasure. The star settled closer and closer until its brightness illuminated the entire forest. Its light was friendly and yet so bright that both Raccoman and Velissa blinked at its intensity. The eerie shadows that it cast left the haunted tentacles of the great trees hovering above the pair like multi-armed monsters. The radiance settled to their very feet and came to rest on the great gem that Velissa had dropped.

"It's Singreale!" she shouted.

She stooped to pick it up, and she held it high above their heads. The Fire was intense, but it did not burn her fingers. "Come, Raccoman," she invited. "Now we shall find the road to Quarrystone Woods!"

This was easier said than done for the trees were tangled and the undergrowth was thick. It was even as the deceitful Parsky had said in his own devious story. Each time they turned in a direction that the Fire did not agree with, the light would dim and offer them scant illumination until they had corrected their course. The trees looked less ominous once the two travelers had grown used to the shadowy closeness of the twisted branches.

They had progressed only a quarter of an hour when they saw the brush clearing away and the trees becoming widely spaced.

"I think it's a road," said Raccoman.

"Indeed," agreed Velissa.

They started to go left, but Singreale grew faint. Quickly they reversed their choice and the Fire burst into brilliance as they traveled forward.

In a little while, Singreale dimmed, for they then were on the road that crossed the Western Highlands. "It is a principle of Singreale that no light is ever to be wasted," said Velissa.

The stars came out.

Estermann had no moon, and on any moonless world, the stars seem even brighter.

"Velissa, I won't be able to stay very long—once I've walked you safely back to your father's home."

Raccoman Dakktare suddenly remembered that his original purpose for going to his uncle's house was yet unfulfilled.

"Metal-working is my life, and I must get back to work—I'm the best you will ever meet."

Raccoman's immodesty had not been diminished by the events of the evening, but Velissa was not quite used to it. Dakktare never considered himself a braggart, only truthful. Being the best in his trade, he saw no sin in saying so. And considering his outmoded equipment, he was, indeed, a fine welder.

They walked most of the night in silence. Velissa suddenly saw a road sign that she knew to be less than a half-mile from her home. "We're almost there, Raccoman," she said.

Suddenly neither of them felt well.

They noticed a red glow in the sky directly ahead of them.

"I'm afraid, Raccoman," she said.

The ruddy glow grew more intense, and when the road turned, Velissa cried aloud.

"The house is gone!"

Neither of them said a word nor suggested what both of them knew to be the great concern. The house was gone and the embers of a great fire smouldered in the ashes. There were deep tracks cut into the yard. A catterlob had obviously smashed the house and the fireplace had erupted in flames upon the splintered beams.

Velissa dreaded to see a form in the red glow.

"The observatory!" Velissa cried. "Perhaps my father is still there."

The building looked very much like Uncle Krepel's observatory with the same conical roof. The blue tube still projected from the roof. Even in the dark, the light from the smouldering house permitted Raccoman to see that the observatory was unharmed.

Velissa outdistanced him to the observatory door. She bounded up the steps, still holding the luminous gem. In the dark interior of the observatory, its light was once again brilliant. It was clear that her father was not there.

Raccoman entered behind her and came to the wide wooden platform inside the building where Velissa's father usually stood to observe the Estermann sky.

"Where's father?" asked Velissa. "And Doldeen?" Outside they could hear the cracking of the final timbers as they fell into the charred remains of the house.

"Father! Father!" She stared into the darkness outside the observatory window. "He's dead," she said. She bit her lip, then wept.

"We do not know for sure," consoled Raccoman. "Maybe he escaped into the woods."

"Or was devoured—" Her voice trailed off.

"But we do not know, Velissa," he offered. "He was always in the observatory at night and may thus have escaped when the house burst into flames."

"What will I do? I have no other relatives this side of Castledome Forest. I am afraid."

Racomman embraced her as she cried inside the dark of the observatory.

"Let us leave at once for Canby," said Raccoman.

It was the first time in the frightening night, a night that had all but passed, that Raccoman had found enough peace of mind to set his discourse into studied thought.

"And if my father should yet be alive?" Velissa asked.

"He will come first to the observatory, so let's leave him a note," Raccoman replied.

It was hope against hope, but Velissa took the quill from the observatory ink stand and dipped it in the well. By the light of Singreale, she scratched a note on a scrap of paper she found in her father's nearby desk:

Father,
    I have fled these woods. Should you seek me, I
will be under the protection of Raccoman Dakktare of Canby.
                                            Velissa

She attached the note to the tube of the telescope.

"My things were all burned in the fire. I've nothing left to take with us." She paused and then asked, "It will be light before long. Shall we go while it is still dark?"

Raccoman nodded.

Neither of them moved for a moment, but as they started to leave, Singreale twinkled erratically.

"The light is trying to tell us something."

"What?" asked the welder.

The light winked again and then flashed the brilliance of its incandescence on the blue tube.

"The moving starfields!" cried Raccoman.

It was as if the twinkling Singreale was speaking directly to an issue that Velissa didn't immediately understand. It was odd that Raccoman did.

"The Star Riders!" he fairly shouted. He could now see that her grief had obscured her thinking. He decided to begin more slowly. "Velissa, I think the light is trying to say that this is the only working star-scope in Estermann—at least on this continent."

"This continent—what are you saying?" she interrupted. "This is the only scope . . . with no star-watcher." She trembled, turned her face to the wall again, and murmured, "Father, Doldeen!"

Raccoman touched her and then embraced her to lighten the burden of her grief. She clung to him tightly as if all her world of security was in his arms. For the first time in all his thousand years of life, his emotions became muddled and a deep hunger rose within him. His mind split three ways. A strange guilt occupied him. Should he dare to desire what he held in his arms when the reasons that she clung to him were not altogether the same reasons that he now clung to her?

He tried to release her, but she clung more closely. He loved it and hated it at the same time. Singreale fluttered its light more urgently upon the great scope, and Raccoman tore himself from Velissa's embrace and hurried to the center of the observatory. Her grief needed the darkness to hide her tears. His needed the darkness to hide the blood that washed his face with the aftermath of his strange new feelings.

Singreale burned steadily in approval that the confused welder was at last trying to comply quickly.

Raccoman turned the great wheel on the side of the tube. Because of his haste, the capstan groaned as the great cylinder lowered rapidly. For the first time, Raccoman noticed the fissure in the cradle that the old astronomer had wanted him to weld. When the tube was nearly level with the outside roof, he adjusted the top rotor and the near-level scope swung three degrees to the side. The welder put his eye to the ocular and frowned. "Where are they?" he complained to the night that was fast giving way to the morning.

"How I wish I'd recorded the vectors and paid more attention to Krepel that night."

All he could recall was the starfields moved barely above the horizon of the southwest quadrant.

"Is the scope low enough?" asked Velissa.

"Maybe not, but it seems to be as low as it will go . . . unless . . ."

"Unless what?" asked Velissa.

"Suspend the vertical rotor!" he exulted in a moment of insight.

Velissa had watched her father do it a hundred times, and she pulled the great pin that disengaged the support shaft. The great scope swung free and dropped three degrees.

"There!" she cried, when the cylinder had dropped.

"The moving starfields!" he cried as he gave Velissa the eyepiece. She gasped in excitement. "Moving stars! Have they been there long? They were too near the horizon—that's why my father never saw them!"

Raccoman nodded. "Perhaps they have been there for millennia. Who knows? Wait, Velissa, they are not just fields of roving stars—look again."

She put her face to the eyepiece and squinted into the moving stars. Raccoman was glad that this scope was more powerful than the one his uncle had destroyed. He knew Velissa would be able to discern the tiny creatures with microscopic men on their winged bodies.

"Raccoman, they are not stars at all!"

He smiled.

"They are little men!"

"Not little men, Velissa, but Titans twice our size!"

She continued looking while he explained his near-encounter during the last season of the tilt winds. He continued talking until she interrupted him.

"They're disappearing!"

He took the eyepiece back and squinted with his free eye, which was an odd indication that his other squinted even more to note the progress and direction of the Star Riders. "They cross the horizon always at that same position," he noted. "Now they're almost under the horizon." He hastily scribbled additional notes of their direction and checked the previous figures.

He returned his eye to the ocular one last time and watched a moment before exclaiming, still staring into the tube of blackness where they lately had been, "Gone—gone back to the land we've never discovered."

He straightened his back and stood erect. Singreale had dimmed now, and Velissa looked beautiful in the soft glow of the diamond she still held. He wanted to touch her again but refrained.

"To the lost land?" she asked, destroying his mind-set. His reverie evaporated.

"Velissa, there's a continent somewhere where these Star Riders dwell. They always fly the same direction and disappear at the same geographic point."

He picked up the same quill that Velissa had lately used to write the note to her father. He plotted the coordinates from the figures he had just scratched down. He made forceful, hasty notes on the disappearance point and computed its triangulation with the great constellation.

Once more he looked through the eyepiece and smiled. He knew the exact direction of the flight. And while he had no idea how far it was, he knew the direction in which he would have to go to get there.

"We must go!" urged Velissa. "Let's check to see if Collinvar is in the stable," she said, suddenly and gratefully aware that the stable had not also been affected by the fire.

"Collinvar?" asked Dakktare.

"My father's centicorn."

"Your father owns a centicorn?" Dakktare seemed doubtful. Since there were only a hundred of these great horned creatures on Estermann, Dakktare could scarcely believe the good fortune of a scientist who had known both wife and daughter and the ownership of such a beast. It seemed unfair somehow to lonely bachelors whose every journey must be made by foot.

Velissa had a secret fear that she might find her father injured or dead in the vicinity of Collinvar's shed, but she did not. As they neared the shed, she tripped over a soft form.

"Doldeen!" she cried.

The serpent was still. Her body was all but severed by a blade that must have belonged to the scarlet rider. Velissa wept as she held the regal head of her lifeless friend. The serpent's beautiful skin was as cold as her silver horns.

"Doldeen, Doldeen," she cried. Velissa's sidelocks seemed to droop in the grief she felt. Raccoman's hand touched the point of her left ear. He wanted so to hold her, but thought better of it.

"Oh, Raccoman, she's—" Velissa could not finish the word. "Raccoman, where's Father? Oh, Father, Father!" As she turned toward the charred house, the dying flames of the burning timbers were mirrored in her soft and grieving eyes. "Raccoman, please hold me."

He did. He held her with affirmation, without the duplicity of the earlier caress. He kissed her neck—and she hugged him all the harder.

They found a crude shovel near the observatory and dug a hasty grave. Doldeen looked so little as they folded her into black earth.

Velissa stood and looked at the grave, and then turned her stare silently toward the first streaks of morning.

At length Raccoman dragged her away. They hurried on to the blue shed.

Collinvar was there and seemed glad to see her. She wondered if the centicorn could talk, what he might say. What horrors had his unbelieving eyes beheld that night?

Dakktare helped her with the double-saddle, and soon the girth was cinched behind the centicorn's forelegs. The Graygill welder mounted the sleek steed in a clumsy and not very heroic manner.

He found himself in the foreseat of the saddle and pulled Velissa quickly into the second seat. Morning was all but upon them, and light was breaking over the shorter trees of Quarrystone Woods. The new light played upon the swirling ashes of what had been Velissa's home and she stared vacantly at the glowing embers. Then she tossed her sidelocks behind her shoulders and remembered Singreale. She still held the great gem in her palm. The light had dimmed with the coming of dawn, and she quickly replaced the stone in the pouch that hung from her neck and pulled the drawstring.

"On, Collinvar!" Raccoman commanded.

The centicorn bolted forward into the dawn nearly dislodging Dakktare, who was unused to the magnificent strength and speed of the centicorn. Their trip was swift, and in two hours they passed Uncle Krepel's house lying in shambles, but still unburned. They decided not to stop, afraid to behold at close hand what had been so recently a Graygill party.

Collinvar sped on.

The trip to Canby would have taken little more than three hours if Collinvar had not slackened his pace. But instead of taking the plains route that passed the lea where Raccoman worked, they decided to take the high ridge road.

It was a beautiful morning and one intended to be enjoyed. The sun was warm and drew the reds and golds from the gaudy terrain of Estermann. The pride Collinvar exhibited in his own beastly prowess added a high touch of exhilaration to the clean air on the high cliff. After only a few minutes on the upper ledges they could see the rough-shingled rooftops of Canby: the little village in the valley sparkled like diamonds on a velvet cloth. The round Graygill houses glistened with their high, conical roofs, and the bright colors made the village a rainbow of discovery.

From time to time, Raccoman could see that Velissa was troubled about her father. But upon the sunny ledges of their trip her muddled expression seemed to clear.

Being more of a mind to enjoy the sun than to reach his small home, Raccoman brought Collinvar to a sudden halt. He drew the silver rein with a firm hand, and the great centicorn tossed his proud head and reared on his haunches. His torso wheeled out over the sunny ledge. Collinvar could have run another hour easily, but Raccoman, being unused to riding, was ready to walk. Velissa was no stranger to Collinvar's saddle, but she, too, was glad to feel the hard earth beneath her feet. The pair walked along the brink of the cliff, leading their white steed by his silver reins.

Raccoman had not sung since Krepel's disasterous party. The night had offered him little but suspense and loneliness and fear. The sun had been long in coming; now they enjoyed it for half an hour in silence. Then they mounted Collinvar, and he galloped in free silhouette against the sun-bleached cliffs.

As the muted thunder of his hoofs rang out over the ledges,

Velissa clung tightly to Raccoman. He began to sing away the images of the dark night that had passed.

"Hah-ho to the sun on the lofty ledges!
Hah-ho to the gold on the meadow floor!
Bring me a centicorn, bring him round, winged for flight
And I shall fly where the eagles soar.
Set him white with a silver saddle,
Silken-bannered wind shall stir,
And we shall fly in the golden sky
On unseen wings of gossamer."

He saw that Velissa could not manage his cheer and, therefore, he reached out with his sunny song again.

"Should there come war to the flowery leas,
Should the dragons bleed in the sunny air,
Then soar with me on a centicorn
Above the fire in the village square."

"No, please," begged Velissa, "don't sing. I cannot bear the song when I remember my poor father. Oh, Raccoman! What has become of him?"

The welder merely shrugged.

They stopped, dismounted, and tied Collinvar's reins to a shrub.

They sat and gazed out above the plains for nearly an hour. Their silence was a most amazing communication. Sometimes Velissa's cheek glistened with her anguish, and Raccoman knew that nothing he could say would stop the pain she felt.

They both knew that life on Estermann was destined for a conclusion. Would all parties on the planet end like Uncle Krepel's? Would all houses burn like her father's? Would all the beasts of the planet become savage like the catterlob that had destroyed Krepel's home? Was the menace only for the isolated homes like hers and Krepel's? When would the beasts come to the villages? Neither of them spoke such questions aloud for now such musings had only silent, dreadful answers.

Velissa looked away.

Her melancholy broke into a bittersweet song of her own. Hers was a lovely yet haunting theme. It was not the sort of tune Raccoman was really good at singing. There was too little that was merry in it. It clung to the soul and caused the mind to grieve life's melancholy destiny.

> *"There was a sunny, sovereign village*
> *Warmed by winsome hearty friends*
> *Who loved their living, laughing world*
> *Too much to see the vicious ends.*
>
> *Heedless of their infamy, their thoughts were nude,*
> *Their joy decayed, their hopes grew lewd.*
> *They danced too near the precipice*
> *And glutted on forbidden food,*
> *Till none at all were free.*
> *Poor Canby Down! Was life too sweet?*
> *Did laughter spring from fetid meat?*
> *Now bolt the doors to bar the beasts*
> *And call your children from the streets*
> *Where preys catastrophe."*

Velissa paused. Her silence was so heavy it seemed the ground would crack. She added but three lines and stopped.

> *"Oh, Castledome! High Castledome! Death lies now at your heart.*
> *Command your silver, leafy screen*
> *To hide our rancid art."*

There was no more music. Her song faded.

"That was beautiful, Velissa. I love you," Raccoman said at length.

She looked down and then away.

"Velissa, would you be my wife?"

"Consent to promise?" she asked.

Now Raccoman looked away for a long time, afraid to look back.

"This is too much at once!" she exclaimed.

He looked away again.

"We've not yet been together one full day and night."

They both sat silent for a moment.

But the welder was firm in his intention. He summoned this little-used strength of character, turned her face to his own, looked into her eyes, and demanded, "Well?"

"I do consent," she said.

"Whoop! Halloo! For the wedding stew!"

As was his custom in exiting moments, Dakktare set about congratulating himself:

> "Dakktare, you're immortal
> While ages shall roll
> The envy of everyone—
> Estermann's goal.
> Velissa is yours,
> You excellent soul!"

He nearly danced himself from his yellow boots and twirled so near the edge of the cliff that Velissa was concerned for his safety. Undaunted by her concern, he continued to congratulate himself:

> "You're consented to promise,
> You refined demagogue,
> You superb poem-maker,
> You excellent rogue.
> Behold the great welder!
> Look, marvel, and stare!
> For he's bringing his bride
> To the Hall of Dakktare."

To call his comical house the Hall of Dakktare was an exaggeration that amazed Velissa, who in her wildest imagination could not begin to imagine what the poetic welder called home.

His eyes twinkled and his mouth was so merry that his overlarge teeth sparkled a white contrast beneath his black moustache. When he had settled down again, Velissa untied Collinvar, and they started on down the high trail. The great beast was more in the mood for running and wanted them to ride, but they had not quite had enough of walking.

Dakktare was happier than he had ever been. The sun could scarcely match the glow that warmed his heart. Women were scarce on the planet, and he not only had one of his own, but the best of all.

Velissa shared his joy.

"Raccoman," she asked, "If you could give up the black in your gills, would you?"

"I'm afraid it will never be, Velissa."

"But would you, if you could?"

"At once, but . . ."

"There may be a way."

"But how?" he asked.

"Singreale is set against black. He hates the dark. Remember how the forest yielded when the star settled downward?"

"Yes, but . . ."

"Could you stand his light directly against your face? It might be painful."

"Oh, Velissa—would it work?"

"I cannot say. Black is a heavy obscenity in a world of color. To be freed of it might hurt."

"Pain is no object if you could give me back the gray."

"There is a high cave upon this very ridge whose ancient entrance faces the pinnacles of Demmerron. My father took me there once to see a spectacular star shower fall above the Moonrhyme cliffs. There is where the gleaming sweeps all darkness with a clean but painful hope. Come, we must turn north and ride for an hour," she said.

Without a word they turned around. Collinvar snorted and half-reared. He was aware he was about to be mounted and ridden.

They climbed to the silver stirrups once again. Collinvar snorted and bolted north.

Raccoman felt Velissa's young arms around his waist. He secretly wished his waist had not been so large, but she held him and he enjoyed the embrace. There were some promises of marriage he waited for and he smiled at the waiting.

In sunny hope Raccoman's rich voice floated on the wind above the heavy hoofbeats of his mount.

"Sing-ho to the centicorn wild and high!
Ride the great star trails into the sky,
Push the horizons into the night,
And the black shall yield to the brilliant white!

Sing ho to hope—sing ho!"

Humans always enter life clawing for their milk and air—
Wailing, comatose existence ignorant of their despair.
But high upon the crags and ledges infant eagles scorn the sod
And children take their clumsy steps while feathers brush
    the face of God.

CHAPTER IX
The Revolt of the Beasts

R ACCOMAN PULLED back on the gleaming strands of silver. Collinvar tossed his head in defiance, but only his head defied the firm hand of Dakktare. Obediently he stopped. It amazed even Raccoman that he was learning so quickly to control the creature.

The afternoon shadow of the western bluffs fell out over the plains and brought twilight to Canby. It would soon be dark on the ridges as well.

The Graygills did not dismount, but they did slow Collinvar to a walk. In a moment they came to the opening of a cavern, above whose yawning orifice was a simple sign that read in the Estermann tongue:

THE PATH OF PAIN AND HOPE.

Velissa knew that they must not be hesitant for the ordeal of change could never be traversed without firm resolve. Dakktare was resolute and unafraid as he turned the centicorn into the cavern.

Centicorns do not like darkness any better than Graygills, and therefore Collinvar stopped almost immediately, for he was reluctant to leave the dim light of evening at his back. Velissa called gently, "On, Collinvar," to urge him forth as she reached for the pouch at her bosom and withdrew the gem. The passageway ahead flooded with light.

The centicorn moved forward.

In the shadows at the edge of the band of light, the rough-hewn walls moved by in eerie silence. For half an hour the ceiling was so low that the great steed had to lower his head, while the Graygills dodged the black stone protrusions hanging from the roof. There were long, dark shafts, perfectly cylindrical stalactites.

After half an hour, the ceiling of the cave vaulted upward and the entire cavern widened into an endless hall. The radiance of Singreale gave them confidence, and Collinvar bolted to a run. The echo of his furious hoofbeats resounded into thunder, and the steel of his hoofs shot sparks of fire into the shadows. On he galloped until Singreale suddenly dimmed and went out. As surely as if Dakktare had pulled at the reins, the centicorn halted and refused to budge.

"It's awfully dark," admitted Velissa. "Singreale must mean for us to stop."

"Can this be the center of the planet?"

"I think not," she replied, "but this is as far as we need to go."

They both dismounted. Neither of them could see a thing, but once they were on the ground, Singreale brightened to a soft glow. There was little need to worry about Collinvar running off on his own into the darkness. He followed them closely as they cautiously explored the great stone vault in which they had stopped.

On one side of the cavern there was a set of four chains that hung from the stone wall. Two chains ended in manacles and two in footlocks, and above them all was a a single word: ENDURE.

"Do you know what these four chains mean?" Velissa asked.

"They mean I must have your help," said Raccoman.

"Then are you afraid?"

"Yes."

"The pain will pass," she consoled, "but remember, black never can be white except for pain."

"I understand," he said as he walked to the first footlock. Velissa walked with him and reached out to take the chain.

"No," he said, "I must do it myself."

He reached down to clasp his feet in the lower chains. The bands would not fit over his boots so he removed his foot gear and quickly snapped the circlets shut. His legs were stretched so far apart by the taut chains that he could not reach the left or right manacle to enclose his own wrists. He laid his wrists on the cold steel.

"Singreale, Singreale,
I beg of you.
Bind my desire to know the dark
Embrace my hopes with chains of iron
The Lord of Light is Lord of Steel!"

The chains swayed upward until their defiance of gravity caused the Graygills to gasp. As if by magic, the manacles obeyed his words and closed upon his wrists. His limbs were pulled taut—both arms and legs.

A large steel band descended from the ceiling of the cavern and settled over his head. He was now unable to move anything more than his fingers and the muscles of his face. Velissa ached to see him bound so unmovably. It hurt her even more to know the pain that would soon be his.

She was not prepared, however, for what did occur.

Raccoman became a personality other than himself. "Let me out of these chains! Call my friend, Parsky," he ordered her brusquely.

"Parsky is not your friend," she countered.

"He *is* my friend. He cooks my meals."

"He murders to make meat. He is evil!"

"No, he is good. Parsky murders, but murder is good!" Raccoman strained against the iron. It held fast.

"It is time to begin," she whispered.

Singreale burned white-hot now.

"I must touch your face," she said.

"No!" he cried. "Please, Velissa! I cannot stand the pain."

"But you want your gills to be gray. You said so."

"No!" he cried again. "I hate gray! I hate you, Velissa!"

She ignored Raccoman's words. She brought the burning fire against his face. He screamed in terror. His head strained against the steel bowl that bound it. If intention alone could break steel, he would have been free. He closed his eyes against the light that passed close to his black gills. It seared his face. There was the smell of burning hair.

"The light must pass your face again—perhaps twice more," she said.

"No! No! No!" His face became hideous. "Burn me again and I'll tear these chains from the wall! Parsky is lord! Murder is love!" His lips were curled in hate.

Velissa brought the white-hot light against his face. She held it firmly across his leering mouth and black moustache. Once more he wailed and his demonic cry resounded through the caverns. Collinvar tossed his head—wide-eyed in fear.

Velissa's face glistened.

"Once more, my love, until all the inner black is gone!"

"Love!" he screamed. "Here is love." His horrible lips pursed and he spat into her face. His eyes were like an animal's and his fingers curled into claws. Velissa saw in Raccoman's hate the power of Parsky's evil. She felt the terror of the last approach. She came quickly to the leering face—he strained against the light as she laid the white-hot flame upon his head.

He screamed and went limp—unconscious from the pain. The steel band unlocked from around his head, which fell forward on his chest. The manacles and footlocks then opened as if by magic, and he crumpled in a coma on the floor and seemed devoid of life. But his gills were no longer black!

Velissa laid Singreale upon the floor, lifted Raccoman with great effort, and laid him across the saddle of the centicorn, who kneeled to make her task easier. He was a trifle heavy for her, but she managed. Last of all, she picked up his yellow boots and stuffed one in each of the silver saddle bags. Collinvar then stood.

She picked up Singreale and then took the silver reins and walked before the great centicorn with the unconscious welder still draped across the saddle. It took two hours to walk to the entrance of the cave, but Singreale was faithful, and his light never diminished.

Velissa did not immediately realize she was at the mouth of the cavern since night had fully settled on the ridge. She could tell by the stars it was near midnight, and she decided to wait for light before she proceeded on down the ridge toward Canby. Singreale softened to a glow. Collinvar went to sleep. Velissa dozed during the remainder of the night, but her unconscious husband never stirred.

As morning began to dawn, Velissa was wide awake and watched the sun come to the valley. As it had from ancient ages, Canby awoke in a rainbow that drenched her colored dwellings in gold and silver. Velissa's eyes wandered to the little river whose meandering intentions were too lazy to move with much speed into the sunny brilliance of the valley.

There was light on the ridge. Raccoman groaned and his first moments brought a little gasp from Velissa. His black gills were gone! Even in the new light of morning, she could clearly see he was gray! She moved nearer to have a better look and smiled.

"How do I make my living?" he asked in a kind of innocent amnesia.

"You are a worker of metals, a welder," replied Velissa in tenderness.

"Will I be able to remember my art?"

"You have not forgotten that, I'm sure. But, my dear Graygill, things have gone ill in Estermann. The Black is coming!"

It was as though Raccoman understood. His new stupor did not seem dense to every truth.

"Look, there in the valley!" cried Velissa.

The alarm in her voice called Raccoman back to the world of Estermann. He looked in the direction in which Velissa was pointing.

"Catterlobs . . ." Her voice trailed off. The sun was now well above the horizon and climbing. Raccoman watched. There appeared to be about fifteen of the large beasts moving toward the village.

"No! No!" cried Velissa. "Not on Canby! Which house is yours?"

"I can't recall. I think none." Raccoman strained to remember. "I live southwest in a country home. It's a maroon, I think."

"Not yellow?" asked Velissa.

Raccoman looked at his jacket and his boots. "Yes!" he cried. "You're right, it's yellow! Now I remember—of course, everything matches my boots.

"Yellow the sun and yellow the pear,
Yellow the house of the welder Dakktare."

He was glad that his talent for poetry had survived his coma.

The beasts were at the outskirts of the village. They could see the Canbies scurrying out the opposite end of the lane that comprised the main street of the village. One catterlob, blacker than the rest in color, knocked the chimney from one of the houses and stepped through the roof. The house broke like matchwood. The other catterlobs, not quite so dark as the first, followed the blackest beast into the town. House by house, the town crumpled as walls and towers toppled and the great claws of the catterlobs tore the community to debris.

In the center of the village was the meeting hall. The great beast tore the tower from the roof and clawed at the brickwork before hurling the entire turret into a cluster of houses. If there were Graygills who suffered from the falling stones, the distance was too great to see. One could feel the uncertain lament of dying in the morning air.

"The shed . . . my work . . . I need rods and silver. We must go," cried Raccoman in broken sentences, remembering everything at once. "Collinvar!" he cried.

The centicorn came quickly to them.

Suddenly, behind them they heard a terrifying roar on the narrow ridge they had just traveled on their way to the high caverns. It was a catterlob on the high ledge. The huge beasts rarely attempted to travel on the narrow ledges. Velissa and Raccoman were both surprised and startled to see one at that altitude.

It flashed through Raccoman's mind that he had once ridden the calves of catterlobs in the meadows where the huge cows grazed. Now the ebony beast that they faced bared its huge white teeth for destruction. Like the deceived Blackgills—it sought meat.

The beast confronting them reared on its haunches and rose to a terrifying height. Even Collinvar seemed small by comparison. Fortunately for Raccoman and Velissa, the centicorn's size had little to do with his speed.

"Our way is blocked," cried Raccoman.

The beast drooled and slammed the iron plates of its tail into the side of the bluff. Huge boulders were dislodged and rolled down in a landslide that blocked the lower ledges. The catterlob swung its foreclaw at the centicorn who, being fleet of foot, leaped free, uninjured.

"There is a break in the ledge ahead. Collinvar may be able to leap it with us in the saddle." The welder had barely said these words when he jumped into the saddle and pulled Velissa up behind him.

The catterlob lunged at them, but its teeth closed on the empty space that Collinvar left as they bolted up the ridge. The catterlob fortunately was much more cumbersome and slow of foot. Twice it appeared to slip from the trail. Its massive torso would scratch the narrow ledge for leverage while its tail hung down, raking the trail below and spraying rocks and boulders and dust into the morning air.

In a moment the centicorn had reached the breach and stopped. The breach was impressive in width, and through the break, Raccoman saw a falcon soaring far below, yet well above the white clouds. Collinvar seemed reluctant to try and leap. The proud steed looked for an instant at the falcon, as if the two of them were friends.

"We've no choice. We must jump," cried Raccoman.

The catterlob was gaining on their position. They heard it bellow and Collinvar turned back on the trail as far as was safe. He beheld the cumbersome catterlob still struggling up the ledge, and turned and began to gallop for the broad lunge. He gathered a speed that Velissa and Dakktare had never before achieved. Velissa held her breath as the great centicorn reached the brink, but cried out a little as beneath the belly of Collinvar she saw nothing but air and clouds. It seemed they hung suspended forever in space, and then the opposite ledge appeared and Collinvar settled gently as though he were floating. He rushed forward a few paces and came to a stop.

Raccoman turned in time to watch the catterlob plunge headlong over the brink and plummet downward into the canyon. The dumb and angry creature moaned as it disappeared into the clouds below and was gone. They could not behold the fall. Even though the catterlobs were now evil, Graygills had no stomach for blood and death.

The centicorn ran in high elation back to the plains of Canby. The trip beyond the ledges was much further than the way they would have returned had the beast not blocked their way.

They rode all day long, and by sundown they passed the ruins of the main village. They dared not enter the destruction. Dakktare was worried to see how well his own small isolated house had fared. After leaving the small town, they came across the brink of a shallow hill. Raccoman was elated. In the distance he could see the barn in the middle of the field, still undamaged, and he was confident that its contents were also undamaged. It had been three days since he had left home, and he was eager to show Velissa his work.

In only moments they rounded the grove of trees that prefaced Raccoman's house. He was ecstatic!

"Look, Velissa, my house—or rather our house—is unharmed."

But his elation was short-lived, for crumpled against the stone porch supports were two Blackgills—his uncle and his one-time friend.

The blind were all gathered to battle, to brandish their swords
  as they chose,
Eyeless enemies of hatred blindly killing eyeless foes.
There were no final scenes of glory, absent were the last hurrahs,
For blood is colorless in blackness and hands unseen resemble claws.

CHAPTER X

Rexel

UNCLE KREPEL'S left leg was broken, and there were several cuts on his forehead and hands. Parsky had suffered no injury.

"We must take care of that leg," said Raccoman, opening the door to his home and gesturing for his two friends to enter. Velissa was unnerved by their presence.

"They say it was a catterlob," said Krepel.

"It was indeed. We had left the party for air and saw the whole thing from outside."

Parsky seemed uneasy at the statement.

As they entered Raccoman's small house, Velissa excused herself to take care of Collinvar. There was a little light left, and she made her way to the rear of the house, leading the centicorn, who still shivered in the excitement of his long ride. The great steed ducked his horns when he entered the low door of the shed. The shelter would work well for Collinvar, though it was clearly not built for a stable. Some of Dakktare's old welding equipment and tools were stacked neatly in one corner, but the remainder of the floor was open and dry and quite an adequate place for the big animal to rest. Velissa thought again of the blue stable where Collinvar had last slept and the home she would never see again.

Velissa unloosed the girth and removed the double saddle from the centicorn. Methodically, she unbuckled the bridle and removed it also. She patted Collinvar on his left haunch and was about to leave the shed when she noticed a piece of paper sticking out from beneath the silver trim of the saddle. She pulled the paper out and read the words upon it:

Beware Parsky, for his gills and his heart are one color—I am wounded by the evil Blackgill, and I feel sure I will not live. He rode from the forest on the neck of a great black catterlob and has destroyed everything. I love you, but I am very much afraid for your future on Estermann. If we never meet again, you must know that I will never cease to love you. Treasure either myself or my memory.

Your Father

Velissa wept.

So perhaps Parsky was a murderer. She wished that her father had written more positively of his own life. How could she know if he had survived, and if so, where was he now? What was the nature of the wounds that the Blackgill had inflicted?

When she came back to herself, she feared for her own future as well. She left Collinvar and returned to the house. She touched the little pouch at her neck. How good she felt to know that the steady light of Singreale awaited her next moments of desperation.

Graygills were incapable of hate, but she now regarded Parsky with a disdain that cried in anguish for the fate of her father.

When she re-entered her new home, she heard Raccoman explain to Parsky, "We consented to promise."

"Where?" asked the Blackgill.

"Upon the ridge over Canby," replied Raccoman.

"And how did you escape the catterlob?"

Raccoman Dakktare was about to answer when he suddenly realized that Parsky was aware of their attack in the high country.

"How did you know about the attack?" asked Dakktare.

Parsky sat silent. Velissa marveled that the Blackgill's hair was so black. Raccoman's new gray gills stood in strong contrast to those of both his old uncle and the deceptive Parsky.

"What of Uncle Krepel's leg?" asked Velissa. For the next hour, they worked at setting a splint for the old man and assured him that in a few weeks he would be strong again.

"Do we have a few weeks?" Krepel asked.

"Who can say? Canby is in ruins. The catterlobs have turned north to the villages of the Moonrhymes. But the Moonrhymes are a hearty group of Graygills—perhaps they can fight," said Parsky.

"The Moonrhymes will not be so easily destroyed as the Canbies," said Uncle Krepel. "They survived the ancient fiery cataclysm before Maldoon."

"Ancient cataclysm?" probed Dakktare. "How did the Moonrhymes survive? I had this vision of horrible fire on the faces of the cliffs."

"Will they return to the steppes to Canby or go on to the east?" Velissa interrupted her husband's tale for it didn't seem to fit the conversation.

"Who can say?" mused Krepel, and then added, "The Graygills

east of the mountains are also house builders. They would not fare well against the beasts."

"At least for the moment, we are free," said Raccoman, changing the subject.

"I would give my strong leg for a bowl of meat stew," said Krepel."

"Well, you will never more have it in this house. I am healed of that dreadful curse!" Dakktare exclaimed.

"Your whiskers would tell us that. You must have undergone the ordeal of Singreale," said Parsky. In his long association with Krepel, he had heard of the strange ritual first performed by Moonrhyme wizards in distant centuries.

"Indeed, I have," replied Raccoman.

"I mean to own that treasure myself, by slaughter if need be! Do you have the Fire, my dear?" Parsky asked Velissa.

"It is mine, given me by my father, as it was given to him by his grandfather," she said.

"You will give it to me," he said, advancing toward her.

"It is mine and I will keep it," she said firmly.

Parsky's raspy demand made Velissa afraid. She dropped back from his evil voice.

Raccoman stepped boldly between them and declared: "I'm afraid I must ask you to leave."

"In the morning," he said.

"Tonight!" declared Raccoman with firmness.

"Very well," said Parsky. "You will be sorry that you have driven me from your house, and you will see, Velissa, my dear, that I mean to have Singreale as my own." He curled his lips in hate.

Velissa felt again the pouch as Parsky leered at it. Then, grabbing his red mackinaw, he ran from the house.

They were relieved to see him go.

Parsky had not been out of the house a moment when Velissa looked at her husband with foreboding. At once they both spoke the same word: "Collinvar!"

Dakktare dashed from the side door of his little house in time to see Parsky enter the shed. Within seconds, he too had reached the door. He was about to command the Blackgill to leave the shed when suddenly Parsky came flying through the open door. The Blackgill had not reckoned with the centicorn's powerful haunches and hooves, and he landed with a dull thud on his back.

Raccoman doubled over in laughter.

He stopped laughing when he saw how angry Parsky was. The look he gave Dakktare was enough to slay any mortal. Still, the sight of the Blackgill's wounded pride and the circumstances by which he had arrived at his predicament set Dakktare to rollicking all over again.

He laughed while Parsky disappeared into the darkness on foot. Velissa came running at the sound of all the commotion.

Krepel hobbled out after her on his newly splinted leg.

Both expected to find Raccoman grieved by the loss of Collinvar to the despotic Parsky. Finding him bent in laughter and rolling in glee left them both dumbfounded, and as Parsky had already fled, they wondered if the welder could be losing his mind.

Several times Dakktare tried to stop laughing and explain what had happened, but he was not able to relate the whole story for several minutes. Krepel looked wounded, but Velissa also found the incident amusing, though she contained her laughter better than the welder. To have seen the whole debacle made it a thousand times more laughable than Raccoman's best description.

"It is difficult to steal a reluctant centicorn," cried Dakktare, at last the master of his hysterical mood, wiping the tears of mirth from his face.

"It is," agreed Velissa. "But do you think Parsky might try to come back later and steal him?"

"Not steal," answered the welder. "Perhaps kill—but not tonight."

Dakktare was not sure why he had made that last remark. Yet he felt it was true. They must be wary of Parsky.

Parsky had declared himself at long last. Still, it was not so much what the Blackgill had become, but what he had been all along that troubled Raccoman. Parsky's threat that he would own Singreale at any cost now set the Graygill's fears to the worse sort of imaginings. There were still so many unanswered questions. Why had Parsky left the party at Krepel's hall before the disastrous attack by the catterlob? How did he know of the attack that the second catterlob had made on the high ridges—or was it the same catterlob?

During their long walks on the upper ridges, Velissa had told Raccoman of the warrior who had driven her from the snowy trail in winter and of the same armored catterlob that both her father and his old uncle had seen leaving the smoky towers of Maldoon. Other questions needed answers as well. Where had Parsky been during the long months of spring and summer? Why had he been so insistent in his argument with Raccoman when they debated the existence of the smoke around the towers of Maldoon? What, if anything, had become of the relationship of his old uncle and the lone survivor of the Flandry Migration? Why did Parsky show such disdain for his interest in the Star Riders and what had caused his uncle to break the lens of his own scope and deny that he had ever seen the moving starfields? But the most haunting question of all had to do with the lengths to which this one-time friend would go to obtain the treasure of the ancient king, the diamond Velissa wore at her neck. Without voicing his doubts, Dakktare re-entered his home, and the others followed.

When they had settled down in the house, Raccoman set himself to cooking stew while his new bride and his uncle set themselves to discussion. Krepel propped his splinted leg on Dakktare's thread-bare footstool.

"You've lots to do to make this house fit to be a home for the two of you," said Krepel.

"Yes," she said, and then at length continued: "Oh, Krepel, are there ever to be homes again, or dancing, or joy? Everything seems so difficult now. There is a foreboding that chills the air and makes me feel like our marriage is over and not beginning. I cannot tell you the terror I felt upon the ridges, for the monster was hideous. Yet we never called catterlobs 'monsters' in days gone by; we rode their calves in the level meadows."

Krepel had known esteem as the wisest Graygill of the western mountains. The Canbies were his friends; the Moonrhymes trusted his wisdom. He had once stood in the light of the King of Maldoon and pledged himself to honor and to keep the king's creed on the upper ridges. He had loved truth, and the greatest truth he felt was in the stars. Like Singreale, the stars were steadfast. Each gave its light from a predictable place and offered a constant answer to those prone to despair that life was unsure of itself.

Krepel had once loved the stars and in centuries past he had hoped that his nephew would leave off his metal-work and learn the keeping of the orange observatory. He knew his nephew loved yellow, but he would have suffered even the changing of the color to see his ancient science saved. Besides, Raccoman also loved the night skies. He watched them in summer and soared through them upon the restless winds of winter. Raccoman would have been the logical heir to his uncle's work.

But now the wizard of Moonrhyme legend had lost his zeal for all that he had loved. His face had become as hard as his gills were black. His interest in the night sky died the night he sampled Parsky's stew, and he had turned to all he once hated and proclaimed it love. Now he killed animals—sometimes to eat, sometimes to enjoy the warm red of the brotherhood he now felt for Parsky. He had not even resented the loss of his hall on the night his party ended in terror and death.

In his changed state, he would do anything for the Blackgill. He knew what Raccoman had only begun to guess—that Parsky had been gone from his little square house on the edge of Castledome for more than half-a-year. He knew, too, that Parsky now had an uncertain residence that served his designs for power in the land of the Canbies. A power the Blackgill would not be ashamed to acquire by any kind of terror he deemed necessary.

The ignorant animals feared Parsky, yet desired to serve him just as Krepel himself did. So passionate was the old scientist's desire to please the evil Blackgill that he permitted himself nothing but unquestioning allegiance. He had resolved himself to this end the night he stood against his fondness for the skies and climbed the barrel of the scope to smash the upper lens with his axe. With that act, the light of the distant stars died in his eyes and he became one with the soul of evil.

Yet Krepel's eyes looked tired as he stared into the fire. A clear tear spilled over his thick lashes and coursed down his cheek. Because he said nothing, Velissa continued.

"Oh, uncle, can it be the meat alone that set this death upon us?"

His face did not move.

After a while, his stone mouth opened ever so slowly. "It was not the meat itself—it was the killing that brought the meat. We were one world of living things until we divided it into two halves—the eater and meat. It is the division that was wrong. Unity was wholeness and strife came when we set ourselves against the oneness of life. The animals have only reciprocated in kind to learn of war. It is their right as it was ours. There is hate and death for one fair reason: all would be eaters; none would be meat."

"There's the error—I am Velissa of Quarrystone Woods. I am being and not fodder."

"All beings are only meat before an eater. Today on the high ridge, you were meat."

"No!" she cried. "A person!"

"As sure as Collinvar had stumbled, you would have been devoured."

"Oh, uncle . . . this is a dreadful world. We must go back."

"Back?" he asked. "Back where?"

"Back in time, back to the place we cuddled congrels and played in the snowy tracks of catterlobs. There was no fear then."

"Yes, but there was no meat, either."

"I have never tasted it. Can it be so good? Good enough for the unholy wrecking of a beautiful world?"

She was still speaking when Raccoman re-entered the room. He was carrying a large wooden tray with three steaming bowls. They each took one bowl and set it before themselves on their short laps. (As Graygills were short of physique, they were also short of lap.) Raccoman had never considered furniture all that important, and his table was a small, yellow surface that could hold only a single bowl and cup.

No sooner were they seated when Raccoman and Velissa lifted their bread and said:

"To the maker of the feast
To the power of loaf and yeast
Till the broth and bread have ceased
Gratefulness is joy."

Krepel looked nervously away. Such blessings were for bread-eaters only. He grabbed a spoon and took a huge bite. Velissa and Raccoman ate placidly, but no sooner had Krepel tasted than he screwed up his face and winced at the bland taste. If his face had frozen at that moment, it would have frightened a gargoyle.

Velissa and Raccoman had expected him not to like it, but their hospitality would never have excluded their uncle from their simple fare—bland though he considered it to be. Their chatter during dinner was light, and they spoke of the sunshine on the ledges, refusing to broach the unpleasant subject of the harrowing experience they had also endured there.

"Uncle," said the nephew, "stay with us."

"The house is small," he said, "and the food is bland."

He did not say he would leave by the morning light, but they knew his intention. Besides, he was too much enamored with the evil Parsky ever again to enjoy his relationship with his nephew.

Velissa picked up the dishes and took them back to the kitchen.

It had been a long day. Raccoman heaped the fireplace with logs, and the three retired. The house had only three rooms and Velissa and Dakktare took the small bedroom where the welder had always slept alone until this very night.

Raccoman kissed Velissa in the ardor he felt for her and they retired to a new kind of companionship both of them needed to complete their security in a desperate and deceptive age.

The love Raccoman felt for Velissa welled up within him as they spent their first night of married life in a real bed. All that he had felt for Velissa was affirmed in the rightness of the love they shared. The fulfillment of their new relationship had warmed a bed left cold for a millennium of bachelorhood. Velissa had come from the sorrow of the great loss of her family to the security of a protector whose love she could not doubt. In this new security they both fell asleep.

It was characteristic of contented Graygills to hum in their sleep. It was an odd sound, but not unpleasant, often resembling a pleasant melody with little variation of tune. Like snoring, humming was an utterance unheard by the hummer himself. Between the Graygill groom and his bride, there was just enough variation of hum that their slumber produced a simple harmony that neither of them would ever hear, for the instant one of them woke, the hum of the sleeper was a solo.

Sometime before day, old Krepel rose, grabbed his orange mackinaw, and stole quietly out of the little house. He was as tempted to steal Collinvar as Parsky had been, but remembering the outcome of Parsky's attempt, he thought better of it. He limped off toward the east country, having decided to walk wide around Canby.

He had gone less than a mile when he heard some savage growling. He turned to see forty or fifty congrels baring their teeth at him. He was unnerved because he was afraid they would attack. He had never seen such a large group of them in one place before, and their vicious faces were small but snarling in hate. He walked on and soon left them comfortably behind.

When Velissa finally awoke, she cried out to Raccoman: "He's gone—our uncle is gone!" She had quickly accepted Raccoman's uncle as her own, for since they had consented to promise, all things that were once his alone were now theirs together.

"Velissa," he said, "let us ride to Canby."

"To find our uncle."

"No, that would do little good. He would never be content here with us. He has spoiled his appetite for decency by feasting on evil."

"Why then ride to Canby?" she said.

"Because I need rod and torch tips. Besides, winter is coming and we must enjoy the days while we can."

"But Canby is in ruins," she protested.

"Somewhere in those ruins I must find the shop of Orkkan the metal-worker, for only there will I find the welding rod and torch tips I need to finish my work."

"Your work will have little meaning if life is soon to be over," she said. "The war will come back, Raccoman."

"But we will survive, you will see. Let us not be gloomy. Come, we're off to Canby on Collinvar."

"But first we'll have bread," she said.

They did, and while Dakktare went to saddle the centicorn, Velissa stuck extra slices in her small, blue knapsack and donned her blue gloves. They matched her favorite riding cape with which she had escaped.

"Husband," she said when she had joined him at the little shed, "do you think the catterlobs will come again to Canby?"

"Yes, but not until they have pushed their war into the north."

"Then let us be free for there is nothing to fear."

Raccoman could not forestall his urge to rhapsodize.

"Velissa, the scent of camaran tree;
Velissa, the fragrance of which life is key!
Let's mount the strong centicorn—and ride the high lea!
By the Fire of Singreale, the day is born free!"

They mounted and rode.

There was a light breeze that stirred the centicorn's forelock and set his wispy, gold mane flying. In no time Collinvar had chased his swift shadow to the edge of Canby.

"I'm afraid to look," said Velissa after Raccoman had brought the steed to a walk. He said nothing, but it was clear he was not eager for a glimpse of the city. The war of the beasts had been destructive. The village was in ruins.

"Can you find the shop in all the rubble?" she asked when the silence had become oppressive.

He grunted in assent.

Collinvar stepped lightly around the fallen timbers and the stone and the debris that the monsters had created in their assault on the town.

"Halloo!" cried Raccoman. "Is anyone at home?"

His voice echoed down the debris-filled lanes. Collinvar's hooves made a ringing, hollow sound on the paving stones as they advanced through the buildings. Here and there they could see that some of the lanes were not damaged, especially the narrow ones, but in most of the streets, the brightly colored tiles from the roofs were strewn in shattered fragments. Beams and shards of glass and splintered wood lay everywhere.

Dakktare turned from the main road and pursued one of the undamaged lanes. Collinvar now looked like a giant, for the alleyway was narrow. He advanced for half the distance of the lane and stopped. Velissa looked up to read the great, yellow sign printed in sharp letters: "ORKKAN OF CANBY." In smaller letters were the words: "Welding Supplies and Torch Tips." Raccoman dismounted, stood before the silent shop, lifted the iron door knocker, and rapped loudly. His knocking resounded through the empty streets, then echoed, and reverberated into silence.

"Orkkan, Orkkan!" he shouted.

There was no reply.

"Shall I break the glass?" he asked Velissa.

"Try the door," she said.

He did. The latch lifted easily and the door creaked open.

"I do wonder where they all are," said Velissa as Raccoman disappeared into the dark shop.

He knew well what he wanted, and thus he was not there for long. Within minutes, he emerged carrying a large bundle of such things as he needed for his work.

"I left money for all that I took," said Raccoman. "I do wish he were here though. I feel like a thief."

"But you paid," said Velissa.

"Still, Orkkan is not here personally to approve the sale."

In a moment he had secured the bundle to the back of the saddle. Then he once again repeated the curious process of mounting the centicorn. The stirrups were a latticework of metal which he grasped to pull himself upward, hand over hand, until he could at last get a foot in the stirrup brace. From that point the effort gained a bit of dignity.

They rode back down the narrow lane they had only lately traversed, and as Collinvar turned into the larger lane, he quickened his step. The silence once again produced a deafening yet casual thunder as his hooves hit the stones. Except for the vacancy of the homes, this particular lane looked as though it could erupt any moment with people, but once Collinvar returned to the main thoroughfare, there was the same grim desolation of war.

Without warning, a stone came flying through the air.

It struck Collinvar on the left side of his proud neck and he reared and settled back, stepping nervously in anticipation of an assault the two Graygills had not expected. The assault came in a shower of stones as the silence of the village came violently alive.

"Death to the animal!" cried a red-faced Graygill who emerged from an alleyway. "Kill the beasts!" cried Orkkan as he suddenly appeared at the front of the crowd.

"The centicorn must die!"

"Kill the brute!" cried another.

All at once the street was alive with little people who converged upon Collinvar with rocks and sticks. The centicorn was bewildered by the instant mob, for he could not run without trampling them. Still, he was determined not to run the risk of hurting any of his little persecutors.

The Graygills all began to chant, "Death to the animal!" and "Kill the centicorn!" They menaced the great beast by jabbing at him with their sticks. The sticks were actually primitive spears sharpened on one end. Several of them punctured Collinvar's beautiful white skin and left ugly prickles of red.

"No!" cried Raccoman.

"Death to all animals!" chanted the people.

"No! No! No!" cried Raccoman.

Velissa quickly undid the drawstring on the little pouch that hung from her neck. Singreale was faithful. The radiance glittered, and even in the sun, the light that glowed from her uplifted hands flooded the angry faces and littered street.

The crowd fell back a little and Raccoman sat erect in the saddle and called out, "Behold the Fire of Singreale!"

The mob shielded their eyes against the intensity of the light as they strained to see the great gem at its source. For a moment, they seemed to forget their attack on the centicorn.

"Your attack on our steed is wrong!" shouted Dakktare.

"The animals have destroyed Canby—now we must destroy all animals!" cried Orkkan, who was clearly emerging as the leader of the frightened Canbies.

"But those were catterlobs—Collinvar is a centicorn!"

The light from Singreale illuminated the crowd and gradually their eyes adjusted. Most looked at Raccoman and Velissa as they spoke.

"All animals are bad and must be slaughtered, for they mean to destroy our village," insisted Orkkan.

"Even if you destroy this creature here, how will you stop the catterlobs when they return?" asked Raccoman.

They had no answer.

"Let us pass in peace, and by the light of Singreale, we shall try to help you defend yourselves against the beasts."

"What have we to lose?" asked one.

"Let them pass," cried another. Orkkan conceded at last.

The crowd fell back and Raccoman gently urged Collinvar forward. Velissa continued to hold Singreale aloft as the centicorn moved on. Then Dakktare called back to the mob:

"Winter begins on the first day of the month of Amadin. Meet me at sundown on the upper rim of the highest ledge, for there a single sentry can watch for enemies. The catterlobs will take at least two months to return if they travel all the way to the cliff dwellings of the Moonrhymes. While you wait, clean the debris from the streets and repair your houses against the coming of the winter."

It was odd that the Canbies responded to his words. Perhaps they were desperate for any direction, but even Raccoman was surprised at his own forcefulness, and Velissa sat back in awe of his ability to take control over a desperate situation. Dakktare seemed to push the words now lest he lose the new control that made him increasingly uneasy.

"When the month of Amadin comes you must be ready in stamina to conduct your war in winter."

"War?" asked one of the older Canbies. "War as our grandfathers knew in the days of the overthrow of Kendrake and the siege of Maldoon?"

"Your ruined houses are the outcome of the first battle. The war is now! But we may turn the war to our favor, for if the beasts return in winter, we will be able to use the elements to our advantage. Catterlobs move sluggishly in snow, and they huddle for warmth in severe weather. It will be easier, then, to track and destroy them."

"But how would we destroy them?" asked a young Canby.

Collinvar had now settled down and was no longer quivering.

A strategy for the defense of the Canby Graygills took shape in Raccoman's mind. Raccoman's father was the brother of the now evil Krepel. In his younger days, he had kept the armory of Singreale before moving to the valley south of Canby. His Moonrhyme father had showed him the plans for the weapons that had come too late to save Singreale's ancient kingdom.

"Orkkan—do you remember the huge spear catapults that once existed on the tower of Maldoon?"

"I do!" replied Orkkan.

"Could you build the frames and make the iron harpoons by the first of Amadin?"

"Sooner than that—but we'd still need someone who knew how to aim and discharge the spears. The catapults would need to be mounted on platforms and wheels—and we would have to pull them into battle position by ourselves since all the beasts are now set against us."

Dakktare nodded and addressed the crowd again: "We must work—for the time to prepare is short and there is yet another enemy—Parsky the Blackgill! Though I cannot tell you why I think so, I now believe he is an even greater enemy than the catterlobs. He may even now be leading the beasts toward the stone pillars of Demmerron Pass, though no one knows for sure his whereabouts.

"For now, there is much to be done. Orkkan, you must build the spear catapults with rollers to move upon the dry plains of winter, in case there is no snow. And you must build them to ride on sledges in case the snow comes. We will hunt the meadows to survive and we must be trained in the use of the great catapult and of smaller spears. In the ancient battle of Kendrake, the brave war-

(154)

riors could blind the catterlobs by hurling little spears directly into their eyes."

Several of the Canbies winced at this barbaric description of the methods of war. Raccoman reminded them that war required a new way of life that met the horror of aggressive wit and offensive that would ultimately stop all slaughter.

"Remember," he said, "prepare yourselves. We meet upon the ridges on the first of Amadin. Build a huge fire, for the great beasts fear light. If there is snow by the first of winter, they will not try the icy ledges at all. There, in the night council, I shall reveal to you a plan that may save your village." Though he had no idea then of any plan he could reveal, he knew he had two months to come up with some strategy. He urged the centicorn forward.

The villagers had a doubtful and hopeful look as they watched Collinvar move down the deserted streets. They were frightened, for many of their number had been lost in the first attack, and now the war would defeat them unless they could find a successful way to defend themselves against the monsters. Raccoman knew they would meet him for the night council—fear alone made them open to his suggestion. But it was two months till the first of Amadin. Till then life was to be full. It was the middle of autumn, and the sky invited both Raccoman and Velissa to enjoy its gaudy blue that reflected off the silvery leaves of the ginjon forest to the south and produced what was called "orontes light" because the sunlight appeared to emanate from a misty helix of blue that summoned to him. This ethereal daylight came only in mid-autumn but it always cast a magic spell over the villages and countryside.

Before long they were in the open country, enjoying the kind of day when Raccoman would have liked to go on riding forever, though the times were too serious to permit that sort of frolic. Still, never was life so gloomy that a Graygill could not find delight in the morning sun, especially when he rode a silvery centicorn through the blue mist of an orontes day.

Velissa hugged Raccoman and pulled him back in his saddle as far as she could while she advanced to the front of her seat. She kissed him behind his pointed ear and raised her hand to touch his chest through his open tunic that the gentle winds of orontes had separated.

Raccoman smiled ahead and treasured her touch. Life was the

brink of disaster for his dying world, but when Velissa touched him, he felt that all danger was silenced in the love that she gave him.

They soon stopped and dismounted, and while Collinvar rested, they lay in autumn mist at his feet. Raccoman drew Velissa's side-locks from her face and kissed her as though she were the only treasure in these troubled times. They waited while the mists of orontes confirmed their love and marriage.

Then they rested longer.

At last they stood and embraced again, kissing in an exchange of ardor that gave them courage to face what lay ahead. Singreale dangled from Velissa's neck and hung in the very center of their embrace, confirming all they felt and giving them hope.

Raccoman lifted her to the second seat of the double saddle and kissed her arm in the passing. He climbed into the first saddle and exulted in a new ballad composed in the ecstasy of orontes and his new fulfillment.

> *"I have married a wife*
> *Who's the light of my life—*
> *Velissa of Quarrystone Wood.*
> *Our day begs the sun;*
> *May our centicorn run,*
> *In the leas where the running is good.*
> *Come to this golden and glorious day,*
> *Warmed by the Fire of Singreale."*

It was indecent to sing only one verse on a sunny day, and so there was another, set to the thumping accompaniment of Collinvar's hooves in the flowery fields. The orontes mists swirled about his song.

"Come, love, let us fly."

At this point Velissa squeezed him with such ardor that she forced the melody forth.

> *"For the light of the sky*
> *Is the light of the love that we share.*
> *And the future is bright*
> *When warmed by the light*
> *That breaks in the late Autumn air.*

"Ohhhhhhh—" he sang and swelled with testimony.

"Come to the constant and glorious day.
Warmed by the Fire of Singreale."

Soon they were at the very meadow where Raccoman had spent
so many of his recent months. Collinvar swiftly arrived at the door
of the old barn and stopped. Raccoman dismounted and, once on
the ground, made this invitation:

"Come, my Velissa.
The day shall declare
The intelligent forthright
Wit of Dakktare."

She dismounted right behind the poetic metal-worker and was
about to follow him into the barn when he turned again and said:

"Close your eyes.
You must close your eyes
And the sun of my genius at last shall arise."

She did indeed close her eyes and her none-too-humble husband
led her through the small door. Once again he walked the dazzling
floor, dancing with sun patches. When Raccoman had her carefully
positioned, he said to her, "Now you may look!"
She did.
And she could barely take in what greeted her!
The craft that greeted her vision seemed a great steel behemoth.
It lay in a long, brilliant blur of shining metal, freckled with spots of
sunlight falling through the leaky roof. It was an ingenious sail
plane, built in the shape of a ginjon leaf. Like everything else Raccoman owned, the odd craft matched his boots, but he did not think
this comical. He thought yellow a most reasonable color, and to
have chosen any other color for his craft would have been illogical
in his own orderly scheme of thinking.
Velissa was stupified by the size of the sleek invention. From
every angle resting on the floor of the barn, it looked round like a
leaf, except that it had two crude seats bonded to the upper surface. Toward the rear of the craft were double foil-fins and a cluster of three rudders steered by an unusual hand lever that came up
between the seats.
Velissa had never seen such a craft before. She had heard that
some of the Moonrhymes living in the cliffs north of Demmerron

had built them, and some of them had even flown, but she herself had never in her one hundred seventy-five years seen one before.

"Will it fly?" Velissa asked, as she stared dumbfounded at the sleek, yellow sail plane.

> *"Will it fly? Will it fly?*
> *It will sail through the sky!*
> *It will lift from this place*
> *And soar into space . . . or at least I think it will fly.*

"But we shall have to wait for the season of the tilt winds to know for sure," he added.

Velissa was impressed. Raccoman's poetry might have been deficient, but his craft, by its very appearance, proclaimed him a worker of metal.

"The idea first came to me as I surfed the winds last winter. It occurred to me that if I could surf with a leaf tied to my underside, why not build a giant leaf and fly as far as the winds will carry the craft," he said.

Velissa looked concerned. "They say south of Kendrake the uncharted ocean begins. Suppose the wind fails and your genius craft lands in the sea? Suppose it doesn't fly at all? Suppose it will not lift off the ground? Suppose your seams don't hold in the first ugly impact of the gales? Suppose it is inverted in mid-air and we fall from the seats? Suppose the guidance system breaks or the stabilizers cannot hold in the upper currents?"

She was raising doubts faster than he could answer them.

"Will it fly if the winds fail?" she asked.

"Look," he said, "at the peddles set below the seats. They depress the rod assembly that gently pull upward on the sides of the leaf."

"Much like a bird flutters its wings in flight," she said and beamed.

"Just as Parsky and I used to raise our arms and flutter the foils on our arms, causing the updraft to lift us higher. I believe it will work, and I need only wait two months till the winds come to test it. Come," said Dakktare.

He led her to a back room. There suspended from a long, silver and blue, steel wire was a tiny replica of the great yellow craft that lay sun-spangled on the floor of the barn. He drew the model to the top of a pulley, which raised it to the top of the barn. He cut the steel thread which held the replica. The tiny craft was so light that when it started to fall, the currents of air inside the old barn caught it and it appeared to fly off into the mock night created by the cascading darkness beneath the high conical interior of the old barn.

In the dark, it appeared that the ship was already in the night air, flying faster and faster through the reaches of unchartered sky. The toy craft raced through starfields constructed by the blips of sunlight bleeding through the split shingles high above them.

Velissa applauded.

"So the toy craft shall teach the bigger one to fly," she laughed. "My dear husband, you're wonderful!"

On that they both agreed. "Yes," he answered.

"I'm the standard that all men should be.
The model, the hope, the ensign, the key."

She laughed in agreement, "The idol deserving of idolatry."

She did love him.

"Come to the real craft," he said as he led her up across the broad lip of the sail plane. He helped her into her seat and tied a crude fiber strap across her lap.

"The strap is here in case the glider should become inverted in a terrible updraft."

"Will you be afraid to ride the gales with me," he asked, "when the season of the tilt winds comes?"

"Never," she replied. "I have never yet known the joy of surfing the winds, and what a way this would be to surf—a great ginjon leaf for two. Raccoman, it's beautiful." Velissa laughed in excitement.

After a suitable period of admiration of the ship, they stepped once more upon the craft.

"Why did you build it with two seats?" she asked.

"When I first began this craft, you see,
I planned to take Parsky or my uncle with me."

He said this, looking ashamed that he had once been so naive as to have trusted either of them.

"Now this is the chair
Of Velissa Dakktare."

She was delighted and quickly took her seat, as Raccoman sat down beside her. They looked out through the darkness of the barn. The sun splotches made them feel as though they were already in space.

"When does it fly?"

"I have a week of welding left," he said. "Then all we have to do is move the craft outside and wait for the winds."

"Where will we fly?"

He knew where, but he waited until suddenly she remembered.

"Will we touch the path of the Star Riders?" Velissa was proud to be in love with the Graygill welder who was soon to make them both Graygill star-surfers.

Outside, the sun passed behind a cloud and the sail plane disappeared in the darkness of the old barn.

"What will you call the craft?" asked Velissa as they walked outside.

> *"I've yet to think of a proper name,*
> *But it must be right just the same."*

She nodded. They both stood blinking in the afternoon sun until their eyes adjusted. Dakktare walked to the patient centicorn who still waited in the sun.

He untied the saddle pouch and found it hard to reach, for he was standing in a shallow trough of ground and could barely touch the saddle, though he strained from the very toes of his yellow boots. He finally managed to lift the bundle of welding equipment he had bought from the empty shop in Canby. He put it inside the barn. Both of them found it difficult to resist a second survey of his life work, but they turned toward the centicorn and were about to mount when Velissa suddenly showed alarm. She grabbed her husband's arm with one hand and reached protectively for Singreale with the other.

"Look . . . there in the thicket!" she whispered. When Raccoman looked, he saw movement but little else. He ran to the thicket and a whole family of congrels scattered from him in fear.

"They were just congrels!" he called back and laughed. Velissa felt ashamed that she had shown such alarm.

But the delightful creatures ran only a short distance before they stopped, sat upright on their haunches, and studied the Graygills.

"I believe they want to be friends," she said.

"Perhaps they are afraid we shall treat them as Parsky would.

Come, friends," Raccoman said. He extended his open hands toward the animals, and Velissa did the same.

The creatures hesitated, then approached cautiously. One of them sniffed Velissa's open hand, then rubbed its soft fur against her arm. She lifted the furry inquisitive animal from the earth and petted it gently. At once the entire family of congrels was happy, begging to be held and cuddled.

"This is paradise," said Velissa. "Can there be evil anywhere in our world?"

"Look, a falcon—it is the symbol of peace," the welder exulted.

In the sky above them, a lone falcon flew in circles, settling lower and lower until it landed on the parapet of the barn. It studied the Graygills and the congrels and then flew to the saddle horn of the centicorn. Surprisingly, Collinvar did not bolt.

Raccoman and Velissa were utterly astounded when the great bird spoke: "My name is Rexel. I have come from the mountains beyond the River Kendrake. I am the friend of all who love Singreale. I offer you my wings and eyes for seven weeks."

"Why should we need them?" asked Raccoman.

"The war on Estermann grows daily, and you will need me," replied the falcon. "I will fly with you tonight and survey the winds of war until the first of Amadin has come and you meet the council on the high ridge." They were both surprised that the great bird knew of Raccoman's plan for the last defense of Canby. "I will not leave you till the season of the tilt winds has come."

The Graygills loved the falcon instantly.

Rexel stayed on the saddle horn as Dakktare took the centicorn's reins and led Collinvar back to the house. Raccoman and Velissa stepped carefully, for the family of congrels scampered and played about their feet.

"This really is paradise," said Raccoman, looking first at the falcon and then at the capers of the congrels.

"That's it!" he cried.

"What?" she asked.

"The name for our ship."

"What are you saying?" she asked again.

"The Paradise Falcon!"

At these words, Rexel spread his giant wings and lifted from the saddle horn. He was waiting on the arched gable of Raccoman's house when they arrived home.

The silver steps of dreamers gleam glistening like wires
Across the empty, blackened voids of great galactic fires.
Their courage sails on nothingness—shrinks light years by its grace,
And denying fears of emptiness, they walk on spongy space.

CHAPTER XI
The Paradise Falcon

$\mathcal{T}$HE GRUMBLEBEAKS knew winter could come early. They left the azure lagoon near Canby, taking their offspring from the cold and icy waters to the frozen air. They lifted their beautiful silver bodies to the icy winds for their trip to the shallows of the ocean that knew the warmer soil far to the south of the River Kendrake.

The days sped by. The brisk air of autumn cooled and then crystalized in frost. The candolet trees grew fiery red. The ginjon leaves gained a new tinsel rattle as the winds came to tear them from their firm resolve to cling to their lofty trunks and branches. The weeks and days were longer, twice those of earth, and their years a perfect cycle of the seasons that were, therefore, also twice as long.

Almost four seasons had passed since Parsky and Raccoman had first met to surf the gales of the previous winter. Those had been days of freer laughter—days, indeed, when life was more sure, when the Canbies knew the luxuries of dancing and singing and berry wine and hot winter stews. Now winter was coming again, and the snows that blew from the frozen pillars of Demmerron Pass would leave the blood of beasts and Graygills in bright stains on the white winter fields.

In but a year, the peace of the Graygill would have inverted itself and left a trail of pain and uncertainty whose steps were first laid down by the lone Blackgill survivor of Kendrake. Now there were Blackgills without number, and their intermingling with those who had not yet tasted meat did not prevent suspicions from growing. Once there had only been Graygills. Now the color of one's hair marked one clearly as a defector or as one who had not succumbed to the murdering of animals for food.

Tales filtered down the trade routes that there were now Blackgills among the Moonrhymes just as there were among the Canbies, though not so many of them. But their defection, while not so great, would spread, for as Krepel and Raccoman had once observed, the intrigue of not knowing the taste of the forbidden had somehow been set free in a world that once had forbidden it. Besides, meat-eating was not an indulgence that was easy to track, for those who tasted meat were not discovered until the changing color of their gills announced their appetite and set them against those who still were gray.

There was a feeling among the Graygills that their Blackgill neighbors had brought on the horrible war. Thus the tension between the meat-eaters and those who had not eaten became intense. It seemed imminent that civil war would soon break out between the defectors and those who still honored the older traditions of a world which only a year before had been one.

Several riots broke out in the streets of Canby, and for some reason, the new Blackgills seemed to be more savage than their Graygill antagonists. Only the constant fear of the returning beasts caused them to endure the day-to-day keeping of a very shaky peace. For even as they repaired their shattered village, they knew they were living out a brief spasm of time before Parsky and the huge catterlobs returned.

Raccoman had only been partly right in his earlier estimate of the direction that the war had taken. It had taken the catterlobs, at their lumbering pace, two full weeks to reach the Red Sentinel Stones of Demmerron Pass. They did move on to the cliff dwellings of the Moonrhymes and, true to Raccoman's prediction, were not able to inflict any real harm on those who colonized their villages high in the burroughs and narrow windows of the cliffs. The Moonrhymes were safe.

What was not safe were their crops, which the catterlobs in but five or six weeks had either eaten or destroyed. Now the winter food of the cliff dwellers was gone and their hopeful harvest never came. By the last week of autumn, the enemy had turned southward and headed once again for the portals of Demmerron Pass, which would admit them to the lower plains where the terrified Canbies waited.

Orkkan had become the soul of the village. His was the last work in the crude repair of the houses against the winter. His wisdom brought stability to the village. He had not eaten meat and his gills were the ensign of his fidelity to the age that had gone before. At the same time, his spirit of tolerance did not condemn the meat-eaters. Because of his remarkable freedom from prejudice, the villagers trusted him and listened to his advice and followed his instructions that would prepare them for the inevitable.

Orkkan had finished ten of the spear catapults, with the help of fifty other villagers who had kept the bellows going night and day to forge the smaller weapons. Villagers not involved in repairing the houses worked in the forging room by shifts. Throughout the long night, the bellows kept the coals glowing red and the ring of hammers on the anvils never ceased. The armory of Canby came to be, and the formidable cache of weapons was stored in the guarded street in front of the welder's shop.

The Canbies under one thousand years of age all trained themselves in hurling spears or turning the windlass that drew the tension on the great spear catapults. They were an awkward but determined army. None in the village had ever before known the hurt of war. Two old men who once survived the siege of Maldoon had reckoned only with marauding soldiers and thus could not give the other villagers much help in dealing with the beasts. Orkkan knew how strategic the large catapults were, and he insisted that those who manned the machines be younger Canbies with stamina and commitment to learn the art of using their devices.

There was little doubt that the catapults would kill the catterlobs if they stuck them in the proper place. For the little men of Canby could wind the windlass so tight that the harpoon would shatter a wooden beam and pierce clean through the porous heart of the furless candolet tree. The problem was that once the missile left the taut ropes, it took a long time to fit the weapon with a new harpoon and wind the tension into the cables once again. Still, the Canbies worked at it as a last and desperate hope for their defense.

While they worked, winter came on in force. The early snow did not slow the production of weapons, but it seriously curtailed the repairs to the village and it caused Raccoman Dakktare a great deal of chilling as he worked in the drafty interior of the old barn. His remarkable sail plane was finished by the third snow and ready to greet the test of the tilt winds whenever they began.

He lamented to himself that it was impossible to see the moving starfields with the naked eye. He did not doubt that he and Velissa would be able to navigate the void across the seas to the unknown continent the Star Riders called home. But he was not sure that once they arrived on the continent there would be food and drink for them to survive.

Most of all, he knew that weight was a factor to the success of his flight. They could take nothing with them if they hoped to reach the upper currents where he had first encountered the Star Riders. His concern with weight had caused him to diet, and by the end of autumn, he was nearly as trim as the Moonrhymes, who were never overweight because of the vigorous exercise they received while climbing the tall vertical ladders that brought them to their windowed apartments inside the cliffs.

A heavy snow fell the day before winter officially began, and Raccoman decided to stay inside with Velissa and enjoy the fire. But his plans had to be laid aside.

Just before midday, Rexel rapped his heavy beak on the frosted glass. He had come from the North, riding the icy gales from Demmerron Pass. The catterlobs were returning, he told them, and within two weeks would be passing the Star Sentinels of Demmerron. Raccoman was glad that the morrow would bring the council with the Canbies on the ridges.

The first of Amadin came wrapped in gray and sailing snow. Dakktare left Velissa with Singreale, and took the centicorn on the snowy trip. He reached the upper ledges just after dark.

The Graygills waited in the night and quailed as they heard hoofbeats.

"Halloo!" cried Raccoman. The warmth of his greeting set the frightened minds of those who waited at ease. He leapt from the saddle where Rexel still rode upon the saddle horn.

"We brought firewood," said the leader of the refugees.

"Then why have you built no fire?" asked Raccoman, bewildered.

"We were afraid the catterlobs might see us."

"Let us build a fire and the falcon will watch the trails from aloft."

Rexel stretched his great wings and fluttered noisily, but for the moment he did not leave the saddle. Most of the Graygills had never seen a falcon so close at hand.

"The catterlobs are still north of Demmerron and making war on the snowy settlements of Canby-Dun. For the moment, we are safe," said Rexel.

"It speaks!" gasped Orkkan of Canby.

They were all amazed.

"There is a greater fear than the catterlobs," the great bird went on like a winged prophet. The centicorn shifted his weight when the falcon spoke.

"What evil could be greater?"

"The Blackgill."

There seemed a sudden chill in the night air at these portentous words. "Parsky of Castledome?" responded the Graygills with uncertainty.

"Yes," Rexel replied. "While he has spurred the beasts to this revolt, I no longer believe he is with them. Where he is, I cannot say."

For a long while there was silence as the Graygills built a fire on the ledge and meditated on the evil Blackgill and his cause. The wood ignited swiftly into flame, and the amber flickerings brought to light the uneasy faces of the crowd.

"What are your women and children doing here?" asked Raccoman, when he suddenly realized that those few men privileged to have families had brought them along.

"Where were we to leave them—alone in the village?" asked Orkkan. "The night itself stalks us with fear."

"Go, Rexel, and watch the ridges.
Circle high enough to see every trail,"

said Dakktare. The snow had stopped by nightfall and the skies were now clear.

The falcon leapt into the air and fluttered only once through the light of the campfire before he rose invisibly into the starry night directly over the snowy ridges.

"Do you have a strategy for survival when the monsters return?" asked Orkkan before the hopeful ears of the villagers.

"We will not allow the beasts to return.
At least we will make it difficult for them,"

said Raccoman. In the two months that had passed, he felt he had come up with a strategy for survival.

"But how are we to prevent their return?" asked a voice beyond the circle of light.

"We must march northward
To Demmerron Pass."

"But that's where the catterlobs are now," objected another Graygill.

"Actually they are beyond there,
But we need to go only where
The cliffs thrust upward into air."

At Demmerron, the floor of Canby-Dun narrowed to a small path between the two high peaks that were towering sentinels of red stone. They were the only gateway in the upper ridges that separated the plains of Canby in the South from the high plains of Canby-Dun in the North.

"There we dig," exclaimed Orkkan, excited that his own logic had moved ahead of the strategy that Raccoman was about to suggest.

"Yes—we'll dig a pit between the cliffs on either side
Deep enough to hold the catterlobs."

"But is there time?" asked another of the Graygill men.

"Who can say?
But it's our best hope to stop the war with little bloodshed."

"What's to keep them from taking the northern roads around the mountains?"

"Nothing," admitted Dakktare. "The catterlobs are only animals and will not know that the pits exist around the mountains. Besides, the trip over the mountains to the southern plains would require weeks. It is more probable that a pit at Demmerron Pass would leave them trapped in the upper valley. Take only the smaller weapons and do not attempt to move the catapults. It would waste valuable time—and we need the time for digging."

"Dig into ice?" Orkkan openly challenged.

"The ground is covered with snow but not yet frozen."

"But when must we go?" asked one of the old ones.

"Tonight, if possible. If you work hard, it will require two days to dig the pit at Demmerron, and there is little time to lose. Rexel will fly ahead and watch from the sky day and night. He can give you warning should the beasts come back early."

(169)

"Will you go with us?" they asked.

"No, I must return home," declined Raccoman.

"Why?" they asked. "We need you, Dakktare."

"Because—well, because."

Raccoman fidgeted, for he simply did not want to disclose the reason for his refusal. He knew his time also could well be running out. If the strategy for Demmerron worked, there was still the very real chance that the monsters would find the road around the eastern cliffs, and they would still have to face them within months.

"We will go," said Orkkan. "Tonight."

"Yes, yes," agreed the others. "We will return to Canby and pick up our shovels and move by dark to the North."

"May Singreale protect you," said Dakktare.

Raccoman led Collinvar to the edge of the circle of firelight and mounted the centicorn.

"Farewell, welder!" they cried.

Raccoman spoke to his steed and galloped away.

The centicorn left hollow hoofbeats hanging in the air that soon grew silent.

Dakktare was off the ridges when Rexel fluttered out of the dark.

"Raccoman!" cried the falcon, "The Blackgill Parsky is heading toward Canby with a flaming torch and a bucket of pitch."

"Rexel, lead me to him!"

The falcon flew before the centicorn. In a swift quarter of an hour, they overtook Parsky. He heard the centicorn approach and turned to face Dakktare.

"Leave me alone, welder!" he shouted, thrusting his torch in a menacing fashion toward his former friend.

"Villain! Extinguish your fire!"

"When I've burned Canby to the ground!"

"Now!" shouted Raccoman.

Parsky laughed in his face.

Raccoman Dakktare spurred the centicorn who flew at Parsky full speed. When Parsky saw that the centicorn was about to trample him, he threw the bucket of oil on the snowy ground and dropped his torch into it. The night exploded with light. The fire burst up before the centicorn, who crashed through the flame and knocked Parsky to the side of the trail. The Blackgill yelled as he tumbled from the trail and sprawled in the snow. Rexel seized the torch and carried it flaming into the air, setting a spectacle of orange fire against the blue-white stars. Collinvar and the welder rode on, not stopping for further discussion with the Blackgill, who stood up to brush off his tunic and spit out the dirt that had clotted his gills with pitch and ice.

Rexel drew a wide arc of fire as he carried the torch aloft. He kept the trail of fire safely away from his wings and finally dropped the torch into the small lagoon near the ruined village. The torch sizzled as it hit the icy water and extinguished.

The falcon returned to join the Graygills enroute to their homes where they planned to stop only long enough to gather tools and provisions before they moved on to Demmerron Pass.

Raccoman stabled the centicorn and was safely in bed by midnight. He snuggled close to Velissa, who was grateful to have him home again.

"Is the light of Singreale secure?" he asked.

"It is," she replied. "And Rexel, is he safe?"

"Yes, he's gone north with the Graygills who will dig a pit at Demmerron Pass."

In the darkness, Velissa smiled approvingly at her husband's plan and then asked, "When do the tilt winds come—in only a week?"

"Maybe a month before the strong winds begin," he said.

"I am eager," she said, "to fly with the Paradise Falcon."

"Doubt it not," he said. "May the tilt winds come early."

"Dakktare, you're the standard that all men should be," she cooed in the dark as she caressed her bridegroom and snuggled close to him.

"Let's face it with candor and brisk honesty.
I'm the heartbeat, the standard, the idol, the key,"

he said drowsily and soon fell to humming. Her softer harmony joined his.

They rose early the next morning and saw that the day was clear. After a breakfast of black bread and red berries, Dakktare was off to work on the Paradise Falcon. He began enthusiastically securing the updraft stabilizers. He checked the rudder rods to be sure that they still moved smoothly. He was not disappointed. At noon Velissa brought him lunch, which he ate hastily, and then he checked the welds as he had done a thousand times.

All afternoon he continued to inspect the seams of the landing skids. Raccoman realized that after the craft's flight, the skids would have to prevent the underside of the light metal from being ripped apart in landing. He had doubled the seam-welds so that the landing skids would be reinforced enough to stand the impact.

Velissa had already fed Collinvar by the time Raccoman arrived home that evening. After dinner, Raccoman told her of Parsky's devious plan to burn Canby and of how Rexel had discovered his treachery.

"But what's to prevent him from returning and completing his vile intention? With Rexel in the North, Parsky will be able to do as he pleases unobserved."

"He will not—for one reason," he said and paused.

"And that is?" Velissa urged him to conclude his statement.

"The women of Canby have stayed to defend
What's left of their town in the absence of the men.
Poor souls,
They were there, torn by fear, on the ridges last night."

"The women were with their men?" interrupted Velissa, who found it hard to be fond of Raccoman's tedious habit of making half-statements.

"Yes, and their little ones, too. Fear—that's what it was: you could see it in the the faces of the children.

"Terror is the Blackgill's delight.
Have you seen a child captured by fright?
Nothing is sadder. Their desperation
Steals all the light and hope from their eyes."

Velissa turned from him with a far-away look in her eyes. She did not mean to ignore him, but she was overtaken by her fear for the villagers. "Will the women be able to hold the village against Parsky?" she asked.

"My guess is that Parsky is on his way to enjoy the war in the North."

"Enjoy the war?"

"What is terror to good men is the delight of the depraved."

They sat silently and meditated on the day as images of the war swam in the dying fire. Dakktare had not done much singing in the recent days, but as he gazed fixedly at the hearth, he began the song that once had been the anthem of Graygill freedom:

"*Let us sing at the base of the ginjon tree,*
That Canby's fields are the fields of the free.
May the sun long rise
And the morning skies
Herald the anthem of liberty.
Come winds, free! Blow so our children may roam,
Through the friendly fields of Castledome.
For beasts and men are timeless friends
In the ageless land of Estermann."

"Raccoman, will it ever be that way again?" asked Velissa.

"Who can say? If the Canbies dig the ditch deep enough, the catterlobs will be gone."

"But forever?"

"I doubt it," he replied after some thought.

"It is not the beasts who are the enemy. It is Parsky," she said.

"Yes, even if the villagers dig their trench in time, Parsky would still lead the beasts back around the eastern road. I am afraid the Graygills cannot endure. Our world is dying."

Velissa remained in melancholy thought while she fluffed their pillows and turned the bed down. They had a second cup of tea and retired as the fire burned blue and nestled into the glowing embers.

The women of Canby stood guard the entire night. As Raccoman had predicted, it was uneventful. Near daybreak, however, one of the women in the southwest part of the village heard a noise in the darkness and went to investigate. She was horrified to see a Black-gill hurry off into the darkness. He was apparently lame, walking with a decided limp. By daylight, she saw his footprints in the soft earth and the decided imprint of crutch-points alongside them.

But what had he wanted in Canby?

She had caught only a shadowy glimpse of the stealthy intruder, and she was unsure of what he might have taken from the little town. Later, after some investigation throughout the village, it was certain that he had broken into Orkkan's shop and taken such welding equipment as he could carry. Once the thief's path reached the stone flats east of Canby, the women were unable to tell which way he had gone.

Dakktare went immediately to the old barn after breakfast and continued work on the sail plane. By mid-morning, three Graygill women arrived at the Dakktare house, just as Velissa returned from feeding and grooming Collinvar.

The women introduced themselves and told Velissa of the strange and silent burglary of Orkkan's shop and the strange footprints.

"It sounds like the Blackgill astronomer," offered Velissa.

"But why would he want welding supplies?" asked the eldest of the three women, running her fingers nervously through her sidelocks into the sideburns beneath.

The question was, indeed, puzzling.

The women soon left, and at noon Velissa took Raccoman his lunch. She loved to come upon him when there was a streak of grease on his forehead and his hands were covered with the grime of his occupation.

She repeated the women's tale of the burglary of Canby. They thoughtfully considered the riddle, but were perplexed as to whether or not the night thief had, indeed, been Krepel and, if so, what on Estermann he would be doing with welding supplies.

After lunch, Raccoman lay in the new snow, with his head in Velissa's lap, and looked out across the silver meadow. There was no wind, and he dozed in the afternoon sun, lying half-awake as she stroked his forehead. Three congrels crept up to them and a small green bird settled on Dakktare's yellow boot. One of the furry animals snuggled under his half-raised arm and a second dozed next to his chin, resting on his short, round chest.

Dakktare's gills were still a handsome gray. His color of gray was so perfectly in harmony with Velissa's that it seemed they might have been brother and sister rather than man and wife. Lying there before the old barn, it was hard for them to realize the kind of devastation that was occurring in the snowy North.

"I think I shall take Collinvar across the eastern stone flats this afternoon," said Velissa. "The snowy field beckons me to go."

"Looking for the Blackgill Moonrhyme?"

"No, at least not specifically, but it is a lovely day to ride."

(174)

Raccoman agreed but warned her about he unpredictable nature of his uncle since he had fallen under the influence of Parsky.

"Should you see old Krepel, keep your distance, for he could be dangerous. If he would trespass and steal, he might also seek to harm you in some way. Besides, I no longer believe Parsky is in the North. He might indeed be with my uncle."

The afternoon was right for a ride.

Collinvar was eager to split the countryside and glide on his powerful legs to the sunfields east of Canby. Velissa hoped to find Krepel and by some chance discover why he had burglarized the shop in Canby.

The terrain east of Canby soon gave way to large, flat fields of stone slabs. It was as though the meadow had been paved. Collinvar's horns glinted silver in the afternoon brilliance and he continued on.

Once across the slab fields, they came to a line of trees and what had appeared in the distance to be a stream. It was indeed a stream, and its sparkling water was a welcome sight to the thirsty centicorn. Swiftly he arrived at the banks of the little rill and lowered his head to drink. Velissa dismounted and crouched down to drink. But when she lowered her head, she caught sight of a footprint in the muddy snow at the edge of the stream. She was immediately intrigued by the appearance of a crutch point as well.

She wiped the cool water from her mouth and looked in the direction the footprints were going. In the remote distance she saw the Castle Maldoon, whose crumbling towers fascinated her. Velissa was adventuresome by nature, and having seen Maldoon from a distance for many years, she now felt it was the perfect afternoon to get a closer look at the castle. Having been raised in Quarrystone Woods, she was unfamiliar with the land beyond the eastern flats. The towers of Maldoon were strange and alluring. They excited her curiosity, reviving memories of old tales she had heard about the fortress, once the ancient home of Singreale. From the tower on the left flew a flag which could be seen even at this great distance.

She felt uneasy that the footprints seemed to go in the direction of the towers. Collinvar's stamina was an easy complement to the afternoon. In less than half an hour, the centicorn approached the castle, and on closer examination, Velissa could see that while the structure was still in ruins, it was occupied. She decided to take precautions in case Dakktare's uncle should indeed be inside. She left Collinvar in a dry creek bed and tied his reins to a berry-nut shrub before she approached the castle's shaded wall.

Against the wall were numerous shrubs that provided cover for her from anyone who might be looking down from the crumbling tower. She moved with stealth alongside the moss-covered blocks until she reached a niche in the eastern wall. Her feet crunched too loudly in the snow.

There was a cleft in the wall where several stones had left their mortar, and through this cleft Velissa could see across a rocky courtyard. Several of the windows that once guarded the inner court of the palace had rotted away, and their rusted hinges bled red-and-black stains on the crumbling stones of the ancient casements.

Velissa saw a huge iron object in the center of the courtyard. It was a metallic black vehicle larger than a catterlob, with a spidery insignia engraved on the side. The menacing insignia was identical to the one she had seen twice before on the armored catterlob: an eight-point star whose every point ended in a barbed blade. And there was a single word written beneath the strange symbol. It read, "H - O - L - G - A." The ugly letters looked ominous and the word itself had not been used much on Estermann, since most considered it obscene.

While Velissa studied the vehicle in the courtyard, a door in the main fortress wall flew open. It was one of the few doors still hanging on its hinges, and through it marched three Blackgills followed by Uncle Krepel. The old astronomer held a barbed pole.

"Holga!" he shouted as he hobbled forward.

The word meant "power," and more than just power, for it also had the force of a command. The three Blackgills moved with quick steps and picked up a large iron girder, which they carried to the armored craft. The girder was much heavier than the wind foils from which Raccoman had built the Paradise Falcon.

After the three small Blackgills had struggled under the heavy metal for a few minutes, they managed to bring it to the right side of the large iron mass and then struggled to hold it in place. In another instant, Parsky himself appeared. The sight of the villainous Blackgill caused her to cry out in surprise. But she was not heard.

Parsky advanced to the small girder held by the three Blackgills and took a torch which Krepel extended to him. He welded the girder at an odd angle to the torso of the armored contraption, which looked like a metallic beetle. There were fierce, knifelike projections that extended from the outer rim of the black, iron circumference, and a large door, crossed by several seams of rivets, opened at the rear of the vehicle. The piece that the Blackgill attached to the body of the iron insect appeared to be bracing for the axle and wheels, which as yet were missing.

When Parsky had welded the girder into place, he stepped back and surveyed his work. He smiled in a fiendish manner and then said, "Krepel, there's nothing that can stop it."

"Nothing," agreed the one-time star-watcher.

Feeding at some distance away was a huge pair of catterlobs. As Velissa studied Parsky's machine, it seemed clear to her that these beasts were intended to power the odd iron contraption. The catterlobs would be secured inside the completed mechanism and drive it forward. Two openings in the iron mechanism would expose the upper torsos of the beasts, and there was an armored canopy under which the driver of the beasts would sit as the machine rolled forward. The instant Velissa looked at the heavy iron plates she realized the catapults that the Graygills had labored to build and trained to operate would be of little use against the advance of such a device.

Parsky would no doubt sit in the control canopy and drive the catterlobs forward, and the weight and size of the plodding steel beetle would crush any of the Graygill soldiers who happened to get in the way. Parsky climbed into the chair, looked at the grazing catterlobs, and threw back his head and laughed. "The Valley of the Graygills is mine!" he exulted.

"Mine! Mine!" he repeated, doubled over in laughter. "All the Graygills!" Krepel smiled. The primitive machine stood like a suit of armor as the Blackgill climbed down from the armored chair beneath the canopy.

"If I cannot burn Canby, I shall grind it up!" cried Parsky triumphantly. "Nothing will stand, all will be destroyed."

Presently he turned briskly on his heel and disappeared through the same door by which he had entered the courtyard. Old Krepel followed him at a slower pace, still hobbling on one good leg and his crutch. Then the three Blackgill drones moved into the same doorway and were gone.

Velissa could not imagine where Parsky had concealed the foundry that had made the iron destroyer. She took a bold step and squeezed through the gap left by the broken stones. As she came close to the iron monster, she felt dwarfed by its horrendous size. She crossed the tiny courtyard and passed through the stone archway into which the Blackgills had vanished. She paused, for it took a moment for her eyes to adjust to the dim light of the castle. When they did, she could see that the hallway she had entered ended in a smoky cavern. The corridor was empty, but she heard activity ahead, so she hurried down the passageway until the narrow chamber opened onto a large vault where she hid herself behind a stone column.

The cavern was a beehive of activity. Some Blackgills held goads and whips, while other worked at smelting ovens, and great cauldrons of liquid iron shot fire and smoke into the hazy room. Sparks cut white showers of light through the red haze. At last Velissa understood the mystery of the smoke that her father had seen around the towers.

In a moment, Parsky appeared on a ledge near the ceiling of the great domed enclosure.

"Holga!" he shouted. "We need more iron to build the heavy wheels of the Iron Destroyer." At the word "Holga," the workers stopped.

"In a week, the death machine will be finished," he cried. "By that time, the catterlobs will have returned from the North and they will join me in bringing death to the Graygills of Canby." Parsky knew that the catterlobs would turn against him sooner or later—when they devoured the last of the Canbies—for he too was fodder to the beasts; but for the moment the great lizard beasts had joined him in an unholy alliance. "In the meantime, we must have a double output of iron to finish the Iron Destroyer. Now! Work! Holga!"

Mindlessly, the workers resumed their tending of furnaces and cauldrons of molten iron.

Stealthily, Velissa left her viewing place and retraced her steps to the outside of the castle. She crossed the courtyard, walked a short swath around the iron monster, and left through the same fissure by which she had entered Maldoon.

Outside the crumbling walls, she turned and was horrified to see that two Blackgills were following her. She chided herself for leaving Singreale at home. She began to run as fast as she could to where she had tied Collinvar, but the Blackgills followed in swift pursuit, rapidly closing the distance.

"Collinvar!" she cried.

The centicorn, still some distance away, heard her cry and broke the frail limb to which his reins were lashed. He reached her just as her pursuers tried to grab her and thrust his huge body in between his mistress and the Blackgills. He wheeled, reared up on his back legs, and became such a fearsome foe that the two Blackgills ran back a safe distance to escape his threshing forelegs. He settled long enough for Velissa to mount, and in a moment, they were gone.

"Canby be damned!" cried Parsky, who had observed the chase from a window in the upper tower of Maldoon Castle. "She has escaped—and she knows of the machine."

Velissa wheeled her mount again on his haunches and looked up at the evil face in the tower window.

"Fear Singreale!" she shouted, and the centicorn bolted north and then west and soon was no longer visible from the ruins of the castle towers.

It was nearing sundown when Velissa again crossed the stone flats southeast of Canby, and thus darkness overtook her before she reached the sheltered road that led at last to the home she shared with Raccoman.

So late was the hour that he had been concerned, and he was greatly relieved when he heard the swift hoofbeats of the centicorn.

Collinvar skidded to a stop in the soft earth before the house.

"Hello, my love!" she cried.

"What kept you?" he asked as she dismounted.

"I have found your uncle and old friend, Parsky."

"Where?"

"At the ruins of Maldoon."

"You went that far?"

"It is good that I did, for I have discovered that the war is worse than we supposed."

Briefly she recounted how she discovered the foundry and the horrible machine, and she shivered visibly even as she related the incident of her near capture.

"It is even too horrible a foe for Singreale," said Raccoman, whose anxiety was too obvious to hide.

"Nothing is too hard for Singreale," said Velissa.

Two weeks had passed. The first of the tilt winds came.

"I thought I was through with the Paradise Falcon," said Raccoman. "But I've discovered that I must reinforce the landing skids."

"How long will that take?" It was clear from the desperation in her voice that she thought Raccoman finished with his work.

"Three days or so, if I work at night, too. The landing skids must be braced with girders and welded to the underside."

"Can it fly without the work?"

"Yes, but landing it might be risky. The skids must be finished. Maybe I can do it in two days," he said with grim optimism that left her unconvinced.

"I'll stable Collinvar," she replied. "Then we shall go back to the barn and work together."

After a hasty dinner, Velissa slipped the pouch containing Singreale about her neck and the two of them walked to the old barn. Once again the bright flare at the end of Dakktare's torch burned brightly and the metal yielded to his flame. Driven by the fear of the unknown perils that lay ahead, they worked to the limits of their endurance.

The night was half gone when Velissa finally convinced Raccoman to retire for the night. He reluctantly doused his torch in the water bucket and the sizzling sound of the steam sent them wearily toward home. They walked across the field and entered their little home and climbed into bed. They drifted off into the dual hum that they had earned by their perseverance.

Just before daybreak, they were startled awake by an abrupt noise outside their window. A fluttering sound exploded against the glass. Raccoman was instantly out of bed.

"It's Rexel!" he cried.

When he opened the window, the falcon fell into the room. His feathers were soaked in the lather of a hard flight. He groaned a doom that dulled the dawn.

"The North is lost! The Graygill warriors are dead—the catter-lobs have broken through!"

The battle was the final hope. They faced it valiantly.
Young soldiers kissed their women hard and spoke of victory.
The war was swift as it was red, and catapulted stones
Gave birth to roaring silence after whimpering and groans.

CHAPTER XII

Demmerron Pass

FROM REXEL, Raccoman learned that Orkkan was the only survivor of the defenders of Canby. He had escaped and had hidden himself in a shallow cave with so small an entrance that the catterlobs could not reach him.

After an early breakfast, the metal-worker and his wife accompanied the falcon outside and continued talking about the war. Rexel believed that the catterlobs would be back to Canby before two days were ended.

"What will the women and children do?
Their strength is small, their number few."

"They will be caught in the jaws of war between the catterlobs from the North and the Iron Destroyer from the South," said Velissa. Velissa quickly described Parsky's terrible machine and was surprised that Rexel already knew of it—but then, the falcon seemed to know everything. "What will the villagers do?" lamented Velissa. "What *can* they do?"

"If there is an answer, it lies with Singreale," said Dakktare.

"The Fire of Singreale is far more than light.
He is the substance and source of all that is best
The terror of free men.
The powerful defender of all those who serve right."

Velissa was pleased to hear her husband speak so confidently about Singreale.

It was himself about which Raccoman was troubled. He had felt his idea of the trench at Demmerron was sound, but the digging in winter had gone too slow. If only he could have thought of the idea earlier. In autumn, it might have had a better chance for success.

Further, though he could not have anticipated it, the Iron Destroyer would render the spear catapults useless against Parsky's advance. It was clear that Orkkan and the women must try to move the weapons to the high ridges where the armored destroyer would be powerless to navigate.

If they could talk the Moonrhyme men into an alliance, perhaps Orkkan and the few surviving Canbies could defend the upper ridges with the spear catapults. The first of the slanted breezes had come, and Raccoman knew that the tilt winds would soon be screaming across the ridges and slamming into the valley floor.

Raccoman's desire to stay and help Orkkan secure an alliance with the Moorhymes was strong, but his desire to commit himself and his wife to the pursuit of the Star Riders was even more pressing.

Whatever the status of the war, he knew he would have to leave soon, even if he felt like a defector, for his ability to keep the Singreale safe could not be assured much longer. The one desire of the Blackgill was to own the treasure of the vanquished king and perhaps to bring it once again to the crumbling throne room of the old castle. If Raccoman succumbed, light would not reign as it had in the past when Singreale had known the protection of the serpent Doldeen. If Parsky owned the treasure, the world would suffer from the terror of his dark desires.

But for the moment, Orkkan was inaccessible, separated from any hope of joining the cause of the surviving Canbies. For now he was freezing in his icy niche in the cliff of the Red Sentinel of Demmerron. And Raccoman knew something had to be done to rescue him.

"The women of the village need Orkkan," said Velissa. "Could swift Collinvar ride to the North and bring him back to Canby before the end?"

"He would never get past the catterlobs. And even if he did, he would not have the stamina required for a swift return to Canby in time."

"Let us seek Singreale!" cried Velissa.

She quickly undid the pouch at her neck. The gem flew out into the air. Its brilliant light spun a golden fire—a flame of filigree, shimmering in the sunlight until it landed upon the head of Rexel. Then, oddly, its light died for a moment only to reappear behind the falcon's eyes.

"Rexel!" cried Velissa. "Are *you* Singreale?"

"Singreale is the power of truth in the face of evil. Singreale is the possessor of any who are not afraid to risk themselves. I am not Singreale, but I contain him and feel him at my heart, and I shall fly swiftly to Orkkan fueled by the power of the life source."

The falcon began to grow. He grew until he was larger than Collinvar. Each of his talons was larger than Velissa's body, and his huge beak looked like the blade of a guillotine. His size was so ominous that both Raccoman and Velissa drew back and were afraid.

"Bring me Collinvar's saddle," boomed Rexel, for as he had grown in size, so had his voice grown in volume.

Raccoman left and soon came back lugging the saddle. It was most awkward for the giant falcon to lie down flat enough for Raccoman to assemble the girth strap and hinge. Rexel flexed his giant wings, churning loose snow into the air with every flutter. Raccoman coughed into the huge feathers of Rexel's upper body, but finally succeeded in tightening the girth strap around the falcon's neck. He rigged Collinvar's bridle around the head of the giant bird and then smiled in some satisfaction.

"Are you afraid?" asked Rexel, standing up.

"Yes," admitted Raccoman. "You have both the Singreale and Collinvar's saddle. I have nothing left to defend my home or my wife—yes, I'm very much afraid."

"Dakktare, you're the standard
The model, the key,
The idol, deserving of idolatry,"

mocked the giantesque Rexel in his basso tones.

Raccoman knew that the times were serious now and braggadocious egotism seemed powerless. He felt ashamed the falcon had reminded him that his Graygill arrogance was no match for the possible rigors of war.

"Come back soon!" he shouted as Rexel took two steps and flapped his giant wings. The cascading air caused snow and dust to swirl around Velissa and Raccoman. The bird rose upward. His wings opened to such a span that their shadow fell all the way across the small house. When the fog cleared, they watched Rexel until he was but a dot in the blue sky and then was gone.

Velissa could barely suppress the urge to go to the women of Canby, but she felt insecure in the knowledge that the Villain of Maldoon knew of her discovery. She was all the more afraid now

(186)

that Singreale flew with Rexel, and she could never hold to the swift Collinvar without his saddle. So she clung to the hope that Orkkan would be rescued soon, for she felt it was his place to break the news of Demmerron Pass to the women and children who remained.

She went with her husband who lost little time in starting to work. Velissa threw back the large door at the front of the barn.

The splendor of the Paradise Falcon glinted gold when the sun danced over the threshold and fell on the large ship. Velissa wanted to stay and marvel at her husband who, in only a few short months, had managed such a beautiful and magnificent feat. Though a month on Estermann was equal to two on earth, the accomplishment was nonetheless a magnificent tribute to the discipline of the lone welder. And he was more than a welder. He was an inventor, a genius whose ingenuity could not be denied.

All was going well, and Raccoman was determined to labor on into the night, if necessary, to see if the last of the work could be finished by the next morning.

Velissa brought the welding rod to her husband, who pulled his visor down over his ruddy forehead and began. He had made the hood out of a yellow alloy, and when he pulled it down over his eyes, he looked already like a traveler among the stars.

By now he had welded the left skid into place and flawlessly connected the bracing to the steel skid that set in the floor of the barn and fit snuggled close and flat to the underside of the Paradise Falcon. Raccoman laid the windfoil in position so that he would be ready to begin work on the right skid after lunch.

Raccoman and his bride walked outside into the meadow. The sun glinted on the tinsel leaves of the distant ginjon trees and the candolet shrubs were heavy with fruit. The snowy lea and the playful congrels had become the last retreat from the growing horror of a war that would soon envelop everything in its path.

"It's hard here to look at all I adore
And believe there is anything evil, like war."

"What do you think went wrong?" asked Velissa.

"The Blackgill did it all. He corrupted Castledome Forest, then moved to the plains."

"Did you never suspect him? He was your friend. You sang and danced a thousand Claxtons. Did his devious nature never cause you to distrust him?"

"In those days,
Estermann was happy.
Laughter was the speech of men.
And then . . . then my long-time friend . . .
I . . . I loved the Blackgill so . . .
How was I to really know?"

His voice trailed off. Velissa thought for a moment and then said:

"He killed animals,
Deceived you with Blackgill stew,
And passed his gluttony to you."

She was unaware that her words had rhymed. In fact, the more she lived with Raccoman, the more she tended to pick up his affected way of speaking.

"And I ate, too—oh, I ate, too," he sighed.

Velissa could sense the shame he felt at his confession. They stopped talking. He held up to the sky the black bread she had brought for lunch and said the familiar words:

"To the maker of the feast
To the power of loaf and yeast
Till the broth and bread have ceased
Gratefulness is joy."

"But where did he come from?" she asked as soon as the bread was blessed.

"Who? Where did who come from?" asked Raccoman.

"Parsky."

"He was a survivor—apparently the only one—in the battle of Kendrake."

"Yes, but he was a Blackgill. Did you never wonder just how he appeared in a world of Graygills?"

"He could sing and dance and, best of all, cook delicious meals. Why should he not have been welcome in the Graygills' world?"

They decided to steal ten minutes for a nap they both needed. They had worked so late into the night that had just passed that their exhaustion had begun to show. As Velissa closed her eyes in the warm sun, she felt the soft fur of a congrel who was snuggling next to her. The green frost butterflies were back for the winter, and the clean smell of new snow continued to blot out the memory of the horrible fate of the little warriors who would never return from Demmerron Pass. The snow was dry and the cold air felt warm on the south side of the barn.

While they slept in the warm sun, Raccoman dreamed of the lovely world he had once found so sure and predictable. In his dream, he walked the meadows and sang his way through the glistening lanes of winter. He laughed and rode upon a catterlob calf and scooped up armfuls of congrels. He made rhymes and danced and drank the grog from his uncle's ale barrels. His dreams were fantasies of joy—the realities of yesterday, now living only in the mind of a man who could remember life before evil. He danced to a clump of wild flowers, picked up an iridescent butterfly, and held it on his finger. He laughed as long as one can laugh in a dream without waking himself, and he sang again the ballad of the centicorn, which he had composed in the joy of the sunny ledges.

"Ho-ho to the centicorn, wild and high!
Ride the great star trails into the sky.
Sing heigh, shout ho, ride on!"

"Holga!" said a loud voice. Raccoman was instantly awake and on his feet.

"Holga!" The harsh word ended all dreams. A huge net fell over the pair. They were captured.

Velissa awoke and her eyes strained to adjust first to the sunlight and then to the evil Blackgill. In the sudden brightness of snow and sun, she couldn't focus.

"So this is your work!" Parsky exclaimed to Dakktare through the webbing of the heavy net. "Were you thinking of going somewhere?"

By the end of his comment, four of the Blackgills who traveled with Parsky had drawn the net so tight around Raccoman and Velissa that the pair could scarcely move.

"Now," Parsky commanded the drones, "burn this barn and then we shall wrench Singreale from the neck of Velissa Dakktare."

"I have it not, Parsky," said Velissa in joy. "Right now it lights the eyes of the great falcon."

"Burn the barn," sneered Parsky. "Destroy the glide plane."

"No!" cried Raccoman. "Please—it's my life work! Please, no!"

"Holga!" shouted the Blackgill.

One of his servants began striking two flintstones together to ignite a torch. The sparks glinted in the yellow sheen of the Paradise Falcon. Raccoman looked through the netting at his life dream—his one hope of tracking the Star Riders and escaping the valley which war now promised to destroy.

Suddenly a whirling of dust and debris flew up around them.

"Rexel!" cried Velissa.

The great bird, with Orkkan in the saddle, grabbed the two Blackgills who were trying to ignite a fire and carried them aloft. They cried out in fear.

Fortunately, Rexel carried them only a little distance from the ground and dropped them to the meadow floor. They lay still for a moment. Then they stirred, shook off their dazed expressions, and staggered away in the direction of Canby.

Rexel returned for Parsky, who drew his rapier and slashed at the talons. It did him little good. The falcon's claws grasped him by his red cape and carried him for many miles before dropping him rudely to the earth. With their leader taken, the other Blackgills scattered.

Rexel returned.

Orkkan vaulted from his saddle, nearly stumbling as he touched the ground because the height from which he had dismounted was so great even after Rexel had landed. In a moment, the sole survivor of Demmerron Pass had cut the netting that bound Velissa and Raccoman.

Rexel and Orkkan recounted the tragedy of Demmerron. Just a few hours before the trench would have been finished, the snow fell and the whole project became mired in a blizzard. Then the catterlobs returned, and though a few perished in the portion of the pit that was complete, most moved through the shallow stretch of the ditch and savagely attacked the Graygills.

Orkkan could not suppress tears as he told of the massacre of Demmerron Pass. Now he faced the tearing prospect of telling the women of Canby the fate of their husbands.

"Within two weeks, the beasts will be back in Canby," said Rexel.

"What of Parsky?" asked Raccoman.

"He will never give up," replied Rexel. "He will return to the Castle Maldoon and gather reinforcements and be back. It grieves me by millennia to realize I once lived there and served Singreale with his excellence, the White Falcon, my brother."

"Your brother!" exclaimed Velissa in astonishment.

"Parsky was more than a Blackgill stew-cook. He incited the rebellion that left Maldoon in ruins. He was afraid Singreale would grant his power to the falcons, for we could fly. Lord Parskon—that is what he was called in those days—slew my brother and left his proud white feathers red! Then, angry that he had failed to grasp the Fire of Singreale from its crystal pedestal before the throne, he fled into Castledome Forest and introduced death to Estermann. It was inevitable that he would one day return to the fortress, for his lust to have the power of Singreale never ceased. He felt that the great stone had somehow been lost in the rubble of the siege. For years he sifted the debris in his fruitless search for the lost diamond.

"He was unaware that your father was keeping it. He did not know that I had taken the gem to Quarrystone Woods, along with the guardian serpent Doldeen, and placed it in the keeping of your great-grandfather. Had he known that, Parsky would have gone there years ago. He only discovered the true whereabouts of Singreale when he found a reference to the ancient fire in a letter your father wrote to Raccoman's Uncle Krepel. As soon as he knew, he went to Quarrystone Woods to retrieve the gem, riding the armored catterlob you saw in the snowy forest."

For the first time, Raccoman and Velissa knew they were hearing the truth about sinister Parsky.

"I felt lonely and afraid without the light force," Velissa confessed. "When you were gone to rescue Orkkan, we longed for your return. Fortune was ours and you returned just in time. Parsky, or Parskon, would have destroyed both us and the Paradise Falcon."

"You can have the light back anytime you wish," said Rexel.

"We will be safe for a while. Keep it till you have seen Orkkan safely back to Canby, for the report must be taken to the Graygill women."

"I must go," said Orkkan.

The falcon again lowered his lofty neck, and with some awkwardness, Orkkan climbed back into the saddle. Churning the air, Rexel once more lifted aloft and winged toward Canby. Raccoman and Velissa watched them and then entered the barn. They had to work. Canby could be under siege before the week was out, and the Iron Destroyer would roll from the crumbling fortress of Maldoon before long. Now that Velissa knew the truth about Parsky's murderous past, she feared him all the more, and so she worked with new zeal and looked to the coming of the tilt winds.

Within a short time, Rexel arrived at the village of Canby. His size so frightened the women that they ran at first. But Orkkan swiftly dismounted, and then the women pressed him for the outcome of Demmerron Pass. Orkkan's brief recounting of the tragedy dissolved the frail hope they had sustained.

"It is the end of Estermann!" cried one.

"How shall we stand against the catterlobs? Who shall defend us now against their advance?"

"Our husbands—gone . . . gone," wept an old woman whose sidelocks were little more than thin wisps beside her wrinkled face.

"There is another horror," said Orkkan when their disconsolate weeping had subsided. "From the foundry of Maldoon there is shortly to come the Iron Destroyer. What the beasts leave standing in Canby, the machine will obliterate."

The women sat silent. Fear camped in their eyes.

"There is but one hope for life!" said Orkkan. "The ridges! Your homes will not escape, but you may. Neither the catterlobs nor the Iron Destroyer can traverse the high ledges. The terrain is too rough. Rexel will watch the enemy, and while he watches, you must gather some of the weapons forged by the men and come. Bring your heaviest winter clothes and follow me to the ridges."

In spite of the evident melancholy, Orkkan continued speaking, "Thanks be to the cliff dwellings of the Moonrhymes. Neither the Iron Destroyer nor the catterlobs can reach their lofty homes. They are secure. Once we are gathered on the upper ridges, I will lead you and your little ones across the mountains to Canby-Dun and we will ask the Moonrhyme Graygills for asylum."

Orkkan promised them his allegiance through the dreadful days ahead. He mounted Rexel and guided him south and east. He had developed a great deal of grace in riding the falcon. Once in sight of the towers of Maldoon, he flew dangerously close, circling low over the courtyard. The huge iron machine with its barbed insignia looked complete. Even to see it from aloft inspired terror. To view it from the ground would inspire more fear than the average heart could endure.

Parsky was not back in the fortress as yet. Hopefully, he would not set the war machine in motion until the widows of Canby were safe on the upper ridges.

In the courtyard of Maldoon, several of the foundry workers were attaching more armaments to the beetlelike machine. They trembled when the shadow of Rexel fell back across the sunny courtyard. Orkkan felt anger as he guided Rexel to a pile of boulders well outside the walls. Rexel grasped a heavy stone in each talon and flew back across the courtyard and dropped them directly over the workmen. The largest of the stones struck the machine with force, but the armaments of Lord Parskon's terror were not even dented by the boulder.

The surprised workmen scrambled.

Orkkan scanned the trail. Some miles from the castle, he caught sight of Parsky and his companions. Orkkan thought he might drop stones on them as well, but he changed his mind as Rexel rose high. In a distance he could see the file of the widowed refugees beginning their long journey. The bent forms seemed frozen against the snow.

By mid-afternoon Orkkan was back with Raccoman and Velissa. They were comforted to see the falcon and the master metal-worker of Canby.

"How are the women?" asked Velissa.

"Well enough to have begun their trek to the highlands."

The weight of the great defeat of Demmerron Pass continued to choke their conversation. The air was so charged with despair that Orkkan intentionally changed the subject.

"When does she fly?" Orkkan asked Dakktare, gesturing through the open barn door to the bright ship now standing firm on her landing skids.

"Tomorrow noon," replied Raccoman. "We need only the winds."

"Come, stay with us and we will show you the glory of the ship by night."

"Tonight I must go to the high ridges and wait with the women. I must not leave them now."

"Then I make you a present," said Velissa.

"What present?" he asked.

"The centicorn!" cried Velissa. "Collinvar is yours."

"Collinvar!" exclaimed Orkkan in delight.

"We cannot take him, and he is swift to his owner," said Raccoman. "He is fleet and sure of foot on the ledges."

"Come, you may take him now," said Velissa.

In the joy of the moment, Orkkan followed Velissa to the shed that had served as the centicorn's stable. She brought Collinvar out of the shed. He needed no bridle and followed them as docilely as a household pet.

"Singreale we must keep," said Velissa.

They walked back to Rexel.

"Singreale, come!" she said.

The light died in the great falcon's eyes; it swirled from his eyes and collected in a single glowing sphere. Then it shrank down and gathered into the diamond of white incandescence. It entered the little pouch that swung free on Velissa's bosom.

She felt secure in the knowledge that Singreale was back again where his nearness could not be doubted.

No sooner had the light left the falcon's eyes than the grand bird dwindled in size. He crawled out from under Collinvar's saddle that only moments before had barely fit his wide neck. The saddle was tightened around the centicorn and the bridle installed.

Orkkan did not immediately mount.

"Stay for a bit," said Raccoman.

The old barn doors were pushed as wide as they could be opened.

Raccoman released two pins that held the Paradise Falcon on each side. The craft rolled easily and gracefully down the rails and out into the sunshine. The skids adjusted the leaf-shaped ship easily into a level position.

Its sleek golden metal made its color appear illuminated in the late sun of afternoon. Collinvar pranced and pawed the earth in the glorious vision he beheld. Rexel soared upward and swooped in glee before settling back to the saddle horn. Velissa beamed in pride for the miracle her husband had created from wind foils and his own determination to be free of Estermann.

Raccoman also beamed upon seeing his creation for the first time in the sunlight. The radial fins swept in clean, sleek lines to the perimeter of the ship. The expert welding displayed a clean, glassy, faultless surface with never the intrusion of a rivet. Raccoman fell once again to egotistic jubilation:

"Here's the pride of our own stratosphere,
The work of a genius artist is here
For all to behold and marvel and cheer!
She'll walk upon stars flung galaxies high.
She'll walk on the winds and inherit the sky.
Marvel, you Graygills, but never deny
That Dakktare created the falcon to fly!
I'll swear I am he—the great Mr. D.
A capable artist as ever you'll see!
I am he who is brilliant, efficient, and kind,
With an artisan's hand and a scientist's mind.
Get in line, wait your turn, behold me and stare,
So you may in good time shake the hand of Dakktare!"

And Mrs. Dakktare could not help but join his sunlit rhapsodizing:

"I am the bride of the
Genius welder whose deeds are untold!
By the sunlight that shines on the ship that you see
I have married Dakktare to become Mrs. D."

There were not any who fell in line to shake his hand that evening, but the ship was a beautiful thing to behold.

This tale is soon brought to completion. Shall it finish in some
   tragedy,
As a saga of regal adventure where dangers resolve happily?
Could it be that this planet's protected, a star system where
   living is fun?
Or is this a world whose best heroes ride epics that crash in the sun?

CHAPTER XIII

Escape

ORKKAN CLIMBED into the fore-saddle of the centicorn. The animal was so tall that he felt a little insecure at first, even after having ridden Rexel. Then he was riding swiftly toward the ridges. Rexel was sent to the skies to watch, since both Raccoman and Velissa were afraid that Parsky would make one last attempt to steal Singreale.

There was no report from the widows of Canby that their situation had worsened. Nor was there any sign of the returning beasts. The sky was not clear enough during the week for Raccoman even once to see Maldoon. The days were gray, without a single evidence that the tilt winds would ever come. It snowed—never hard, but constantly. Rexel fluttered in and out of the snow with never a report of trouble. It was almost as though they had imagined the war and life was once again as simple as it had been in earlier days.

A week passed.

Velissa put aside the food and clothing that they would need on their trip and felt uneasy about the quiet days. Raccoman himself waited impatiently for the tilt winds and nervously inspected the ship from day to day. Both of them were so busy that neither took time to watch for anyone coming from Maldoon to complete the mischief they had earlier begun.

By nightfall, it was still snowing and Raccoman knew there was little chance of a tilt wind, for the winds never came during times when the sky was overcast. On the ninth day after Orkkan's departure, they heard a rumble in the northern sky behind the remaining conical towers and spherical roofs of Canby. But it was not the coming of the tilt winds. Even before Rexel arrived to confirm their fears, they suspected that the rumble was raised by the return of the catterlobs.

Rexel ventured out into the thin snow and flew far to the East and was surprised to see that the Castle Maldoon had most of its southern wall destroyed. The wall looked as though it had been chewed to splinters by an insect. It took the falcon a while to locate the Iron Destroyer, which was now outside the walls. The death machine was frosted with ice crystals and covered with a layer of snow which softened its evil appearance. Even the sharp eyes of the falcon had difficulty locating Parsky's creation in the snowy terrain around Maldoon. The deadly insect was propelled forward by two huge catterlobs whose armored, ugly upper bodies shot columns of hot vapors into the fresh air as they drove the crude machine forward. It was now not moving in the direction of Canby but toward the home of Raccoman and Velissa. Rexel noted that its motion was steady and determined. Fortunately, it did not move fast. But even at its plodding pace, two days would bring it to the field where the falcon now rested in the snow. Dakktare had been careful to keep a complete and consistent surveillance of his elegant glider. He constantly brushed the snow from it and used a soft torch-tip to burnish away every hint of ice buildup. He was now in a race against time, and when the winds came, he wanted nothing to encumber the flight of the Paradise Falcon.

Raccoman never doubted that she would fly, though it may only have been his arrogance that forbade such doubt. After his years in the skies, he knew the winds and he knew the secret of navigating them. He knew his ship would soar as easily as he had done through the seasons. His certainty was transferred to Velissa, who never permitted doubt to interfere with her dreams.

Rexel flew to Dakktare to report the position and direction of the death machine. His surveillance told them it would be arriving before two days had passed.

"Two days!" exclaimed Velissa. "What will we do?"

"We can do nothing," said the welder, "unless the winds come." It was hard for Raccoman to admit that he could do nothing unless the winds came.

The depressing snow continued to fall and, at midnight, became heavy.

Raccoman was glad, for he knew that the deeper the snow, the harder the catterlobs would find the work of driving the Iron Destroyer to the lowlands. The terrain from Maldoon was rough and the cold snow and rough earth would slow the beasts in their progress.

Raccoman stayed up all night, cleaning the Paradise Falcon of snow and ice. After midnight Velissa decided to take him a steaming kettle of candolet tea to cheer his toil. As she took the tea to the welder, she thought she saw something in the bushes behind the barn. She gave no outward sign that she had noticed anything, but mentioned her fear to Raccoman. He signaled to Rexel to have a look about. The falcon took to the silent air and winged quietly away. In a moment he was back with the confirmation. Someone in the bushes watched them as they brushed the snow from the ship. Since Orkkan was with all the other Graygills on the sunny ledges, they could only assume the watcher was one of Parsky's drones.

"Why here?" asked Velissa, although she knew the answer.

Raccoman slipped silently into the darkness with a piece of steel in his hand. He measured his steps quietly until he had circled the little break of bushes at the rear of the barn. Once behind the break, he moved slowly, scanning the thicket, trying in vain to see the figure Rexel had reported.

There was no one.

Could both the falcon and his wife have been wrong? He continued looking. He started to walk back in the direction of the barn when he felt a sharp blow on his head and his mind swam in a blue-and-white delirium of pain before he crumpled unconscious in the snow.

Velissa soon became very uneasy that Raccoman had not returned. She didn't know whether to leave the falcon and search for him or wait. She decided to wait.

Again Rexel flew from his parapet above the door. He circled silently. He saw one form lying prone—apparently unconscious— and the other form still staunchly watching the ship.

He was almost sure that the prone form was Dakktare. He decided to take a closer look, and so he landed, folded his wings, and walked over to the unconscious welder. A falcon's eyes are better at night than by day, and his superb vision caught sight of a bulk moving toward him in the dark. He flew just in time to escape a blow from the great club that had just laid Dakktare out in delirium.

Rexel returned to the ship to report Raccoman's fate, and his own close escape, to Velissa. Velissa knew it was Singreale that her husband's assassin was after, but she found herself in a dilemma: should she abandon the ship or stay with it and abandon Dakktare?

She reached into the pouch at her neck and pulled out Singreale. The familiar light flooded the little meadow around the ship and fell with intensity on the trees. Velissa moved in the direction of the short trees with a quick, courageous pace. Just as she approached Dakktare, a dark and hooded form dashed from the thicket, raised a short heavy stick, and struck her a glancing blow. She was struck with such suddenness that she stumbled and lurched forward into the icy grass. Singreale rolled from her hand, melting the snow and sinking into the frost where it landed.

The hooded figure grabbed the brilliant light.

He held it high and exulted with a wild laugh.

His hood fell away from his face.

"Krepel!" cried Velissa.

"Yes. I have Singreale!" shouted the evil Moonrhyme.

At that precise instant, Rexel completed a fast drop and fastened his talons in the astronomer's scalp. The pain of his own torn flesh and the impact of the large bird when it came screaming out of the darkness sent the astronomer staggering into the meadow. His head, badly bleeding from the falcon's talons, struck a rock as he fell and left him unconscious in the foliage at the edge of the thicket. Singreale rolled free again and Rexel seized it. The falcon rose quickly into the air—ready for a second go at the villain should it be necessary.

But Krepel did not move.

Velissa ran quickly to her husband. He was alive. She held his face in her hands.

As consciousness returned, Raccoman asked, "Singreale?"

His mind was still muddled from the blow he had received.

"There," she replied. "In the talons of Rexel."

Gazing upward, Raccoman smiled. Even through the falling snow, the aura of light fell outward, illuminating the snowflakes like a downy cascade of tiny stars.

As soon as Raccoman was able to stand, he and Velissa walked over to the silent form on the ground. Velissa knelt in the snow. By the light of Singreale, she could see that things were not well.

"Your uncle is dead," she said. "Killed by his own villainy."

Raccoman stared down in silence. Besides his father, Krepel was the only relative he had ever known, but he could not find it in his heart to wish him alive again. He knew that this was perhaps a better end than his uncle might have had if he had lived to follow the villainous Parsky. Raccoman felt sure that once the usefulness of the old star-watcher was through, the evil Blackgill would have disposed of him in some way.

"Holga!" said Raccoman as he looked again at his dead relative. "This is the end of Holga! Power is a lost illusion that dies a frigid death in the greed of its own pursuit." The snow blew through Krepel's black hair and collected in his orange collar.

"Holga," repeated Velissa as she slipped her arm around her husband's waist. Her blue sleeve gained an illumination as it snuggled up to the yellow mackinaw that Raccoman customarily wore. The coat hung loose on her husband whose cares had stolen from his zest—he was no longer as plump as he had been in the days before Parsky's deception. Raccoman's thousand years felt like two thousand.

Rexel settled on Raccoman's shoulder. This added weight caused the welder's tired frame to bend a little more. Rexel's free talon extended the Singreale to Velissa, and the light cast by the gem into the snowy dark made the falling white seem a magic world.

"Singreale is the only answer to Holga," Velissa told her husband. A snowflake stuck on her eyelash and he kissed it away. She held the huge diamond close to his face—a face whose kindness had become wisdom and whose merriment had learned the pain of tears. But it was a strong face still bright with hope, for his eyes never doubted what they had seen nor gave up their adventure with time unborn. He kissed her as Singreale bathed their dazzling world of falling snow with hope.

They knew that, somewhere in the dark, Parsky drove the black catterlobs with a huge whip as the beasts shoved against the cold steel yokes that pushed the Iron Destroyer toward the snowy meadow. This unspoken image made Raccoman and Velissa pray for the coming of the winds.

Once more they looked at Raccoman's uncle. Now the snow was covering his orange sleeves and welding his black gills together in clots of ice. They turned to walk away.

"Tomorrow when there is light, I will bury him as best I can," said Raccoman.

Velissa did not reply.

Raccoman thought of the days when the Moonrhyme wizard had

been the friend of all who sought his wisdom. For a thousand years, orange had been the color of hope for all who sought its counsel. Krepel's orange scope had scanned the night skies of Estermann and the constellations had been his passion. Now orange was a hopeless and treacherous color, freezing in a dead silence that would never stir again. The ancient keeper of the highland observatory was dead—as dead as the serpent Doldeen.

"Can't we sleep for an hour?" asked Velissa, at last breaking into her husband's reverie.

"I'm afraid not," said Raccoman, picking up his brush and sweeping the snow from the outer edges of the Paradise Falcon.

The candolet had grown cold.

Velissa put Singreale back into the pouch at her neck and returned to the house to warm a second kettle of tea.

Separated by the night, Collinvar was now standing silent by the huge fire that Orkkan of Canby had built on the high ledges. The night had been darker than any night the new widows of Canby could remember. Their children clung to them. Several hundred of them waited for the dawn. Among their number was a group of boys, youngsters whose suffering was contained in the silence of their hearts. They were too soon men—yet not ready to be what their age demanded. Still, the sight of their grieving mothers united these children in their zeal to defend them.

The night passed slowly and the sky toward morning began to clear. The stars before dawn had replaced the snow and lit the northern mountains and the lower plains with brilliance. The Grand Dragon coiled in cold, white stars above the silent roofs of Canby far below. As the skies cleared, however, the cold deepened, and the chill of the winter air cut the refugees to the bone. Orkkan could not see very far beyond the fire that flickered on the faces of those whose fate he both directed and shared.

He tried to make his mind look up, but it was the double prisoner to grief and darkness. At last, he began to sing softly and with a bravado that defied the face of his circumstance. His husky voice moved slowly over the crackling of the burning embers:

> "Let us sing at the base of the ginjon tree,
> For Canby's fields are the fields of the free.

May the sun long rise and the morning skies
Herald the anthem of liberty.
Ho! To the light, may our children roam
Through the friendly fields of Castledome.
For beasts and men are timeless friends
In the ageless land of Estermann."

He stopped singing and his words clung to the dark cliffs that towered above him, truncated by the heavy dark and the smoke of the fire. In the starry darkness, the refugees huddled into oneness.

As dawn came, their worst fears were confirmed. The catterlobs, lumbering through the new snow, could now be seen making their way through the distant plains north of Canby. Throughout the morning, the Canbies watched their plodding progress through the snowfields. The great beasts were forced to stop and rest after they crossed areas of rough terrain. While their advance could not be called swift, watching it became the nervous occupation of those refugees who loved their cold and fireless homes below.

On a typical winter day, one would have seen coiling smoke rising above the conical roofs of Canby. Now nothing rose above the village.

The sky was clear, and by mid-afternoon Raccoman dared to believe that the first of the tilt winds might come by night. Velissa felt a growing need to visit the women of Canby one last time. She talked to Raccoman about taking Rexel imbued with Singreale and making a flight to the ridges. Raccoman agreed to the visit if she would be back by nightfall. He reminded her that this was perfect weather for the coming of the winds.

"Before you leave, survey the area to know the progress of the Iron Destroyer. Remember," he further cautioned, "come swiftly back in case the tilt winds come."

Velissa did not have a saddle since it was now with Collinvar on the high ridges. But she felt that she would be able to cling tightly to the feathers of the great Rexel, who was all too eager to know again the empowering of Singreale.

She took the diamond from its pouch and the swirling of light was even brighter than the glistening of the midday sun on the snow. The light swirled in illumination till, like a hurricane of light, it penetrated the head of the falcon. Again his eyes glowed and he grew to an immense length; he was half-as-long as the Paradise Falcon.

Velissa made her way up onto Rexel's broad wing, which he courteously extended and moved to a position where she could cling in comfort to his strong neck. She grasped his large feathers and gently urged him off the ground.

He obeyed, but not gently.

It was not that he meant to be disobedient. It was just that there is no logical way that a falcon can take off in flight gently. The mere stretching of the wings and the force of exertion required to leave the ground must be accompanied by a violent lurching and a leaping into the air.

Velissa, who had looked forward to the adventure, nearly fell as Rexel stretched his proud neck toward the bright, cold sky. His first leap came with such violence that it frightened her into a little outcry.

"Hold on tight!" cried Raccoman, seeing the alarm in her face.

Velissa did not need his encouragement. She clung as tightly as she had ever done. She leaned forward, clasping her legs close to the falcon's powerful wing muscles. Beneath her, she felt the rippling power of these muscles pulling like hard steel pinions in the first rigors of flight. The stinging air moved around Rexel's head and burned Velissa's eyes. The bird's great beak looked like the yellow metal of the Paradise Falcon. Rexel's powerful wings churned the thin air to confident flight.

Velissa's knuckles turned white.

At last, the long wings stretched out beside her and eased the tension she had felt. Rexel's heavy muscles still rippled beneath the feathers of his upper body, but now the rippling was more gentle. Cautiously she opened her eyes wide to peer over the edge of the huge wings.

Instantly she gasped aloud and closed them again.

It was some time before her tension eased again. Once more she peered out beyond the falcon's neck. Far below her, she saw the hall of Dakktare, the barn and the yellow sail plane lying in bright contrast with the white field. Velissa began to enjoy her lofty perspective. She waved good-bye to her husband from her airy mount as the falcon turned east.

In a swift half-hour, Rexel circled low across the edge of the Castledome Forest and Velissa saw the sluggish Iron Destroyer. It was still crusted with ice from the storm of the previous day. The black catterlobs labored inside the huge machine as it wallowed through a heavy thicket. The trees bent or were cut down by the knifelike projections in the iron circumference of the war machine. The beasts seemed undaunted by their work, and while Rexel circled overhead, they propelled their heavy burden through the trees toward a more open path. Velissa urged the falcon lower till she could see Parsky's face beneath the canopy of steel. He uncoiled his whip and laid the long lash to the back of one of the catterlobs. The whip cracked in the cold air and the beast that Parsky had struck lunged forward. The other catterlob, fearing the same, picked up his pace as well.

Rexel flew over the catterlobs' armored heads. The tusks beneath their great jaws shook as they struggled against their yokes while trying to catch the talons of Rexel in their crushing jaws. Never had Velissa seen their ugly heads so closely. Rexel flew ahead and circled back. He dove at the iron canopy where the red-clad Blackgill shouted and shook the haft of his ugly whip at them.

"Come, Velissa, and my beasts will feed on your falcon!"

Velissa was unsure of what Rexel would do next, and she was too frightened to answer Parsky. Rexel landed at a safe distance from the Iron Destroyer. Velissa, who knew the roughness of the falcon taking to flight, felt even more the trauma of landing. The bird seemed to draw back his wings and stop all at once. She felt as though she were going to pitch over his head and fall to the ground. She had barely recovered from the landing when Rexel grasped the shaft of a broken tree and lurched to the sky again.

She became apprehensive. She was not sure she could maintain her grasp on the falcon while he continued these antics. Rexel flew again over the canopied Parsky and swung the shaft of the tree at him. It glanced from the plated roof of the Iron Destroyer and ricocheted into the body of one of the catterlobs.

The beast was infuriated by the stabbing pain from the blow. He lurched at the passing falcon, roaring his displeasure. Again the ugly tusks slashed the air and the hot breath around the vicious teeth of the catterlob made Velissa tremble.

Rexel seemed content with his harassment of Parsky, and his

wing beats evened out to a slow, rhythmic cadence that carried Velissa on an easy ride across the plains.

She was glad that Parsky was making only slow progress across the southern plains toward her home. She felt that her husband would be safe for at least a day or so. Even if Parsky were to leave the Iron Destroyer and try to get to the house on foot, it would take him the rest of the day. Within the hour, Rexel was gliding on the upper drafts and settling into the camp of Orkkan.

On the high ridge, the sun seemed especially warm once Rexel had landed. The refugees gathered about the huge falcon who lowered his proud neck so that Velissa could dismount. When the Canbies had last see him, he had not been so terrifying. Now they approached him cautiously, torn between their fear and their intrigue with the monstrous falcon. Velissa straightened her blue coat and turned to speak to the women of Canby.

"Raccoman and I are leaving Canby if the tilt winds come in time," she said.

"On the falcon?" asked one of the women.

"No. Or—yes, on the Paradise Falcon, at least," she said, then explained Raccoman's vision and his creation of the Paradise Falcon.

"Velissa," they pleaded, "please don't leave us."

From the day that Velissa and Raccoman had revealed the Fire of Singreale to the Graygills, they had become symbols of hope in an imperiled age. More than she had guessed, Velissa was the standard of hope to the widows now gathered with their children on the upper ridges. She was the owner of Singreale, and the presence of the treasure that Velissa carried seemed to be the only reason for the women of Canby to talk of the future.

Velissa was moved by their esteem for her and, for a long while, said nothing. Then, at last, she gave them the very kind of explanation her husband would have given, saying it exactly as he would have said it.

"There is nothing more for us to do,
Except to seek a world that's new.
If we stayed one season more,
Would we turn life to hope for you
Or stop the terror of this war?"

She knew what they were thinking. The issue of their own desolation would not be answered by her statement. To them, it seemed that Raccoman and his wife were abandoning them just when their presence would have been a reason to hope.

"You leave us without hope!" challenged one of the women.

"Untrue! I am not your hope. Your survival lies in the North. Hope is the exodus. Stay on the high ridges and you will live. The beasts will not come here in winter. The Moonrhymes will take you in and you will be safe. If the tilt winds come in time, Raccoman and I will be gone."

"That's all right for you," said someone in the crowd. "But what of us? Can we reach the cliffs of the Moonrhymes in time?"

A loud wail rose from another woman.

Velissa moved to gain control of this growing hysteria.

"No—there is hope," she said. "We cannot leave you without a hope. Come, Orkkan."

Orkkan approached.

"Collinvar—I must see Collinvar for one last time."

The shopkeeper smiled. His gratitude was obvious.

Velissa walked to Collinvar and patted his nose just ahead of the silver horns.

"Good-bye," she said simply. She took the centicorn's reins and led him back to the fire in the center of the camp. Then she handed the reins to the kneeling Orkkan.

Velissa extended her hand and lifted Orkkan to his feet and said:

"To Orkkan, the Defender of Canby! Follow him,
For the exodus is the hope!
Orkkan is worthy. He may be trusted.
He once fought with your husbands at Demmerron Pass.
He is the knight of the confident sword.
He is the light in the castle of glass."

The women seemed to trust Velissa again; their anxiety passed even as she spoke. The fear left their faces and confidence stiffened their new resolve.

Orkkan took the reins. He did not seem to see Velissa as a defector, nor Raccoman as a traitor. "May Singreale guard our migration!" he exclaimed.

He placed his foot in the high stirrup and swung his body into the saddle.

"To our future," cried Orkkan, "in the land of the Moon-rhymes!"

"To the hope!" shouted the women and children. "To the exodus!"

Velissa stood silently for a moment before Orkkan and Collinvar.

"Farewell," boomed the giantesque Rexel.

"To Singreale!" cried Velissa.

She walked to the falcon. The survivor of Demmerron began to sing.

"Let us sing at the base of the ginjon tree,
For Canby's fields are the fields of the free."

Orkkan gestured with his upraised sword and some of the women joined him in the anthem.

"May the sun long rise and the morning skies
Herald the anthem of liberty."

The firelight blazed with hope as all joined in.

Velissa mounted the bird's neck and waited for him to lunge into the sky. Remembering the fears she had earlier felt, she looked at the icy ledges below and clung tightly to Rexel. They leapt into the icy sky.

As she rose, she could still see the defender of Canby with his sword raised, mounted on the stately Collinvar. Beneath the red sky of late afternoon, the Graygill women and children still sang.

"Ho! To the light, may our children roam
Through the friendly fields of Castledome,
For beasts and men are timeless friends
In the ageless land of Estermann."

At last the sound of their anthem died away in the upper air, which became stiff and silent and ominous.

Now the wings of Rexel leveled into a gentle glide as he soared upward above the ridges. The clear skies were cold and Velissa moved in a closer embrace of the neck of her winged mount, for his feathers were warm. She reached with her gloved hands around him as far as she could reach and brushed her cold cheek against his warm body.

Far below, she saw an isolated house next to the lowest of the ridges, and she wondered about its inhabitants. It looked like the house she shared with Raccoman and was a good distance from the village of Canby. She couldn't help but wonder what had happened to the residents of these lonely dwellings after the war with the beasts began. She wondered how many of these outlanders, if any, had died at Demmerron. There were many such homes scattered here and there across the land of the Graygills, and their loneliness, she thought, may have spared them the initial attack of the beasts. Best of all, she reasoned, there most likely were men in those homes—alive and perhaps able to help the defender of Canby, if only they could be located and gathered. Then, too, they might be only despairing men whose discouragement over the present war had not yet learned of the hope of the exodus to the land of the Moonrhymes.

Her reflection on these matters was suddenly interrupted when she became aware that Rexel was turning around in flight. Gradually he was altering his course. He had left her to her reverie for a long time, but now his booming voice spoke out briefly in words that trailed off into thin atmosphere.

"Hold on," the falcon warned. "I'm turning back toward the ridges."

"Why?" asked Velissa.

But he didn't need to answer. For as she listened for his reply, she heard a thin whine in the air. She had never lived in the valley nor experienced the tilt winds, but Raccoman had described how they would come. The clear sky, the whining of the air, the groaning of the heavens, the shudder, and then the screaming volleys of invisible gales.

The air was clear and cold and crying.

She clutched Rexel in a death grip.

Suddenly the air moaned and shuddered.

The falcon wisely faced the new breeze that was tortured by the heavy mass of power behind it. Suddenly the screaming wind hit them.

All forward motion stopped, and they appeared to be flying backward. Violently the falcon shot backward and skyward. Velissa's stomach felt weak, and fearing that she would faint and fall, she determined to keep her eyes open, even though the winds were burning them terribly. It seemed the updraft would not quit. Rexel's long wings looked as though they would be torn from his body.

At last, the pressure of the winds eased. When Velissa looked down again, she could barely see the world of the Graygills. And yet she was seeing all of it at once—fields, mountains, ridges, all white with snow and tortured by the powerful wind that had fallen like a hammer on the still earth. Velissa was tormented by one thought alone: "Raccoman!" she cried.

Things could not have gone worse for the metal-worker's plans. He felt the stiffness in the breeze and instinctively ran to the Paradise Falcon. Now he was confused. The air was moaning as his short legs and bright yellow boots crunched through the new snow. He pulled on his yellow hood and then his gloves, running as he had never run before. Just when he reached the Paradise Falcon, the air began to roar and he leapt up to the edge of the craft. He moved so quickly he took no time to brush off the snow. It fell from his boots and then slid off the slightly convex surface of the sail plane as he moved into his seat and quickly buckled the fiber strap across his lap. He pulled the buckle tight, took the rudder control firmly in his hands, and braced his feet on the stabilizer rods. The skies groaned and screamed. He looked at the empty chair beside him and cried in anguish, "Velissa!" The shrieking wind buried his words.

The invisible hammer of air hit and seemed at first to have driven a huge nail through the round, broad leaf of yellow metal on which Raccoman sat. It was pressed tightly to the ground. Raccoman felt cheated. This marvelous invention seemed doomed to be stuck to the snowy earth. The wind pressure on his body made every movement an effort, but he pressed his yellow boot firmly against the stabilizer bar with all the strength he had. He raised the right side of the ship off the ground. The craft shuddered as the pressing winds moved underneath the left side of the ship. Quickly he stomped the right stabilizer bar and the wind moved under that side as well. The sail plane jerked upward radically. First it seemed to hang as though it would settle back again. Raccoman released the stabilizer bars—the ship flattened to a large leaf and steadily began to rise.

Raccoman grasped the rudder and turned it in such a way that, as the craft rose, it gradually turned toward the ridges. Like Rexel, the sail plane faced the roar of the screaming skies. The listing of the ship corrected itself and its tendency to roll stopped immediately. Now the speed of the upward motion increased. The barn and house quickly dwindled into black dots in the snow and finally disappeared altogether. The Paradise Falcon shot vertically into the sky. In an hour it would be dark, but the red sky and the white snow turned all the world pink. When Raccoman looked over his right shoulder, he saw the smoke of Maldoon, and when he looked to his left, he saw the endless silver sea of Castledome Forest. Ahead and to his right were the sentinels of Demmerron Pass. Finally he rose so high that all he saw was sky.

The fiery red of the sinking sun grew hot as Rexel and Velissa traveled with the wind. She felt the warm sensation that always came whenever there was some change in the direction of the wind. She found it hard to believe she had missed being home at the crucial hour when the winds had come. She couldn't help but blame herself for leaving Raccoman on a clear day. The coming of the winds was the moment for which he had worked so long—and she had missed it.

Rexel turned lazily in the high, thin air.

She wondered if the Paradise Falcon had flown. And if indeed Raccoman had made it to the sleek craft in time. She wondered if the glider had left the ground in one piece, or if it had left the ground at all. She hoped that Raccoman would forgive her for not having been home when the tilt winds began. She shuddered to think that he might not even be alive to forgive her if there had been a mishap in the launching.

"Not alive to forgive me," she sighed. The sky around them was now so quiet she could hear herself perfectly. "Oh, Raccoman, Raccoman!" She felt so much guilt she could hardly bear the burden of it.

The falcon turned again and rose on a strong column of air. Velissa no longer knew which way she was flying. She clung closely to Rexel. All she could think about was the disappointment she had caused her husband. For the last year she had prided herself in the fact that she had never eaten meat. Now she realized there were other kinds of wrong as well. Her pride over having escaped Parsky's deception was a snare. She realized that her own pride in her purity had become a barrier to her humility. She wished herself free of self-righteousness, and she also wanted to be free of the guilt of her selfishness in leaving her husband at the hour of his lonely triumph.

"Please don't be dead," she said foolishly yet sincerely to her absentee husband.

They flew for a long time. Only her sense of guilt made any noise, and it thundered all about her.

If only she could be forgiven. If only she could return to the cave on the upper ridges where she had touched Singreale to the face of Raccoman. Only his face had been black—now all her inner sense of fidelity cried out for the cleansing light of Singreale.

"Raccoman," she whispered in the deafening silence.

It was almost dark, and yet there was a kind of brightness about the upper light where they flew.

"Look!" said Rexel, and his command sounded like thunder.

"Where?" she asked as she squinted toward the sunset, only because the falcon's head seemed locked in that direction. In vain she tried to see.

"Your eyes are too good for mine," she said.

The falcon fluttered his long wings gently and Velissa was aware that they were moving steadily into the sunset. Then she saw a black blip in the red air. Rexel continued to fly toward it, and his approach made the spot grow. Before long, the spot in the sea of cold sunlight loomed large and soon became a long, dark silhouette of a single rider on a dark blur.

"Raccoman!" Velissa shouted.

They flew gently toward each other.

The sail plane turned and they flew alongside each other.

"Velissa! You're safe!" cried Raccoman.

Velissa realized that all the concern she had felt for her husband was matched by his concern for her as well. He, too, had worried if she had been able to stay astride her winged friend, or if, indeed, she had been lost in the first onslaught of the powerful winds.

Now their flights were as parallel as their joy. Gradually Rexel eased above the Paradise Falcon. The twilight was as magic as the evening sky, red and deep blue mingled together with the first faint hint of starlight bleeding through the clear night. In a moment Velissa understood why Rexel was hovering just above the Paradise Falcon. She released her grip on the falcon's neck and slid along his sleek feathers to the front of his right wing. She sat there as still as the air around her. The falcon brought his left talon forward, slowly and gracefully, until he held it in an unnatural attitude under his wing where Velissa was sitting.

In a moment of daring, she slid off Rexel's wing into his large claw. There was not the slightest disturbance in the glass air. The talon was scaly and easy to sit upon, but had a rough and demonic appearance she had never noticed before. Only a few feet below her in a smooth flight path, Raccoman was studying the big falcon's maneuvers. Velissa watched the utter stillness of the great floating leaf beneath her and was filled with admiration for the lone pilot.

The falcon brought his claw slowly downward until it was directly above the empty chair beside Raccoman. Raccoman released the stabilizer rod till the edges of the leaf were flat—the great sail plane rose up gently. Velissa felt the sky-yellow surface brush her feet. Rexel slowed his flight just a bit and brought her directly over the empty seat again. She slid from the rough talon into her chair beside Raccoman. As her weight came directly onto the Paradise Falcon, it dipped a little and then leveled smoothly. Rexel fluttered his wings softly and pulled away. The drop had been as easy as slipping into a chair at home. Quickly she buckled the fiber strap and turned and smiled at her husband.

"Hah-hoo!" he cried. "I love you!"

He leaned over and kissed Velissa. For a moment he even released the controls and kissed her again.

"Hah-hoo! Hah-hoo! Hah-hoo!"

Rexel moved well out ahead of them. They watched him and were puzzled by his maneuvers. Suddenly Singreale exploded like a nova against the darkening night, and out of the fireball that enveloped the great falcon, a much smaller falcon flew. Rexel, back to his normal size, was carrying the glowing diamond in his claws. He turned and settled down on the surface of the Paradise Falcon. He extended Singreale to Velissa and she took it and put it back in the pouch at her bosom.

"Mind if I ride with you for a while, Velissa?" he asked.

"Not at all, Rexel," she laughed.

"Hah-hoo!" said Raccoman, whose elation at the largeness of life lifted his delightful craft to the lowering of stars.

They turned away from the sunset and slipped upward in the cold starlight. They moved silently across the skies, always looking for the moving starfields that they never saw the first night. The strong wind blew throughout the next day, carrying them even higher.

By the afternoon of the next day, Parsky's machine finally reached Dakktare's meadow. The sky was a blue dome over the eastern hills. Parsky drove the black catterlobs on in a horrible path of destruction. Snow and frost covered the beetle. The machine moved to the side of the barn and cut its way through the wall, which fell like paper before the Iron Destroyer. Parsky looked out through the windows of the steel canopy with a disappointed expression. When the Iron Destroyer should have reached the Paradise Falcon, it did not. It rolled on through the vacant interior of the barn without even the crunch of steel on steel. Steadily it moved through and out the other side of the barn with still no encounter of metal.

"The Falcon is gone, Lord Parskon," said one of the drones in the chamber below him.

"Kill the centicorn!" shouted Parsky.

The iron beetle rolled to a complete stop.

Parsky leapt from under his canopy and shouted his orders to a squad of four Blackgills who hurried out of the heavily riveted door at the back of the Iron Destroyer. The drones were frightened before him.

"Search the area," said the Blackgill, "If anyone remains on the grounds, bring them to me. Check the shed they have used as a stable. There is a chance they have left the centicorn behind. Holga!"

The soldiers spread out in the diminishing light of afternoon. In a few moments they were back with the discouraging report.

"The house and stable are both empty."

Parsky grew angry. His red face was distended by the blood pounding in his temples.

"Destroy all!" he shouted. "Then we shall move on Canby. Holga!" he cried in fury, pointing to the door of the war machine.

One by one the warriors marched with a clipped step and filed back into the little den at the back of the cold steel beetle. Once Parsky was back under the canopy, he cracked his whip and drove the two great catterlobs forward. The Iron Destroyer advanced through the shed and then the house and then turned north toward Canby. Only splintered wood marked his snowy path of destruction.

Raccoman's once-pleasant meadow greeted the dim light of evening with nothing more than a ruined scene of scattered timbers and stones.

Once more Raccoman and Velissa watched the turquoise sky grow red and then a pale blue. They were now close to the quadrant of sky where Raccoman had been the night he had collided with the moving starfield.

The blue gave way to black and Raccoman looked anxiously through the stars. There are times when every vision must be tried. He knew now that the time had come to test the reality of the vision he had experienced during his night flight one year earlier. He would not despair. Hope was his. His vision was a reality, and that reality was a continent never discovered or discussed in the valley of the Graygills. Reality was the titan Star Riders. In a moment of unparalleled excitement, his vision was confirmed.

"Look, Velissa!"

"Where?" she asked.

"There," he said, pointing into the warm, black sky.

Sure enough, a field of moving stars were clearly visible. The stars were coming directly towards them on their way to the horizon. He took his hands from the controls and embraced Velissa in excitement. Naturally, Raccoman congratulated himself.

His egotism swirled about the sleek ship and floated on the constellations through which they soared. There was little to do now but wait for the Star Riders to come. It looked as if he would have just enough time to congratulate himself, and he never wasted such an opportunity.

"Sky prince, you're the best of all those who fly,
You superb, silver-rider, who tames the wild sky
I'll swear you're the standard that all men should be,
The model, the hope, the ensign, the key."

Velissa kissed him and smiled. After all, how could she disagree?